Forever and Other Lies

Sherri Storey

I would like to dedicate this book in memory of Tasha. She left this world too soon, a kind soul whose light was dimmed by addiction. Her love for her children endures beyond time. May she find the peace that eluded her here.

This book is also dedicated to anyone battling addiction or other demons. Don't give up. What feels hopeless today will make you stronger tomorrow.

I would like to thank Sue and Sandy with heartfelt gratitude for their support, keen eye and insightful guidance. You have helped polish to manuscript into a book that I'm proud of. Thank you both so much.

Books by author

Callaghan's Rescue - debut novel

The Blythe Landing series

Where The Sunflowers Touch the Sky
The Night the Stars Fell Down
I Still Drive Your Truck

The What If series

If She Didn't Love Him
If Love Didn't Hurt
If Hearts Didn't Break

The 3 Is series

Forever and Other Lies
Soulmates and Other Apparitions-releasing 2025
True Love and Other Delusions -releasing 2025

Forever and Other Lies

by Sherri Storey

Introduction

Welcome to Blythe Landing.

In this quirky small town, everyone knows your business—and now, you'll know theirs! Here's your insider's guide to the lives and loves of the people who call Blythe Landing home.

'The 3 Js' series continues where the 'What If series' left off. But don't worry—'Forever and Other Lies' is designed to stand on its own. This cheat sheet will help you dive right in, whether you're a longtime fan or a new visitor.

Now, let's meet the key players;

Derek Brennan. The quintessential 'player'—a civil engineer and farmer's son, Derek is one of five siblings. He's a confirmed bachelor with zero plans to settle down... or so he thinks.

Jayna Sutton. The female 'player'—a skilled nurse, heir to a family fortune, and one of the legendary 3 Js. Jayna's ready to settle down, but her reputation has other plans.

The 3Js;

Jamie Whitney. Blonde and otherworldly. Owner of the quaint Yesterday and Tomorrow shop, and a reluctant psychic.

Jessica Ambers. Blonde and classy. A psychotherapist now volunteering her expertise in Sierra Leone, adding a global touch to this small-town tale.

Jayna Sutton. Blonde and sassy. She's about to have her entire world shaken up.

The Brennan Siblings;

Ian. The oldest brother, who takes after their father in more ways than one. He is married to Vanessa with two children.

Tommy and Derek. Fraternal twins with vastly different paths —Tommy, the perfect son, and Derek, the bad boy.

Kylie. The only sister, who's always tried to keep up with her brothers.

Ben. The youngest, who loves nothing more than stirring the pot with his older siblings.

Secondary Couples;

Nick Taylor and Piper Reynolds. Nick, a police officer and best friend of both Derek and Tommy, is engaged to Piper. She is a schoolteacher and close friend of Leighton. Their relationship is on the rocks and Kylie may be to blame.

Tommy Brennan and Leighton Gray: Tommy, a soldier presumed dead, returns home after three harrowing years as a prisoner of war. Leighton, his fiancée and a cosmetic chemist, owns the successful Notion for Lotion. Their relationship is also on the rocks and Derek is definitely to blame.

Kylie Brennan and Jovanny Grotta.   Kylie is good friends with the 3 Js. She is a nurse who volunteered in Sierra Leone, meeting movie star and philanthropist Jovanny Grotta there. Jovanny followed Kylie to Blythe Landing, buying the house across the road and started a charity and non-profit store in town. Their relationship has a lot of hurdles to overcome starting in the 1st book 'Where the Sunflowers Touch the Sky' and altered in 'If She Didn't Love Him'.

Supporting Cast (and yes, there is a lot of them, but it's a small town where everyone knows everyone!):

Burke Winston – Local police officer who has recently moved to Blythe Landing. He attended Ontario Police College with Nick Taylor. There's never been so many single women dropping off baked goods or filing reports since he started with BLPS.

Lance Roman—The new paramedic and Jayna's latest crush.

Greta Cochrane—A nurse and the woman who is standing between Jayna and her crush.

Norm and Rose Brennan—Derek's grandparents.

Earl Taylor—Nick Taylor's grandfather and Norm's partner in crime.

Harriet, aka Harry—Derek's maternal fun-loving grandmother.

Stan and Marion Brennan—The parents of the boisterous Brennan siblings.

Bianca Grotta—Jovanny's older sister and Ben's unrequited love interest.

Vanessa Brennan—Derek's sister-in-law and owner of Vanessa's Scissory.

Ophelia Meddler—The town hall clerk and head of the gossip tree.

Shamus—Landscaper, bagpipe enthusiast and Ophelia's feuding neighbor.

Connor—Ben's friend and Jayna enthusiast.

Maisie Whyte—Jayna's frenemy.

Sonny Mitchell—Head paramedic.

Ivy—Server at Patty's Pub.

Talia—A single mom struggling with addiction who Jayna offers a lending hand.

Derek Ainsley—Blythe Landing's up and coming daredevil.

Duncan—Busboy at Patty's Pub. He's kind of sinister.

Mario Flavia—Derek's boss with rumored ties to the Mafia. He's definitely sinister!

Nash Logan—Movie star and friend of Jovanny Grotta. He's married to Calla, a doctor and friend of Kylie. He is the founder of the TL Village in Sierra Leone.

Sam Marek—Billionaire cameraman and co-founder of TL Village.

Heidi—A volunteer doctor in Sierra Leone.

Sufta—The driver for TL Village and friend of Derek.

Now that we've got the cast all straight, let's dive into the story. Hope you enjoy it!

Part 1

Chapter 1

Jayna

"Forever Love" blasted from the speakers, and Jayna groaned, slapping the mute button. She loved Reba's badass songs like "I Am A Survivor" and "Consider Me Gone" had practically become her anthem. But this sappy love song? Hard pass. She wasn't buying it.

True love, soul mates, happily ever after—forever; it was all one big lie. This over-romanticized garbage filled books read to impressionable young girls. Hollywood perpetuated the fallacy further, painting the world and love in such unrealistic hues. It was cruel. And now Reba, her idol, was singing the praises of forever love. She might just have to switch to the heavy metal station.

Maybe she'd buy into the whole 'til death do us part' belief if she had the type of mother who read bedtime stories. Or a romantic father who showered unconditional love on his wife and child. Instead, she'd been blessed with a selfish breed of parents. With their substantial wealth, they hired staff to raise their only child while they traveled the world, searching for meaning in their unfulfilled, entitled lives.

Instead of growing up hopeful, Jayna grew up jaded. Rich and jaded, but not spoiled. She liked to think she was a step ahead of the women who desperately clung to the promise of forever love. Not that she faulted them. They held onto the illusion for stability in a world that could be so cold. But Jayna chose her own path. She'd pretty much raised herself, so it was second nature to continue on this solitary road. No man was needed to define or protect her. She could buy her own damn stuff.

Letting someone in who could break her heart? Not a chance. She preferred to be the heartbreaker. Not that any hearts were at risk. She never dated seriously. She was not looking for Mr. Right, just Mr. Right-now. Jayna Sutton was fine on her own. She always had been, always would be. She was an independent, modern woman.

However, she couldn't shake off her small-town roots, no matter how hard she tried. Six years in the big city hadn't helped. Pickup trucks and country music were in her blood. Now she was back home, and her brand-new, fully loaded Ford F150 Raptor was her way of thumbing her nose at the men in town. Just to be sure they got the message, the bumper sticker on the back window, "Silly boys, trucks are for girls," slammed it home. Next to that sticker, another read, "Trauma Nurse—your stupidity is my job security." Sadly, that one was all too true, especially now that she'd taken a job in the ER of her hometown hospital. The boys in this community aged but never truly grew up. Stupid stunts were a rite of passage or simply a way to waste a Saturday night.

Jayna slowed as she approached the bridge, waving to Graham and Amanda Willard, who strolled along the sidewalk walking a Golden Retriever. The couple had dated throughout high school and married right after graduation, buying a small house in town. Starting their family with a puppy, they now had their first baby due in a couple of months. It was the dream of so many girls she'd grown up with; the matrimonial fairytale of building a life with someone, making a home, raising a family. But it wasn't for everyone. It wasn't for her.

Hitting the right turn signal, she pulled onto the ornate bridge that led to the downtown core. Nestled beside a river, the main street of Blythe Landing was the epitome of old-fashioned and quaint. In December, the landscape transformed into a serene winter wonderland as it became blanketed under a pristine layer of snow. The partially frozen, fast-flowing river slowed, meandering at a more graceful pace past the picturesque town. Along the riverbanks, the bare tree branches were adorned with a light cover of ice that sparkled in the sunlight. They glistened even more magically under the enchanting glow of the moon.

With only three weeks left before Christmas, a sense of tranquility and tradition had descended upon the cobblestone streets and historic limestone buildings. Blythe Landing could be a serious contender for the next Thomas Kinkade painting. The one-of-a-kind shops brought tourists in by the droves in summer. Tonight, though, the street was empty. It was past 6 p.m. on Friday, which meant the sidewalks had been rolled up. Next Friday, though, was Midnight Madness, which would bring all the tourists back searching for that unique Christmas gift for the hard-to-buy-for.

Her gaze shifted to the vacant windows of Yesterday and Tomorrow. The store belonged to her close friend Jamie Whitney. Having bankrolled the enterprise, Jayna held the title of silent partner. However, it was Jamie's skill and vision that had turned the second-hand and refurbished furniture shop into a thriving business, and she was happy to give her friend free rein to run it. Although Jayna was not so silent when it came to the Christmas Window Display contest. They had yet to win it. But this year, she was determined to change that.

As she drove past, two guys sitting on the edge of a tailgate waved. They were both cute but far too young, which made them off-limits. She may date ruthlessly, but she did have standards. A frown creased her face, replacing her smile. Had moving back home just drastically reduced her dating pool?

Finding male attention had never been an issue. With long flaxen blonde hair, thickly lashed cornflower blue eyes, and a curvaceous figure, she had her pick of men. The challenge was finding one who didn't bore her after a few dates. Returning to a town of only 7,998 people would make the feat even harder.

The lights turned red at the only set in town, and she pressed the brake pedal, coming to a stop. "I'm the only vehicle on the road," she muttered.

The digital clock on the dashboard blinked 6:20, signaling her usual tardiness. Jamie was not going to be happy. They'd made plans to meet at Patty's Pub at 6 to toss around ideas for the Christmas window display. As a bonus, they could spy on Jessica, the third blonde in their trio, fondly referred to as the 3 Js.

Tapping her freshly manicured nails on the rhinestone-crusted steering wheel, she let out a frustrated breath. It may be the only set of traffic lights in town, but it was seriously the longest-timed set of lights anywhere. Finally, the green light flashed, and she hit the gas. Two minutes down the road, she slowed again and pulled into the parking lot behind the pub, killing the engine. Jamie sat on the tailgate of her battered truck and made a point of pulling up her coat sleeve to look at her wristwatch.

"I know, I know. I'm running late yet again." She hit the key fob. Locking her truck was not necessary in this town where everyone knew everyone, but a habit she developed after living in Toronto.

Jayna flashed her bright blue ombre nails. "But look at these beauties." She'd driven back to the nail salon in the city for a fill. With a nod to Jamie's chipped and paint-stained fingernails, she continued, "You should join me next time."

Jamie shook her head, the pixie cut barely moving. "No point, wouldn't last five minutes in my line of work."

A large armoire that had seen better days was secured in the truck bed. However, it would look better than new once Jamie finished with it.

"Where did you find that monstrosity?" Jayna asked her. "Exactly how do you plan to get it from the truck to the shop?"

"It's not that heavy, just awkward," Jamie smiled sweetly. "I was hoping I could entice a couple of friends into helping."

"Well, this friend wants her nails to last longer than a day, and your other friend probably won't be speaking to you after tonight."

Jamie shrugged. "Can you blame her? I wouldn't be speaking

to us either!"

"Hey, he might end up being a great guy and she'll be thanking us." Jayna playfully nudged Jamie as they walked toward the bar.

Jamie pulled open the door, and Jayna stepped inside, scanning the tables for Jessica. Their friend sat at a cozy corner table, across from a man in an expensive suit.

"Look, a stuffed shirt. Just her type," Jayna nudged Jamie again.

"By the pained expression on Jess's face, I'd say he's far from it," Jamie groaned. "We are in so much trouble."

Jayna's eyes landed on a table near Jessica's. Derek 'Dare' Brennan, the man, the myth, the legend—at least in his own mind, she thought bitterly. What probably annoyed her most about him was his equally low opinion of her.

She didn't recognize the woman he was with, but she fit the typical Derek mold: bleached blonde, painted-on jeans, low-cut top, hair teased to an inch of its' life. Stacked, sexy, and short-term. Exactly his type. The woman seductively sucked on her cocktail straw, offering Derek no challenge. He had the attention span of a hound dog with even lower morals. No way would Blondie get a second date.

Why did it bother her to see him out on a date? She had zero interest in Derek Brennan. Being Kylie's older brother already put him on the off-limits list. The fact that he was a womanizing, conceited ape added him to the don't-touch-with-a-ten-foot-pole list. Sure, there had been those fleeting five minutes in high school when she thought he was a great guy and was madly in love with him. But he had cured her of both delusions. In fact, he'd cured her of any lingering romantic fantasies. He'd been her one and only crush, and she'd never forgotten the sting of that lesson.

"There's Kylie," Jamie pointed out, bringing Jayna's attention back to the present. She forced her gaze away from Derek and onto his sister instead.

Kylie Brennan was the fourth in their group and the only

brunette. They had all met that first day in kindergarten and had been inseparable ever since. It had been one of Kylie's four brothers who had dubbed them 'the 3 Js' and the nickname had stuck.

"She's sitting with Bianca. Wow, Bianca is as beautiful as her brother is handsome," Jamie said as they walked toward the centre table. Kylie had recently become engaged to Bianca's movie star brother and it still felt surreal to Jayna that her friend was about to marry such a famous man.

"And Leighton Gray is with them. Just my luck," Jayna moaned adding in sigh and an eye roll.

Leigthon was the fiancée of Kylie's brother Tommy—Derek's twin and Jayna could not stand the woman.

"Mind if we join you?" Jamie asked, grabbing a vacant chair from a neighboring table.

"Not at all, please do," Leighton answered with a sweet smile.

Jayna clenched her jaw as she took the only vacant chair beside Leighton. Accomplished, kind, and undeniably likable, Leighton was the type of person everyone adored. But despite her efforts, Jayna couldn't shake the deep disdain that prickled within her whenever Leighton was around. It was a feeling she hated but couldn't ignore.

Kylie lifted her wine glass, the giant diamond on her finger catching the light and Jayna's attention.

"Wow, that rock is the size of a skating rink," Jayna whistled. "I still can't believe you're going to be Mrs. Captain Heroic."

The entire town had been shocked when A-list movie star Jovanny Grotta showed up on Kylie's doorstep. The two had met while she was on a nursing mission in Sierra Leone, and he'd followed her home.

"He's not as big of a deal as he and the world think," Bianca offered. "Trust me. He's just a typical man. He was the most annoying little brother. Still is."

"Speaking of brothers, how's Tommy doing?" Jamie asked.

Kylie sighed as she set down her wine glass. "Good, considering all he's been through. The surgery on his leg went well, and the PTSD treatment center is doing wonders."

"I can't even begin to imagine," Jamie said softly, then turned to Leighton. "It must be shocking to learn the fiancé you thought had died is still alive."

Leighton shifted uncomfortably. "Nothing compared to what Tommy's been through," she replied, her voice barely above a whisper. "Three years in Taliban captivity... it's unimaginable."

"Where's Jessica?" Kylie abruptly changed the still painful subject. It was going to be a long road to recovery for Tommy Brennan and his family.

Jayna pointed to the corner. "Over there, on a blind date. We're here to offer moral support—or run interference, depending on how the date goes."

All eyes swiveled toward Jessica.

"He doesn't look like her type," Kylie observed.

"He's a corporate lawyer. He's perfect for her," Jayna defended.

"How did she meet him?" Bianca asked.

"Online dating," Jamie said with a cringe, nervously tousling her platinum blonde pixie cut. The style suited her, highlighting her delicate features perfectly.

"Really?" Leighton's brow furrowed. "Jessica doesn't seem like someone who would use an online dating service."

Jayna giggled. "She wouldn't. Jamie and I signed her up. She needs to change her email password. It's way too easy to guess."

"Oh, you didn't!" Kylie exclaimed. "She must've been furious."

"She was," Jamie sighed, rolling her eyes. "And this date isn't going well. We'll hear about it for a long time."

"How do you know it's not going well?" Bianca asked, sneaking another peek.

"Jamie knows everything," Kylie teased. "It's unnerving how accurate she is. I keep telling her she should set up a tarot card booth in her shop."

"Laugh all you want, but don't come to me for advice next time," Jamie retorted, used to the ribbing.

Jayna's phone dinged with an incoming text, pulling her

attention away. "Oh, that's not nice! Jessica just called us a couple of assholes."

Another ding. "S.O.S.," Jayna read aloud. "Is it a level one or a level ten emergency?" she typed back.

"Level ten," she giggled, reading the reply. "Oh, we are in so much trouble!"

Ding, ding. Jayna covered her mouth, trying to stifle a laugh. "Jessica says her date just told her he's wearing a bright purple thong under his suit. Apparently, he loves to be spanked."

Kylie groaned. "You two are the worst friends. Jamie, how could you not see this coming?"

Jamie held up her hands defensively. "You know I can't read anyone close to me."

"After this, Jessica might not be close with either of you," Kylie said, clearing her throat. "I'll make sure she knows I had no part in this."

"Poor Jessica," Leighton added. "You have to help her out."

"Yeah, we should," Jayna agreed, her eyes drifting back to Derek. He was still at the neighboring table. "It looks like your brother is about to take one for the team," she told Kylie. Pushing back her chair, she stood. "And I'll save Blondie from heartbreak while I'm at it. No way she'll make it past one date with him."

Rolling her neck, she straightened her back and walked toward Derek Brennan. A devious smile lifted the corner of her lips. This was going to be fun!

She raised her voice. "Derek Brennan! I can't believe you! The minute I tell you I'm pregnant, you stop answering your phone. Then you go and hook up with the first blonde bimbo you find!" Jayna settled her hands on her hips and turned her attention to Derek's date. "No offense. I'm sure you're not a real blonde."

Derek leaned back, his eyes narrowing. "Who's the father? Why would you be calling me?"

"Seriously? Who's the father?" Her voice cracked effectively, and she forced a hiccup before pressing her lips together.

Waving a pointed finger toward him, she continued her tirade. "You damn well know that you're the father. And that dose of chlamydia was an added surprise I could have done without. You're going to need a round of antibiotics to clear it up."

She leaned down closer to him, "On second thought, don't bother. I hope it falls off!"

Derek straightened in his chair, forcing his gaping mouth shut. He spun around, probably checking for his younger brother Ben, who lived to prank him. He turned back, aiming an angry scowl directly at Jayna. "Are you drunk? Did you fall and hit your head?"

With a theatrical gesture, she covered her mouth with her right hand. It was more to hide the laugh caused by the confused expression on his stupid face. She bit the inside of her cheek, forming tears in her eyes. After this performance, she should join the local theatre group.

His date stood, letting her chair scrape loudly on the concrete floor as she shot a death stare at both Derek and Jayna before stalking toward the bar. Jayna stifled another laugh, hoping it sounded like a sob. She lowered her hand and blew Derek a discrete kiss before turning toward Jessica's table.

"Jess, I can't believe he's done this to me!" She took two steps toward her friend. Jessica sent her a grateful look that she quickly changed to one of concern before jumping up out of her chair.

"Jayna, are you alright?"

"I'm so sorry to interrupt your date, but…" she sniffled loudly and shot a hurt look over her shoulder in Derek's direction. "But I thought he loved me. I thought he wanted this baby as much as I did. Oh, what a fool I've been."

Jessica draped a comforting arm across her shoulders. "You're not the fool, he's just no good! He certainly doesn't deserve you." Jessica glared in Derek's direction.

"You both are too much!" Derek grumbled. "Are you on drugs?"

"I hate to interrupt your date," Jayna continued to blubber

and apologized to Jessica's date. "I can't be alone right now."

"Todd, I am so sorry." Jessica grabbed her purse and jacket off the back of the chair. "But my friend needs me."

"Uh, sure. No problem." He stood up. "I could wait around. I don't mind."

Jayna began to sob uncontrollably, grabbing onto Jessica's arm.

"Oh, no. This will take some time." Jessica steered Jayna to the bathroom.

"Do you want to reschedule? Maybe tomorrow night?" Todd called after her.

"I'll have to get back to you," Jessica spoke over her shoulder, then hissed in Jayna's ear. "You are so dead."

"Jayna, what the hell?" Derek yelled after her.

"I think you'll have to get in line." Jayna let out a loud snort.

After lectures and laughter in the bathroom, Jayna swore upon her life to never mess with Jessica's love life again. She did it with her fingers crossed behind her back, so it didn't technically count. How could she promise that? Messing with her friends was so much fun.

Jovanny Grotta and Ben Brennan had joined their group, pushing two tables together. So had Derek. Jayna chose a chair close to the actor, and far from Derek.

It was surreal to be sitting at the same table with an A-list movie star, sharing a beer and a pizza like it was just any Friday night. But it was just a regular Friday night, and somehow the actor had become a part of this close-knit community. Admittedly, when he'd first shown up at the Brennan farm, she'd been more than a little starstruck. Okay, more like completely awestruck. What woman with a functioning libido wouldn't have been?

He was Captain Heroic, saving the world and stealing hearts everywhere he went. The man was freaking gorgeous. He had been blessed with every good-looking gene there was. Dark, smoldering eyes of melted chocolate, and whiter-than-white teeth with a 100-watt smile. And can we talk about those impossibly deep dimples? Then there was his hair, styled to perfection, begging for fingers to get tangled in the silky strands. With washboard abs, broad shoulders, and toned thighs, he was every bit a movie star. Of course, Hollywood would have noticed him.

And here he sat, in small-town Canada, at a knock-off Irish pub wearing a ball cap and an ordinary black T-shirt like every other guy in the pub. Except, unlike all the ordinary men, Jovanny didn't look ordinary. He looked as good in regular clothes as he did wearing a tux on the red carpet. The man was beautiful.

But how did Derek Brennan, sitting next to such a handsome man, still look so damn good-looking? Wearing a black T-shirt as well, he was all biceps and black ink peeking out. With that bad boy attitude, he could very well be one of Jovanny's co-stars. One of his hot co-stars.

Now admitting that left a sour taste in her mouth. Pouring a glass of beer from the pitcher in the center of the table, Jayna cautiously side-eyed Derek. Hopefully, he wasn't upset that she had run off his date. She couldn't help but notice that he hadn't shaved today and the black T-shirt he wore belonged in the rag bin. Seriously though, if the date this evening had been well, serious, he would have at least shaved and worn a decent shirt. One with buttons and a collar, minus the holes.

As she set the pitcher back on the table, her eyes collided with his. Derek's violet-blue ones flashed dangerously in her direction. A slow grin lifted the corner of his lips and popped the dimple on his left cheek. He was too good-looking for his own good and knew it. And she hated that she noticed. Not that it made a difference. Good-looking or not, he was still a world-class jerk. A shave, a haircut, and a dress shirt would not change that. He was in dire need of a personality transplant.

"Jayna," he spoke her name, in a slow menacing drawl.

"Derek," she used the same intonation he had, holding his penetrating glare. Never let the enemy sense fear. Or was that for dogs? Either way, it worked for Derek Brennan. He was her archenemy and a low-down, no-good dog.

"Should I be handing out cigars?" Ben chirped. "I'm going to be an uncle again!"

Derek shot his younger brother a scathing look before turning it back on her. "Do you mind telling me what that was all about?"

"Well Derek, I was helping Jessica get out of a bad blind date." A smirk played across her lips.

He leaned forward, slapping both his open palms on the table. "A bad blind date?" He repeated her words, slowly and concisely. Lifting his right hand, he pointed his index finger in her direction and stabbed the air with it. "Let me get this straight. You ruined my date so she could get out of hers?"

Jayna shrugged indifferently. The muscle twitched in his jaw. She had really pissed him off. Derek was always intense, but when he was angry, it came off him like crashing waves. Tonight, his anger was a storm heading straight in her direction. She squared her shoulders.

He is an insensitive womanizer, she reminded herself. There was no need to feel guilt over ruining his date. "It's not like you don't have another date lined up for tomorrow night. If not, just pull out your phone and swipe right on the first big boob bimbo you see."

Derek narrowed his eyes. "What makes you think I wasn't planning to see..." he paused. Was he attempting to remember his date's name? "Tanya Simms tomorrow night?"

Jayna let out a snort. "Right, okay! If you were really into her, you would have showered, changed your shirt, and brushed your hair."

"Her name is Tonya Zimmerman," Ben interrupted. "I went to school with her."

Jayna snorted again, louder this time. "Ha, you didn't even know her name. And she's way too young for you."

"I was close. And she's old enough to drink and vote, so she's old enough to date," Derek challenged and glanced down at his t-shirt. "What's wrong with my shirt? I showered, brushed my hair, and even put on deodorant." He lifted his left shoulder to his nose and sniffed. "It's still working!"

"Whatever!" She dismissively raised her hand, waving him off.

"And it's not like you're all dressed up." He pointed at her T-shirt. "Superpower? Yeah, right! More like super-pretentious."

Jayna glanced down at the rose T-shirt with the bold gold lettering; 'I'm a nurse. What's your superpower?' Lifting her chin, she glared in his direction again. "I didn't have a date. So, what's your superpower, Derek? The ability to stink up a room even after you've showered and put on deodorant? I can smell you over here. You smell like bitter regret and failure. Oh, look," she laughed, pointing to the door. "There goes your date with Jessica's."

Derek let out a loud grunt when he turned to watch Tonya stroll arm in arm out the door with Jessica's date.

"Jayna, I hear you started working in the ER at Blythe Landing Hospital." Leighton forced a change in the subject. "How are you liking it?"

She kept her gaze trained on Derek's face, watching his angry expression soften as he turned to look at Leighton. He apparently still had a thing for his brother's girl. And it caused that weird sensation to swirl in her gut like it did the first time she noticed it in high school. Maybe that was the cause of some of the animosity she felt towards Leighton. Maybe it was jealousy.

No, impossible!

She was not jealous over the fact that Derek had feelings for a woman he had no business having feelings for.

"Loving it," she finally answered Leighton.

Forcing her attention off Derek, she turned toward the stunning woman. While Derek's demeanor softened when Leighton was around, Leighton had a completely different reaction to Derek. She truly seemed to be uncomfortable around her fiancé's twin. Just what had happened between them to cause so much tension? Something definitely had. She'd bet her life on it.

The pub door opened, and Jayna turned her head, watching the new paramedic walk in. Now there was one fine male specimen. Just when she thought she'd limited her dating options by moving back home.

"Speaking about loving it, there's the new paramedic. Even his name is hot. Lance Roman," Jayna cooed.

Derek spun around in his chair before he turned back and stared directly at Jayna again. "You should ask him to join us."

Her head snapped back, her eyes narrowing. "Oh, no! You just want to administer a little payback."

"I would never," he let out a sardonic chuckle, raising and lowering his eyebrows. The smile on his lips was anything but friendly as he tapped his index finger on his chin. "Remind me again just what it was you needed antibiotics to clear up."

"You are such an ass!" Jayna hissed.

"Oh, that's too bad. Looks like Lance Romance is already taken." Derek pointed toward a table where a pretty woman sat. The paramedic walked straight toward her, dropping a kiss on her lips before pulling out a chair.

Jayna frowned as she followed his stare. Greta Cochrane had already sunk her claws into him. Damn, that had been quick.

"Who is she?" Jessica asked.

"A nurse I work with," Jayna sighed. "She's a new hire as well. And nice." Maybe not that nice. Jayna had liked her, but that was before the woman swooped in and stole the most handsome and eligible man in town. Yet another man off limits. The dating pool in Blythe Landing was drying up before her eyes.

"Let me get this straight. Jayna, the man-eater has ethics? You won't steal a man from a friend or a co-worker?" Derek leaned forward, sneering at her.

She flipped him the bird and scooped a slice of pizza off the center tray. "I'll wait until she's finished with him. Then he's all mine! Until I'm finished with him."

Derek leaned forward, pointing his index finger at her again. "It's disgusting the way you treat men."

Jayna dropped the pizza slice on a plate and lunged forward. She grabbed his finger and squeezed hard. "Look down at your hand, Mr. Perfect. Three fingers are pointing right back at you," her voice raised in anger. "You treat women the same way I do men. But it's okay because you're a guy?"

He yanked his finger free, scowling. There was nothing that she hated more than this double standard. Was it her fault that every guy she went out with bored her to tears? She was not going to lead them on or waste her time. And to be brought to task for it by the biggest womanizer himself had her seeing red.

Derek's eyes narrowed. She narrowed her eyes as well, not breaking his intense stare. It was a standoff. Granted, he was 'Dare Brennan'; risk-taker, no dare too stupid or dangerous for him to resist. But she was Jayna Sutton, a woman who never backed down from a fight or a staring contest.

Jovanny loudly cleared his throat. The tension between them was palpable. They were not only making each other uncomfortable, but the entire table. Still, there was no way she was going to let the big jerk think he had won.

"Okay, kids," Kylie imitated her mother, "play nice!"

"Oh, I always play nice," Derek stated, smiling at his sister before turning that lopsided grin back on Jayna.

Jayna sucked in a breath, sitting back in her chair. She imagined what would happen to the cocky grin if she smashed her fist into his chin. It took all her willpower to stop herself from finding out. Instead, she listed all the reasons she shouldn't; it would ruin her manicure, possibly injure her hand, and he was Kylie's brother. It would be assault. But damn, it would feel good!

Forcing her attention off him, she turned her eyes on her long-time friend. Kylie had been acting strangely for a while now. Jayna could attribute some of Kylie's odd mood to learning that her brother was alive. But there was something more. For a woman newly engaged, and to a movie star, no less, she didn't appear happy. Why was that?

Observing relationships of people around her was one of Jayna's favorite pastimes. Scrutinize was probably the more accurate word. She was always looking for proof that her jaded beliefs about love were wrong. So far, all she'd found was reassurance that she was correct; forever was a lie. Knights in shining armor were a fallacy, exclusive to the fairytale realm. Remaining single was a smart choice.

Her gaze shifted back to Derek. If he had one redeeming quality, it was that he didn't pretend to be a good guy. He didn't bother hiding his flaws from the world. Probably because he had so many flaws.

Chapter 2

Derek

Derek was aware of his many flaws. He didn't need Jayna to point them out. Like she was so perfect! Exiting the pub's parking lot, he cranked the stereo, letting Pearl Jam's "Animal" blast through the speakers. He sucked in a deep breath, letting it hiss out between clenched teeth.

While he'd been raised on Johnny and Waylon, he much preferred 90's head-banging music. Not that he couldn't appreciate a country song about a good ole boy drowning his sorrows in the local honkytonk over his dead dog, broken-down truck, and cheating ex. But loud, angry, heavy metal ironically soothed him. The louder and angrier, the better.

Initially, he'd been drawn to hard rock bands as an act of defiance. Being the paternal twin of the perfect son was difficult, so he chose to be the complete opposite of his flawless brother. Over time, listening to hard rock music became more about personal preference than rebellion; he had grown to truly love it. The music relaxed him, allowing him to blow off steam. Tonight, though, it wasn't helping lower his blood pressure or ease his anger.

Jayna! He slapped his palm against the steering wheel and cursed. That woman was a thorn in his side. Normally, she wouldn't have been able to sneak up on him like she had. It wasn't that he had built-in Jayna radar, although that would be helpful. Normally though, the minute Jayna entered the room everyone knew it. She was loud and obnoxious, sucking all the oxygen out of the air. Tonight, though, his attention had been diverted.

He blew out another long, frustrated breath. He had a date with an extremely hot woman, but his attention hadn't been on her either. No, as always, it had been on the one woman he could never have. And shame filled him just like it had for the past decade.

Not long after he and his date had sat down at a cozy table in Patty's Pub, Leighton Gray had breezed through the door with his sister and Bianca Grotta.

What kind of guy lusted after his brother's girl? And not just any brother, but his twin. He did! He was low-life pond scum.

However, it had always been there between him and Tommy, this competition. Maybe at first, Leighton was just one more thing to compete over. Until she became so much more.

Leighton was different from any other woman he'd ever met. She was sweet, classy, and so beautiful. And beyond his reach. He was also that guy who wanted what he couldn't have. Yes, he was truly that flawed and knew it.

Tommy was alive. The brother he thought had died three years ago in Kandahar had been held captive all that time. And for those three years of captivity, his brother had known that he'd betrayed him. That for just a brief, stupid moment he'd crossed that line, taking what wasn't his.

Last month, he and Ben had flown to the hospital in British Columbia, where Tommy was recovering from his ordeal. Tommy wouldn't look him in the eye.

Soon his brother would return home, and he had no clue how to fix this mess he'd made. Why the hell had he taken it so far that night in the cornfield, the night before they thought they'd lost Tommy? Why had he kissed his brother's girl?

In that moonlit field, he had run into Leighton and literally crossed the line. He could blame it on the accidental run-in, too much whiskey, and the magically lit corn maze, but all his good intentions dissolved in that moment. He bent and kissed those sweet lips like he'd been imagining doing for so long. With that one kiss, he ruined everything. Now, Tommy couldn't look at him. Leighton despised him and he hated himself as well. That was more than likely the cause of his anger tonight. He was pissed off at himself, and Jayna was just the tangible person he could direct it at. He smashed his palm against the steering wheel again.

"The Gentle Art of Making Enemies" by Faith No More came on and he groaned. This song should be his anthem. He was so very good at burning bridges and pissing people off.

The yellow light flashed and turned red. He hit the brake and slowed to a stop, glancing down the side street. Jamie's old truck was parked at the curb, behind Yesterday and Tomorrow. The three Js stood in the truck bed, attempting to lift out a large piece of furniture. His eyes focused on Jayna again, and even more irritation filled him. He wasn't so much annoyed that she'd run off his date, but more that she'd been right. Tanya, no Tonya, whatever her name was, she had been a distraction, nothing more. And lately, distractions were not helping to distract him.

The light turned green, and he hit the gas pedal. He barely made it five feet before he cursed again. Glancing in the rearview mirror, he lifted his foot off the gas and cranked the wheel to the left, pulling a U-turn.

If only his mother hadn't instilled such strong values and a deep sense of responsibility in him. Then there was the strong work ethic of his father. Neighbors help neighbors, friends support friends. You showed up when you lived in a small town and offered a lending hand whenever needed.

He hit the right turn signal at the intersection, where Yesterday and Tomorrow hugged the corner of Main Street and Second Street. Pulling up to the curb, he sat for a moment, watching the three women as they struggled to lift the cumbersome armoire.

Standing near the edge of the tailgate, Jayna barked out orders that Jamie and Jessica completely ignored. The other two women stood at the far end of the truck bed, and when they lifted the armoire, they nearly toppled Jayna. She screamed and Jessica dropped the corner she held, cursing loudly as it hit her knee.

It was like watching an episode of 'The Three Stooges'. The armoire was proving to be a formidable opponent, as the three women tried various techniques to move it. They tried shifting their positions. He laughed aloud. It was the most awkward dance he had ever witnessed. What he was enjoying the most, though, was the exaggerated facial expressions as they heaved and pushed. Yet the piece of furniture refused to budge. He chuckled again, which turned to a groan as red lights flashed.

Derek glanced out the back window. A police cruiser pulled in behind him. The cop put on his hat before stepping out. This was seriously not his day. His frown immediately changed to a grin as the officer stepped closer. Burke Winston was Blythe Landing Police Service's new sergeant and a former colleague of his best friend, Nick Taylor. Just last weekend, they played poker. Burke had cleaned up.

"Hey Burke," he said once his window rolled down. "Are you pulling me over for all the broken hearts I've left behind? Or for just being too damn handsome?"

"Nope. But we have gotten a lot of missing person reports on you. It seems you vanish into thin air after a couple of dates." Burke shook his head. "But that's not why I'm pulling you over. It's because of that illegal U-turn you just performed."

"Seriously?"

"License, registration, and proof of insurance, please." Burke held out his hand, his voice professional.

"Seriously?" he repeated. Reaching into the glove box, he searched for the requested documents.

Burke chuckled and shook his head. "I'll let you off with a warning. I'd suggest that you give Winona Clayton a call before she sends out a search party."

"Oh, yeah, that's not going to happen. For our third date, she invited me to dinner with her parents." Derek's eyes grew large. "I don't do dinner with parents."

"I heard you don't do third dates either," Burke chirped him.

Jayna let out a loud yell, nearly toppling off the tailgate again.

"While you're here, maybe we should help out Larry, Curly, and Moe before one of them breaks their fool neck," Derek suggested, opening his door.

The two men walked to the truck just as Jamie and Jessica shoved the armoire forward. Jayna lost her footing again, falling backward. Derek lunged, his arms wrapping around her. He stumbled backward but managed to maintain his footing. She was lighter than she looked and smelled damn good for such a pain in the ass.

He pulled her tighter, his chin dropped, and he buried his nose in her soft golden hair, inhaling. Strawberries and cream. He stiffened. This was Jayna. The woman he couldn't stand, and he was... He wasn't quite sure what he was doing. But what he needed to do was put her down.

Her head lifted, and she met his eyes.

"Get your hands off me, you big buffoon," she muttered.

"You love it," he whispered in her ear before lowering her feet to the ground and stepping back.

"I didn't need saving," she said through clenched teeth as she turned to face him.

"I'll remember that next time." Why had he even bothered?

Chapter 3

Jayna

Why had he even bothered? That man was no one's hero, least of all hers. So why had he stopped to help last Friday when they'd been unloading the armoire? Gritting her teeth, Jayna pushed Derek out of her mind and focused on the armoire that now stood for sale in Jamie's storefront.

How did Jamie refinish it so quickly? It looked amazing. But as Jayna stared at it, all she could visualize was Derek Brennan holding her in his arms.

The man was an ape. A great smelling ape.

She blinked and forced her focus to the armoire once more. Jamie had outdone herself with this piece. She'd repainted half a deep blue and the other half white. Where the blue met the white, she painted blue and white flowers that blended the two colors in such a unique way. Simply stunning.

'You love it,' he'd whispered in her ear when he caught her mid-fall. Yeah right! She blinked again. A week later, she still couldn't get him out of her mind. So not a hero. More like a zero.

Stop thinking about the ape.

Tonight was Midnight Madness and the annual Christmas window display contest. She turned her attention to the two front windows of the store. Wow, both windows looked incredible.

Last weekend, she had scoured the stockroom, looking for inspiration. And there she found it, nestled in the far corner, covered in dust and spider webs, an unexpected gem—a replica leg lamp from the beloved classic, 'A Christmas Story.' Why had Jamie kept this hidden away? It was perfect and sparked what she hoped would be the award-winning idea.

They recruited Jessica to help and spent the entire day on Sunday executing her idea. The left window would transport shoppers into the cozy living room of 'A Christmas Story', while the right window would pay homage to the second most iconic Christmas movie. In her opinion, that could only be 'Christmas Vacation'. Amidst the carefully curated scenes, Jamie's refurbished furniture would shine and hopefully not only win the contest but also boost sales.

The leg lamp cast a warm glow from its perch atop a small, cherry wood table in the cozy ambiance of the first window. Nestled beside it, a beautifully refurbished armchair invited guests to sink into its' embrace. Jamie's craftsmanship showed in every detail, from the refinished electric fireplace to the restored vintage Persian rug. A towering Christmas tree stood beside the fireplace adorned with glittering ornaments and beneath its' branches sat the familiar red foil box. It was the gift Ralphie had been obsessing over—a Red Ryder air rifle.

While the first window captured her initial vision, it was the second display that held her heart. Paying homage to the chaotic charm of 'Christmas Vacation', they had set a beautifully refinished oak harvest table using key pieces from the dinner scene in the film.

Jessica had DIY'd a remarkably lifelike deflated turkey out of Papier-Mâché. Using silicone, Jamie had painstakingly recreated Aunt Bethany's infamous green Jello mold. She had even included the embedded cat treats. The branches of the second tree had been stripped and spray-painted brown, mirroring the burned tree from the movie, with a stuffed squirrel and a cat nestled underneath its' boughs.

She opened the front door and stepped onto the sidewalk, eager to see the storefront from a customer's perspective as Jamie pulled off the brown paper that had kept it hidden. The countless hours spent perfecting the window displays were evident, and excitement and pride surged through her. They had truly captured the magic of the holiday season. No amount of money could buy the deep satisfaction she felt; it was all a result of hard work and dedication—something her mother and father would never understand.

Her parents had both been born into wealth, marrying in their early twenties. It had been an arranged marriage that had not been written in the stars but had been featured in Forbes magazine. The union had joined two powerful families. They had dutifully produced an heir, unlocking both of their trust funds. Unlike her parents, Jayna had no interest in accessing her substantial bank account. The money felt tainted, having turned her parents into stereotypical trust fund babies, a fate she was determined to avoid.

Normally, Jayna never touched her trust fund except to make charity donations, but she dipped into it to finance Jamie's dream of becoming a business owner after several banks rejected Jamie's loan applications. Jayna provided all the funds needed to start Yesterday and Tomorrow, a very wise and satisfying investment. Winning the contest tonight would bring yet another kind of satisfaction.

In the tight-knit community of Blythe Landing, the annual Christmas window contest was the holiday season's Super Bowl. The quaint main street transformed into a winter wonderland, with dazzling lights and storefront windows showcasing over-the-top, imaginative themes. Shop owners were determined to out-sparkle the others and the competition turned fierce and secretive. Brown butcher paper covered the windows, which would not be unveiled until the eve of Midnight Madness. Everyone had their eyes on the same prize: the highly coveted title of 'Best Christmas Window'.

For Jayna, the annual competition was more than just spreading holiday cheer or attracting new customers. She poured her heart and soul into every tiny detail, driven by an intense desire to win. The thought of losing yet again churned in her gut like a bad fruitcake. This year, she was determined to leave her rivals in a cloud of tinsel and glitter, proving once and for all that she was the queen of Christmas displays. She wanted first place so badly that she could taste it.

Strolling both sides of Main Street, she surveyed the competition with a critical eye. Everyone had upped their game this year. 'Notion for Lotion', Leighton's store, boasted a very impressive display, as did 'Frank's Ice-cream and Sweet Shoppe'. However, it was Frank's window that set the bar. He won every year.

Scrutinizing his display, she wrinkled her nose in disdain. It was the same scene that he always showcased, merely adding new pieces. Frank had designed a miniature village that was an exact replica of Blythe Landing during the holiday season. This year, he had introduced a skating pond with tiny skaters who actually glided across the ice. She rolled her eyes and begrudgingly admitted that it was an incredible display.

She glanced at her watch as she crossed the street. Ten to six, almost time to open. A group of four individuals, each holding clipboards, ambled down the sidewalk, pausing at each storefront. The judges. Her eyes widened. Ophelia Meddler was among them. Since when had she become a judge?

"Red alert! Judges are two stores up, and the Meddler is one of them." Jayna was breathless as she rushed into the store.

"Yeah, I heard that," Jessica said, pausing as she filled a shelf with antique snow globes.

"Why?" Was the universe out to get her?

"What happened to Earl Taylor?" Jayna's frown increased. Nick Taylor's grandfather had a great sense of humor. He would fully appreciate their window displays.

"Earl and Norm got creative, turned a riding lawnmower into a snow plow and Earl was thrown off it," Jamie answered, looking up from changing the cash register tape.

Norm Brennan was Earl's partner in crime. The two old men were notorious for their hare-brained ideas which often landed them in the emergency department.

"Is he okay?" Jayna leaned against the checkout counter.

Absently, she started rifling through a wooden box filled with antique Christmas cards. Jamie found the most incredible, unique items for the store.

"I think he just hurt his leg or back, nothing serious. But he had to step down from the judging panel this year, and somehow Ophelia got his spot." Jamie closed the lid on the cash register.

"Great!" Jayna exclaimed and then pointed. "Heads up! There they are."

The four judges stopped in front of the Christmas Vacation window, making notes on their clipboards.

"Just look at her," Jayna dramatically blew out her cheeks. "She hates it! That woman wouldn't know a good window display if it bit her in the ass."

Ophelia sported an intense frown, shaking her head back and forth as she scribbled notes.

"Can't you cast a spell over her? Give her a sense of humor." Jayna turned back to Jamie.

"You know I can't do that."

"Then how about putting a curse on her?" Jayna implored.

"I can't do that either," Jamie laughed.

"Where's the benefit of having a witch as a friend if she can't turn your enemy into a toad?"

"I'm not a witch!" Jamie exclaimed.

Jayna waved her hand. "Witch, empath, medium. It's all the same."

"It's not all the same!"

"Could you believe Derek Brennan last Friday?" Jayna changed the subject as she continued to rifle through the cards, pulling out a couple that she wanted for herself. "I don't treat men badly."

Jessica chuckled as she stepped behind the counter to set a couple more snow globes on the display shelf. "Yeah, okay."

"I don't! Come on Jamie, defend me here."

Jamie coughed loudly.

Jessica turned back around. "You two are so much alike."

Jayna's mouth dropped open. "Pardon me? Are you saying that I'm like two-date Brennan?"

"A little bit?" Jamie grimaced as she said it.

"Not just a little bit, she's the female version of him," Jessica stated bluntly.

"You're both the worst," Jayna barked out.

"Speaking of the worst best friends, and last Friday night," Jessica leaned her palms on the counter, the teasing tone leaving her voice. "Can we discuss what you two were thinking? Todd has been lighting up my phone all week!"

"I'd change my number if I were you," Jamie offered.

Jessica's head snapped to the left. "Change my number? If my FRIENDS hadn't signed me up for that dating site, then I wouldn't need to! And that's another thing," Jessica snapped her fingers. "My email is full of dating requests."

"Maybe you should change your email and password while you're at it," Jayna giggled.

"It would probably be easier to change my friends," Jessica grumbled.

"Oh, now that I would not recommend," Jayna said and reached for Jessica's hand, squeezing it. "Without us, your life would be miserably ordinary and terribly boring." Jayna's life would be empty as well without these women in it. They were her family.

"Oh, a girl could only dream," Jessica sighed.

"Okay, on your best behavior now." Jamie strolled from behind the counter to flip the open sign as holiday shoppers filled the street. "It's 6 p.m. Time to open."

Midnight Madness ran from six to ten. Why it was called 'Midnight Madness' was a mystery to Jayna. However, '10 p.m. Madness' didn't have the same ring. Despite the inaccurate name, it was certainly popular. The door chimes rang continuously, and the new cash register tape almost ran out. A successful evening for Yesterday and Tomorrow. Their window display had been a big hit as well. Jamie sold all the displayed furniture and more from inside the store.

An unexpected warm front had settled in earlier in the week, dispelling the usual December chill, which likely was the reason for the largest crowd they'd ever seen. At 10 p.m., they flipped the "closed" sign, marking the end of a very lucrative event.

"It's such a lovely evening," Jamie said. "And still quite warm. It would be a shame to waste it. I have firewood in the back of my truck. We should have a winter bonfire by the river."

"Oh, that's a great idea. I'll run home while you close and grab marshmallows," Jessica offered.

"Whatever," Jayna grumbled.

"Come on, it will cheer you up." Jamie gently nudged her. "And we did win third place."

"Third place is not winning," Jayna pouted. First place went to Frank again, and Leighton's store took second. "Ophelia seriously has it out for us."

"I agree. But Frank and Leighton both had incredible window displays as well," Jamie offered, always the diplomat. "We should ask Leighton if she wants to join us."

Jayna held in the groan and her breath while Jamie called Leighton, praying that the other woman would decline.

"Leighton's in too." Jamie grinned.

"Look what I found." Jessica came out of the back room with thick moving blankets and a bottle of ice wine. "Here, take these." Jessica shoved the blankets and wine toward Jayna. "I'll run home and grab some plastic glasses and extra gloves as well. Meet you there."

"Great! Ice wine and the ice queen will both be joining us." Jayna scrunched up her nose at the way-too-sweet wine. "Perfect!"

"Why don't you like Leighton?" Jamie asked her as they walked out the back door to her battered truck.

"Why do you like her?" Jayna shot back.

"She's nice."

"Never said she wasn't." Jayna pulled open the heavy rusty door. "You made decent money this year. Why don't you buy a new truck to replace this bucket of bolts?"

"Shh, you'll hurt Bessy's feelings. She is a great truck."

Jayna shook her head and hid the smile when it took three tries to get Bessy running. "You have questionable taste in friends and trucks."

"That's what my dad always says every time you're around," Jamie shifted the ancient truck into drive and headed to the parking lot beside the bridge where Jayna had left her truck earlier. "Thanks for all your help tonight. The display was first-place worthy, regardless of the judges' opinion."

"Yeah, yeah," Jayna grumbled.

The unseasonably warm evening air was filled with the sound of crackling wood along with the laughter of Jamie and Leighton. The scent of the burning wood mingled with the earthy aroma of the riverbank. It was pure magic.

Jayna leaned back on the log, staring up at a sky filled with a thousand twinkling stars. In the city, with its relentless lights and smog, the stars were lost.

For years, all she could think about was escaping this small town's suffocating bubble of familiarity and resistance to change. She had done exactly that, heading to school in Toronto. She'd shared an apartment with Kylie while they both earned their nursing degrees. When school finished, she took a job in the busy ER of Toronto Hospital.

It had been the big adventure she'd always craved, a place where anonymity reigned supreme. However, the novelty wore off quickly, and she found herself missing the simple pleasure of being greeted by name on the street. She even missed the scent of manure and green grass in the summer. It was a stark contrast to the overpowering odor of exhaust fumes and burnt street meat from the bustling carts lining the busy streets.

The sweet smell of Blythe Landing wasn't the only thing she missed. She missed the silence. In her city apartment, falling asleep had been a challenge, with the constant noise of honking horns and loud sirens. Yet, back in her hometown, with her bedroom window open, she realized it wasn't silent after all. The country had its own symphony: the sound of crickets in the fields, the rustle of wind through the cornstalks. It was the soundtrack of her childhood.

"Look who I found," Jessica announced, emerging from the path, waving her arm behind her.

Ben Brennan, Nick Taylor, and—just her luck—Derek the ape-man appeared behind Jessica. What had she ever done to karma to deserve this kind of payback?

Jessica flashed her a knowing smile. Okay, maybe signing Jessica up for the dating app had earned her a little payback.

"Well played," she mouthed to Jessica.

Ben opened the cooler and started passing around beer cans while the men settled around the fire. Jessica poured out her syrupy sweet wine into glasses. Jayna took one and dumped it out after two sips. It tasted like cough syrup, except cough syrup tasted better. She leaned back on the log, her eyes travelling around the gathered group she'd known since kindergarten. It truly felt good to be back home. But instead of contributing to the conversation she found herself observing.

Who needed reality TV when real life was more interesting? Last week at Patty's Pub, she had observed Kylie and Jovanny closely. Now she found herself staring at Nick Taylor across the flickering flames. The cop had called off his wedding to Piper Reynolds, Leighton's best friend. He insisted it was just a postponement now that Tommy had been found alive. He wanted his best friend to be there when he tied the knot.

But was that really the whole story? Nick's eyes held a haunted look, which was hardly surprising. Every day, as a city cop, he faced trauma. Jayna knew the difficulty of disconnecting after a long shift, fighting against heart-wrenching images that haunted her sleep. However, there seemed to be something more troubling him.

Nick looked miserable. He had ever since Kylie had started

dating the movie star. Was Kylie's engagement the cause of the perpetual frown Nick was sporting?

While rooming with Kylie during nursing school, she'd been aware of the brief fling between her friend and the cop. And it ended badly between them. There was a reason why a brother's best friend was off limits. When the relationship soured, as they tended to, the guy was still around. Kylie seriously should have known better. And Jayna should have had the same insight when she'd taken up with Kylie's brother in high school. Seriously stupid move.

However, the person that she truly felt sorry for was Piper, the sweet schoolteacher. Judging by Nick's current state, the woman was in for a world of hurt. Jayna wondered if the wedding would ever be back on.

There it was. More validation to add to her oath of remaining single.

Jayna turned her gaze to Derek Brennan, perched on the log next to Nick, and memories flooded back, blurring her vision. Suddenly, she was fifteen again, sitting in this very spot. Derek's eyes had met hers across the fire. He'd looked straight through her, as if denying that just the weekend before, she had been the girl on his arm, the one he'd been kissing. The girl he'd rejected when he learned she was still a virgin. He couldn't get out of the back of his hand-me-down jeep fast enough.

Derek Brennan didn't do virgins.

He also didn't do feelings.

Never in her life had she felt so humiliated. She'd never hated anyone before.

With Lacey Bellamy by his side, he sat there with his lips all over the new girl. Lacey, with her blossoming modeling career and effortless beauty, had made Jayna feel so small and inadequate. Yet, even with the popular Lacey next to him, his attention had been diverted. As always, it had been on Leighton, his brother's girl.

For years, Derek had been the guy she wanted, the boy she had dreamed of. Her crush on him had been huge, and then he'd crushed her.

It was the last crush she'd ever had. He was the last guy she'd ever chased.

Having lost her virginity to a guy in twelfth grade who meant nothing was something she deeply regretted. And she blamed Derek for that. Derek had changed her that night when he'd acted like virginity was the plague. He'd made her feel unworthy, which then caused her to place such little worth on something that should have been so special.

"Nick, how's your grandfather?" Jessica's voice pulled her out of the past. She blinked away the painful memory.

"He's doing okay," Nick answered.

"What exactly happened?" Leighton questioned.

"Well, he and Norm decided to strap the oversized box from his new flat screen on the front of the riding lawn mower. Then they attempted to plow the driveway with it."

"Hey, that's a great idea," Ben said.

"It would have been if the snow had been lighter," Nick chuckled. "But it had been a heavy wet snow and, well, Grandad went flying. Luckily, he landed in a snowbank, but he tweaked his back."

"Those two," Jayna laughed, forcing her mood to lighten. High school was ruined for her by Derek Brennan. She wasn't going to allow him any more power over her life.

She pretended he wasn't seated across from her. It helped that he was ignoring her as well. Despite the ape-man's presence, it turned out to be a wonderful evening. She loved sitting around the fire, enjoying the unseasonably warm weather with good friends. It was great to be home.

"Congratulations on second place," Jamie said to Leighton.

"Thanks, and congrats on taking third place." Leighton held up her glass of cough syrup in a toast.

"We were cheated!" Jayna exclaimed, and her great mood vanished just like it had when Derek walked down the path. "The Meddler has it in for us."

"Not that you didn't deserve second place," she quickly

added, meeting Leighton's shocked expression at her sudden outburst. "But Frank wins every year with the same display."

"Your window display was just too imaginative for Ophelia," Nick offered. "Which should be taken as a compliment."

But the compliment just wasn't enough. Jayna had wanted to win this year. She hated coming in second place and definitely third place. What she hated most though, was that she still noticed that Derek only had eyes for Leighton. More than she hated losing, she hated not being seen.

Jayna trailed behind the group, making her way toward the parking lot. Only her truck remained, along with Derek Brennan, who stood in the center, scratching his head.

"Looks like Nick forgot he was my ride home," Derek said and shrugged.

She tossed the moving blankets into the back of her truck and let out a loud snort. "Your best friend forgot you? That's classic!"

"Classic Nick these days," Derek agreed. "He's been really distracted."

After hitting the key fob, Jayna opened the driver's door. "So, I'm guessing you need a ride home?"

"Looks that way," he said, staring at her. "Thanks."

How sour did thanking her taste in his mouth?

Derek opened the passenger door and jumped in. "You haven't had too much to drink, have you? My mom warned me to never drive with anyone under the influence."

"Not nearly as much as you!" He'd been pounding back the beer at the bonfire.

He raised a skeptical brow.

"I had half a glass of ice wine," she made a face. "I have no idea how Jamie and Jessica drink that. It tastes like cough syrup."

She fired up the engine and snapped on her seat belt. "So, why is Nick so distracted?"

"No idea." Derek fastened his seatbelt.

"You haven't asked him?"

"Why would I?" He turned, gaping at her.

"Because he's your best friend. And that's what friends do. They listen, offer support and advice."

"They do?" Derek scoffed. "Is there a friend's rule book that I missed reading?"

Now she scoffed. "I'm forgetting who I'm talking to. You'd need a soul to be that kind of friend. Nick's better off, actually. Any advice you'd offer wouldn't be worth taking."

"Ha ha." Derek leaned forward and changed the station on the radio.

"Hey!"

"Country music sucks," Derek grumbled, settling on a rock station.

"Says no one ever. At least no one with taste."

Derek shook his head. "Less than a minute, and you've called me soulless, a bad friend who offers terrible advice, and now tasteless."

"Yeah, I must be slowing down," Jayna laughed.

Derek reached inside her purse which sat on the console between them.

"Hey," she snapped. "And without boundaries. Didn't your mother teach you that it's bad manners to rummage through a woman's purse?" How had she drawn the short straw and got stuck chauffeuring Two-Date Brennan home?

"And I have bad manners with no boundaries," he chuckled, holding up a foil-wrapped package. "Why do you have so many glow sticks?"

"I bought them to hand out to the kids who came into Jamie's store tonight."

"Ah." Derek reached into her purse again and pulled out a handful. "Turn right," he instructed.

"Why?"

"Do you want to administer a little payback to the Meddler?"

"Always." She paused at the parking lot exit, looking left at the bridge that led towards his home, then glanced right.

"I have an idea."

"Like Nick, I'm also too smart to listen to any of your advice or IDEAS," she emphasized the last word.

"It's a good one!" he waggled both brows.

"A good one?" Jayna snorted again. "I don't think you've ever had a good idea in your entire life!"

"True story," he admitted. "But tonight, I have an absolutely brilliant one. Come on, you must be curious, otherwise you would have turned left by now."

"Derek, your ideas, brilliant or not, always end badly. Someone ends up bleeding or needing a trip to the ER to reset a broken bone. Nine times out of ten, the police are called."

"Not this time, I promise." He held up his right hand, which was filled with glow sticks. "No risk of bodily harm or property damage. No police. I swear!"

Her eyes narrowed again. Good thing she had great wrinkle serum because five minutes in Brennan's presence could cause permanent crow's feet.

"I'm listening." She couldn't believe she just heard those words pass her lips.

Another five minutes later, Jayna parked her truck a few feet from Ophelia Meddler's house.

"Pull ahead," Derek instructed. "You're under a lamppost."

She shook her head. This was not going to end well.

He tossed her mitts at her as they climbed out of the truck.

"Oh, nice to see that Nick made it home!" Derek's voice was laced with sarcasm as they walked up the sidewalk.

"I still can't believe he built a house across the street from Ophelia."

"Land was cheap."

"That I can believe!" Jayna paused beside Derek, staring at Ophelia Meddler's darkened house. "What is this brilliant idea of yours?"

He crossed the road and stepped onto the front lawn. "Come on," he whispered.

Crouching down, he began to form a mound in the snow.

"We're building a snowman?" Jayna bent down beside him.

"That's how I'm getting back at her?"

"Not just a snowman, but snow aliens. Come on, help me. We need three mounds."

When had she last built a snowman? Probably when she was around twelve. But she had never done it as a prank. Derek hadn't lied. There would be no bodily harm, property damage, or police involvement in this prank. She was just failing to see how this would qualify as a way to get back at the Meddler. Three mounds of snow on the busybody's front lawn? Derek was known for his bad ideas, but this was just lame.

After digging out two eyes on each snow mound, Derek tore open a glow-stick package and gave it a snap. Setting it inside one of the eyeholes, Jayna suddenly understood his 'prank'. She grabbed two glow sticks, activated the chemicals, and placed them inside the eyeholes of her mound. Stepping back, she giggled. The three mounds with glowing eyes did indeed look kind of spooky.

"Okay, now go knock on her door and run." Derek pointed to the dark front porch.

"Why me?"

"Because it was my idea. Besides, you're the one dishing out the revenge," Derek answered and then waggled his eyebrows again. "Come on, Jayna, you're not chicken, are you?"

No one had called her chicken since she was twelve either. However, the taunt still had the same effect; her back stiffened and her chin jutted out. "I am not chicken!"

With determination, she brushed the snow off her knees and marched up the driveway toward the front porch. Nicky-Nicky-Nine- Doors was another thing she hadn't done in a very long time. With three loud pounds against the heavy wood door, she added two taps to the doorbell and ran like her life depended on it.

"Come on, Brennan," she called as she raced past him down the sidewalk.

Derek caught up and seized Jayna's arm. He pulled her into the bushes bordering the adjacent property. They crouched down, peering through the branches as lights came on in Ophelia's house.

Ophelia swung open her front door and let out a shriek. The woman placed a hand against her fuzzy housecoat, just over her heart. Her gaze fixed on the glowing eyes of the three snow mounds on her front lawn. "Who's out there? If that's you again, Bobby McDermott, I will call your mother. You know I will!"

"She definitely will, poor kid," Derek whispered.

The porch lights of the house they hid in front of switched on. Jayna sucked in a breath.

As Shamus stepped out onto his front porch, he spotted them. Derek greeted him with a swift wave before holding a finger in front of his mouth.

With a nod of understanding, Shamus turned his attention to his alarmed neighbor. "What seems to be the trouble, Ophelia?"

"Look!" She pointed to her front lawn.

Shamus let out a loud guffaw. "I see the mothership has sent down drones to retrieve their queen."

"Are you saying that I'm an alien queen?" Ophelia braced her hands on both hips.

"Well, it would explain a lot. You are far from human."

"I'm far from human? You're the one who's not human. You're a caveman!" Ophelia yelled in her grating voice. "A bagpipe-playing caveman and a bad one at that!"

"A bad one?" Shamus bellowed back. "I'll show you a bad one!"

Shamus slammed his door as he stomped back into his house.

"Let's go," Derek grabbed Jayna's hand again and made a dash for her truck. The sound of doors slamming followed by bagpipe music filled the air.

"Shamus, you stop that incessant noise right now!" They heard Ophelia scream as lights came on in the surrounding houses.

"We just woke the entire neighborhood." Jayna moaned. "And reignited the Ophelia-Shamus feud."

"Mission accomplished," Derek held up his hand for a high five and she punched him in the arm instead.

They reached the truck just as a police cruiser turned the corner. It slowed and came to a stop. The window rolled down and Burke leaned out, shining a flashlight on both of their faces. "Well, well, well. I shouldn't be surprised, yet somehow, I am!"

"What's up, Burke?" Derek inquired, all innocent-like.

"That's what I was about to ask you." The cop's eyes narrowed.

"We're just out for an evening stroll," Derek maintained eye contact.

"Is taking an evening stroll illegal?" Jayna stepped next to Derek.

"Dispatch received a complaint from Mrs. Meddler. Apparently, someone built menacing snowmen on her front lawn."

"That's against the law as well?" Jayna's brows shot up.

"No, but disturbing the peace is. She said that same someone also banged loudly on her door."

"We wouldn't know anything about that," Derek deadpanned. "Like we told you, we were just out for an evening stroll."

"I thought you two hated one another?" Burke continued the interrogation. "And if you weren't involved, then why are your knees wet?" He shone the flashlight down, illuminating Derek's wet jeans.

"Jayna pushed me into a snowbank. Like you said, she hates me." Derek shook his head. "She's real mean."

"Why are her knees wet, too?" Burke moved the flashlight over her legs.

"Because he returned the favor," Jayna answered. "He's such a brute."

The bagpipes grew louder, as did Ophelia's screeching. Burke let out a loud, annoyed sigh. "Now I have to deal with Shamus too. If you two join forces, this town will not be safe."

After rolling up his window, Burke continued down the street.

"No police will be involved, I swear," Jayna imitated him. "Get in the truck before I leave you stranded. Last time I ever listen to you."

Chapter 4

Derek

"Last time I ever listen to you," Derek mimicked Jayna's voice, hitting the haughtiness dead-on. Ungrateful, that's what she was—on top of being annoying, argumentative, and abrasive.

No good deed goes unpunished, his grandmother always said.

Case in point. It was Monday morning, and he was still fuming over Jayna's lack of appreciation. It had been the prank of the century. Okay, maybe not the century, but it had been pretty creative. Ophelia had screamed, and the cops had shown up. What more could you ask for?

What he needed to do was forget about Jayna. She wasn't constantly around his parent's house now that his sister was older and engaged. Though it was a small town, it wasn't so small that he couldn't avoid her.

Turning onto the bridge, he headed to the new coffee shop. He had meetings downtown today and was dragging his ass. A strong espresso was exactly what this morning called for.

He loved his job as a civil engineer with the new build construction company. From designing the blueprints to the smell of freshly turned soil on the first day, he enjoyed the hands-on aspects. The hum of heavy machinery as the numerous trades turned the vision into reality was such a sweet sound. However, he loathed the meetings. And there were so many meetings: architects, project managers, surveyors, urban planners, government officials, health and safety inspectors, contractors, and subcontractors. Meeting after meeting, the list seemed endless.

Today's meeting, though, was with the worst of them all—the investors. Securing funding for projects was a necessary evil. But schmoozing with wealthy investors to sell the vision of turning a simple farm field into a mini village made his skin crawl. He felt out of place in the polished conference rooms, surrounded by people in expensive suits more interested in profit margins than the quality of construction. His head already started to pound at the thought of today's discussions about budgets, timelines, and returns on investments. He should get a double espresso.

As he drove through town, he almost gave himself whiplash. It wasn't an uncommon sight to find his grandfather on a bench with his best friend, Earl even on a cold winter morning. However, this morning, they were not alone. Jayna was snuggled between them, a large takeout coffee in her hand.

He slowed and pulled into a parking spot, killing the engine. The two men were notorious for getting into trouble on their own; they certainly didn't need help from the likes of her. As he shoved open the door, he heard their laughter.

"Hey, Pops. Morning, Earl. If she's holding a gun on you, blink twice."

"Ha, ha," Jayna chuckled. "Good morning to you, too. You're obviously not a morning person either."

"Either?" Derek's forehead creased.

"Well, you're a grumpy jerk at night," Jayna lifted the steaming paper cup to her lips, taking a sip, and held his stare over the plastic lid. "And apparently, morning brings no improvement to your personality."

Norm let out a loud guffaw. "She's got your number, my boy." He held up his cup. "Jayna bought Earl and me one of those fancy coffees from the new shop that just opened."

Earl held up his cup as well. "Pretty tasty! It has that fancy foam milk on top."

"Oh, here she comes!" Jayna sat forward and pointed to the sidewalk across the street. She pulled three glow-sticks out of her purse and snapped them, handing one each to Earl and Norm.

"Jayna was filling us in on your adventures the other night, or should I say misadventures?" Norm chuckled and wrapped the glow-stick around his coffee cup, as did Earl.

"We didn't have an adventure," he grumbled. He'd only helped her administer a little payback. It didn't mean anything. It certainly didn't mean that he liked her. Now she was about to get the two troublemakers into even more trouble. They didn't need any help!

"Morning, Ophelia," Earl called out, holding up his coffee so the woman could see the glow stick wrapped around it.

Ophelia paused at the bottom of the stairs leading up to City Hall, where she worked as a clerk. She turned and glared across the street, her mouth dropping open at the sight of the glowing bands on the coffee cups.

"Heard you had some strange visitors the other night," Norm deadpanned.

"I should have known you'd be involved." Ophelia pointed at Jayna and then moved her finger to Derek. "And of course, you as well, Derek Brennan. You were probably the mastermind behind it!"

Ophelia spun around and stomped up the stairs.

"She's so calling your mom," Jayna snorted, turning her stare back at him.

"Sure is," his grandfather agreed.

"Well, gentlemen, and Derek." Jayna snorted again, "It's been a pleasure, but I have City Hall business to conduct."

She stood, fishing inside her purse, and pulled out a white ticket. "Seems Shamus was issued a noise violation for playing his bagpipes after 11 p.m., and I told him I'd take care of it."

"Don't look directly into the Meddler's eyes," Earl warned. "She'll turn you into stone."

"I'll be careful," Jayna waved as she crossed the street.

"That girl's a hoot," Earl commented.

"And not too hard on the eyes." Norm gave Derek a pointed

stare. "Why aren't you asking her out?"

Derek stared at his grandfather. Seriously? Ask Jayna out. Was the old man losing his mind? "Because she's Jayna Sutton! My little sister's most annoying friend."

"She's rich," Norm continued. "It's just as easy to marry a rich girl."

"I'm not looking for a girlfriend or a wife!"

"And that's a damn shame. Some lucky guy will scoop that girl up and you'll be one sorry ass when it happens," Norm said sternly.

"You'd never have a dull moment with her," Earl added.

"Well, I need to get my sorry ass to work," Derek changed the subject. The coffee Jayna brought the men must be spiked because she was as far from wife material as he was from becoming someone's husband. Not even if she was the last woman on earth.

Chapter 5

Jayna

Not even if he was the last man on earth. Eleven hours later, Jayna was still seething. Where did Derek Brennan get off acting like she was the troublemaker instead of him? He was the biggest hell-raiser this town had ever seen.

Forcing her mind off him, she tried to concentrate on the charting for her chest pain patient. Her blue ombre nails tapped rhythmically on the keyboard as she typed in her nursing notes. But as she stared at the monitor, all she could see was Derek's stupid face.

He had stood there, arms crossed over his chest, looking down his nose at her like she was about to corrupt his grandfather and Earl. Like the pair needed any help. They were the original hell-raisers of Blythe Landing.

Derek had even ruined the enjoyment of messing with Ophelia Meddler. When she walked into City Hall to pay Shamus's noise violation fine, Jayna had still been angry.

"You can't pay someone else's ticket," Ophelia stated in that nails-on-the-chalkboard voice.

"Where does it say that?" Jayna had shot back. "I see 'issued to' and 'payable to,' but I don't see anywhere that it states the ticket can only be paid by the person it was issued to."

Ophelia had let out a loud harrumph before handing over the debit machine. And if Derek's high and mighty expression hadn't still filled Jayna's mind, she would have been able to enjoy the pissed-off expression that had taken over Ophelia's.

The sliding doors opened from the ambulance bay. Lance and

his partner, Sonny, wheeled in a teenager. Jayna closed out the patient's chart and stood, a sudden smile replacing the frown. Lance was the perfect distraction to rid her of images of the Neanderthal. The paramedic was just simply perfection.

But he's taken, she reminded herself. With great effort, she contained the eye roll as she watched Lance make goo-goo eyes at Greta across the room.

Lance and Sonny carefully transferred the injured boy onto the hospital bed, and Jayna grabbed a blank chart. Her gaze fixated on Lance as he reassured the frightened teen. There was just something about the man that drew her in. She had nothing in common with the men she dated and that had been fine because it wasn't like she was looking for something deeper. But casual dating was losing its appeal. With Lance, she would be able to have a conversation about work, he'd understand the exhaustion, the heartbreak, the adrenaline rush of a trauma case. He'd know.

It truly impressed her just how good he was at his job already for being fresh out of school. He was a good paramedic but would end up being a great one. There was something about the way he talked to his patients and kept a level head when things were falling apart. He was not just some good-looking guy. There was something... real about him. And maybe that's exactly what she needed. Someone who would challenge her not only emotionally but intellectually. Lance could be the very one to force her to look inward, pushing her to confront her fears about commitment. He could be the one who she could create a deep connection with. He could take away the loneliness.

If only he would look at her the way he did Greta. Instead, he saw her the way most men did. Jayna was the good time girl until they met the woman to settle down with.

"What do we have here?" she asked, forcing away the hurt.

Sonny grinned. "Meet our future Olympian. Once, of course, barn-roof skiing becomes a recognized sport."

Jayna raised an eyebrow. "Barn-roof skiing?"

"He tried skiing off the Fraser barn roof. If he hadn't caught so much air, he would have landed in the hay bales at the bottom," Lance explained.

Jayna knew the farm. The barn had a steeply sloped roof that did kind of resemble a ski jump.

"What's your name?" Jayna asked the teenager.

"Derek Ainsley." The teen grimaced in pain when she touched his swollen and bruised left leg.

Jayna grimaced at the name. It figured that Blythe Landing's latest daredevil would be named Derek. "Well, Eddie the Eagle, let's get you to X-ray." No way was she saying his name out loud.

"Eddie the Eagle?" The teen scrunched up his face in confusion.

"Seriously?" Jayna glanced up from the clipboard where she marked off triage items one by one. She ticked off an X-ray that nurses had the authority to order. "I would have thought that movie would be one of your favorites."

"It's one of mine," Sonny chimed in.

"Never heard of it," Lance added.

Jayna's head snapped up again. The hot medic just lost half a point. Now he was a solid 9.5.

"You'll have lots of time to catch up on movies while your bones are healing." Sonny gave a gentle squeeze to the boy's shoulder as the porter wheeled the stretcher to the diagnostic department. "Not sure about my partner, though. I may need to add movie education to his orientation list."

Sonny turned, staring at Lance, shaking his head. "How have you never seen that movie?"

"Not much of a movie buff," Lance shrugged again and dropped another half point.

Not a movie buff? Movies were one of Jayna's passions. Lance met her eyes with his thick-lashed hazel ones. Wow, the man was dreamy. The fact that he wasn't a movie watcher was not a deal breaker. She still had her best friends for Sunday movie night. He's taken, she reminded herself yet again. She had no business rating or dreaming about the dreamy paramedic.

"Congratulations, Sonny. Hear you're a grandfather." She turned her attention back to the older medic.

Sonny smiled proudly and whipped out his phone. Jayna barely contained another eye roll. She'd only mentioned it to be polite. Now she would have to gush over pictures of a newborn who most likely resembled an old man. But she really liked Sonny. He suited his name. Every time he entered the ER, he brought in positivity. He was a ray of sunshine.

Lance walked over to Greta and this time her eyes did roll.

"The kid is lucky that he didn't break more than just a leg," Sonny pulled her attention back.

"Let's hope the X-ray agrees." Jayna ordered not only bilateral leg X-ray but spine and neck as well.

Hopefully, the teen learned his lesson and outgrew his daredevil tendencies. She prayed that was the only trait he shared with his namesake. That he wouldn't become an adult who fearlessly risked his life while terrified to show emotion—a man who bailed when life got real or complicated.

Chapter 6

Derek

Derek wasn't too proud to admit that he bailed when life got too real or complicated. It was his M.O. Facing danger? No problem. Working hard? Piece of cake. But when emotions were involved, he walked. Hell, he ran as fast as his legs could carry him in the opposite direction. Or he skulked in hallways like he was now.

Tommy was home from rehab, and still angry. Angry at the world and even angrier with Derek, who had no idea what to say or how to make it right.

Ben leaned on the door frame of Tommy's room, flashing a bright, easy smile. And here Derek was, skulking and eavesdropping as Ben said all the right things to Tommy. All the things Derek should say to his twin. But nausea churned in the pit of his stomach, burning back up his throat, causing a lump filled with regret and guilt. It made speaking impossible. Words were beyond him.

The guilt was becoming all-consuming. Derek should never have bailed on Afghanistan. They had planned to sign up for the armed forces together. He should have been at his brother's side, having his back instead of staying home, and stabbing him in it. And by the hostility he saw in Tommy's eyes, his brother agreed.

Derek may not have shown it at the funeral they had thrown for Tommy, but he had been irrevocably shattered by his twin's presumed death. Now, miraculously, Tommy was home and had survived a nightmare, offering them both a second chance.

However, it felt just as insurmountable as death. Tommy was alive, and now Derek was the one dead to him.

A lifetime of memories assaulted Derek as they sat round the large harvest table for Sunday dinner. The good, the bad, and the unimaginable. It should not feel so unnatural and awkward.

Countless times they had sat at this table, angry at the other, sometimes even sporting a black eye or fat lip. Other times, they joked around, and made fun of each other. It was all the normal fighting and teasing that was brotherly love.

Yet it was the dinner in October, three years earlier, that stuck out the most in his memory. The dinner two men interrupted, delivering the devastating news that Tommy was lost in an explosion and presumed dead.

He pushed the food around his plate, forcing that memory away. His eyes drifted across the table. Tommy appeared just as uncomfortable and refused to look his way. His brother's silence cut deeper than any insult could have and hurt more than a hard and fast punch to the nose.

That first Sunday dinner was pure torture. When the following Sunday rolled around with Leighton invited, he pulled a Derek and bailed. If last week was torture, this one with Leighton sitting at the table would be combustible.

This was probably one of the very first Sunday dinners where he sat at Patty's Pub ordering the Guinness stew. If he couldn't enjoy his mom's pot roast, then this was the second-best option.

"Isn't it Sunday?"

His head shot up, the spoon halfway to his mouth. Jayna Sutton. Karma had it in for him.

"Yeah, so?"

"So, your mom always cooks a feast. One you never miss!"

He lowered the spoon, setting it in the steaming bowl. How he wished there was another restaurant in town. Sure, there was the steak house by the river. However, he'd dated the chef who worked there. More like they went on one date, and he stood her up for the second. Apparently, she was still holding a grudge. Last time he'd been there, he ordered a medium rare T-bone and a baked potato. The steak had been burnt crispy and the potato was undercooked. "Compliments of the chef," the server had smugly told him when she set his plate in front of him.

He glared up at Jayna. "For someone who claims to have zero interest in me, you sure are keeping close tabs."

She pulled out a chair, and his eyebrows shot up. "Oh, please sit down. Or don't! I was enjoying my stew and beer."

"Don't let me stop you," Jayna gave him a toothy smile.

"You're ruining my appetite."

"I didn't want to mention it, but you're getting pudgy around the middle. It probably wouldn't hurt to skip a meal and lay off the beer."

His jaw clenched. "I am not!"

Setting her elbows on the table, she placed her chin on a closed fist, staring at him. Did the woman never blink? It was creepy.

"What?" he used his best grumpy old man voice.

"Why aren't you at home with the rest of your family?"

"No reason. I just wanted some alone time." He emphasized the word alone.

"I heard Tommy's home. How is he doing?" Jayna failed to catch his not-so-subtle hint to leave.

"He's doing okay," he answered evasively.

"Kylie mentioned Leighton was invited to dinner tonight." Jayna lifted her chin and then slapped her hands against the table. "Oh, that's why you're here!"

"Why would that be the reason?"

She scoffed loudly. "Come on Derek, it's painfully obvious that you're hung up on her."

"I am NOT. Ivy, can I have a takeout container and my bill, please?" he asked the server. What was painfully obvious was that Jayna was a pain in his ass.

Chapter 7

Jayna

It was painfully obvious that Derek was still hung up on Leighton. Jayna wasn't quite sure why it bothered her. It just did.

Because it was wrong, that was why!

Leighton was Tommy's girl. His brother's girl! Did the man have no loyalty? Or morals?

She heaved a heavy sigh. When had she developed a moral compass, or cared what others were doing? Was she becoming one of the small-town busybodies who always poked their nose into everyone else's business?

Damn, she hoped not. But she was on the fast track to becoming a bitter old maid. Did people still call single, childless women old maids? Whatever the term was now, she felt like she was staring it straight in the eye.

The door chimes jangled loudly as she pushed open the heavy metal door of the hair salon.

"Hey, Nessa. I need more shampoo." Jayna stepped behind the counter and helped herself to a bottle from the shelf. Vanessa was pulling a straightening iron through a blonde woman's hair. "Hey, Piper. Wow, that's quite the sexy cut."

Piper glanced over her shoulder, eyes huge and panicked.

The phone rang and Jayna answered it. "Vanessa's Scissory. You grow it, we mow it."

"Jayna!" Vanessa moaned from behind her.

Flipping the pages of the scheduling book on the counter, she picked up a pencil. Jayna had spent enough time in this salon to be familiar with the procedure. "Next week for a cut and color. How about Tuesday around two? I need your name?"

Speaking of old maids, she recognized that nasally voice instantly. "Can you spell that, please? O-P-H-E-L-I-E." She messed up the spelling on purpose.

Ophelia sounded annoyed as she corrected Jayna.

"What, E-A? Oh, I-A. And what's your last name? Metter?" She messed that up, too. "Sorry, Mettler, with two T's?"

Ophelia snapped back with the correct spelling of her last name.

"Got it, Meddler." Oh, this was too easy.

She caught Vanessa's shocked expression and tried not to laugh.

"So, you said you wanted a cut and color? Did you want blue highlights or green?"

Oh, that got quite the reaction, along with a gasp from Vanessa.

"Are you sure? So maybe purple instead?"

She held the phone receiver away from her ear as the piercing voice intensified. "No, just your regular color, which is bright orange?"

Jayna smirked and raised both eyebrows at Vanessa. "Really ma'am, that's not nice. There is no need to yell." She paused and listened. "No, I'm not new. I've worked here for years."

Now Ophelia was demanding to know her name.

"Uh, Jamie." She threw her friend under the bus. "Yes, I still own my store. I just moonlight here sometimes. And you should really consider the purple highlights. Hello? Hello?"

Jayna hung up the phone. "Well, I guess Jamie will get an earful next time she runs into Lady O."

"Jayna." Vanessa had both hands on her hips and wore an exasperated expression. "I'll be the one getting the ear full."

"What? It was only the Meddler." Her hands went up in the air. "Do you know how many times that woman got me in shit when I was a teenager?"

"It was probably well deserved," Vanessa shot back.

"I have that day off. Can I come in and help? I could mix the hair dye for you." A vision filled her mind of Vanessa spinning the chair around so Ophelia could see the finished cut and color. A bright vibrant green that would contrast well with the red of Ophelia's shocked face.

"That is very tempting," Vanessa couldn't contain the laughter any longer. "But no. I run a professional salon."

Vanessa pulled the cape from around Piper's shoulders. The shy woman had a brand-new look.

"Wow, Piper. Seriously, wow!" Jayna whistled.

Normally, Piper kept her hair tied in a neat, low bun. Vanessa had cut in bouncy layers with angled bangs and added caramel lowlights to the light natural blonde. The schoolteacher was smoking hot. Or she could be if her wardrobe wasn't so conservative.

Piper moved to the counter, pulling her wallet out of her purse.

"Do you have anywhere you have to be right now?" Jayna asked her.

"No, why?" Piper's newly shaped brows furrowed.

"Do you have much credit on your credit card?" Jayna tapped the card in Piper's hand.

"Yes."

"Let's go, hot stuff. Or almost hot stuff." Jayna grinned.

"Go where?" Piper's voice held a hint of terror.

"You remind me of Ms. Brown, the second-grade teacher. Is she still teaching?"

"No, she retired last spring. I took over her class in the fall."

"Did the position include her wardrobe?"

Piper glanced over her shoulder in confusion as she swiped her credit card. "No, why?"

"Because," Jayna answered honestly. "You dress exactly like her."

Piper frowned, looking down at the pink sweater set she wore. "I dress work appropriate," she defended.

Jayna snorted. "Maybe it's work appropriate, but it's not age appropriate. And it certainly does not match that sexy new haircut."

Vanessa shot an apologetic look Piper's way, followed by another exasperated frown in Jayna's direction.

Jayna shrugged. She wasn't being mean to Piper. Not on purpose. She was trying to be helpful, but tact was not her strong suit. She softened her tone, grabbing Piper's arm.

"Come on. Let's finish this makeover."

Jayna steered Piper through the door and toward her vehicle. She'd driven her red jeep today and hoped there was enough trunk space for the bags. Piper's wardrobe was in serious need of an intervention.

"Buckle up, buttercup. We're going to do some damage to that credit card." And when Piper's card was maxed out, Jayna would pull out her platinum card. This was a worthy charity.

They spent the afternoon at the nearby mall, visiting store after store. Standing in front of the changing room mirror in jeans and a zip-up magenta jersey knit shirt, Piper was gorgeous. Who knew underneath the loose-fitting clothes that the meek teacher was hiding curves and cleavage?

"Jessica sent a text. Everyone is at Patty's. Let's pay and head over there."

"Everyone? Who is everyone?" Piper looked like a deer caught in the headlights.

"Everyone who counts," Jayna chuckled. Nick Taylor was going to lose his mind when he caught a glimpse of his new, improved fiancée.

"Okay, I just need to change first."

"Nope, not a chance. Those old clothes are getting burned." Jayna steered Piper toward the checkout, ripping off the price tag from the back of the shirt.

Half-price wings and a hockey game always filled up Patty's Pub. Jayna was happy to see that it also brought in Nick. He sat at a table with his cop friend, Burke Winston, and Derek. She held in a groan. Life was never perfect. The good always came with some bad. Tonight, that bad came in the form of Derek Brennan. The ape was everywhere.

Piper stiffened beside her. The woman looked so nervous and unsure. Jayna's heart broke for her. Piper's childhood had been so difficult. As a young girl, she'd been taken from the neglectful care of a drug-addicted mother and placed with a grandmother she'd never met. When she first moved to Blythe Landing, the kids at school had not been kind to her.

Jayna strung her arm through Piper's. "You are going to knock his socks off. I mean, seriously, who could resist this? Piper, you look stunning. Nick won't know what hit him," she whispered as they walked towards the table. "Hey men, and Derek."

Nick turned and his jaw dropped as his eyes landed on Piper. Mission accomplished. The man was in need of a wake-up call. Piper had mentioned that he seemed distant lately and non-committal about resetting the wedding date.

"Wow, Piper," Nick blinked rapidly. "You look so good."

"You do look fantastic, Piper." Derek raised and lowered both eyebrows. "If you get tired of waiting for this guy, I'm available."

"She'll never get that tired." Jayna snorted and took the only vacant chair beside the Neanderthal. She motioned to Jessica who was sitting at the bar. "Burke, can you grab another chair for Jessica?"

Derek was outright ogling Piper. Damn, men were so predictable. Her eyes moved to Piper. The transformation was incredible, but she was still the same woman underneath the new clothes and hairstyle.

As the night wore on, Piper looked increasingly uncomfortable, and Jayna began to feel guilty. She knew she could be pushy, often disregarding boundaries and pushing people out of their comfort zones. Had she done that with Piper today?

While Piper and Jessica went to the bathroom, Jayna shifted her focus to Nick. He was staring at the bathroom door. How did he feel about the new and improved Piper?

She snagged a few French fries off his plate.

"Here, take them all." Nick shoved the plate toward her.

"I'm not hungry," she said around the French fries in her mouth.

"That's because you've been grazing off everyone else's plates," Derek grumbled.

Sticking her tongue out at him, she then turned her attention back to Nick. "So, what do you think?"

Nick's brow furrowed. "Think?"

"About Piper 2.0? Doesn't she look fantastic?"

"I like Piper 1.0. Although the new hair does look good. It's just the rest. The clothes aren't her."

Jayna narrowed her eyes. "I think the question should be, is she for you?"

He shifted, visibly uncomfortable by her question. "Of course. Why would you even ask?"

"Well, Nick Taylor, even she doesn't know. How much longer are you going to keep leading her on?"

Nick glared at her. His eyes moved back to the bathroom door, his expression changing to concern. She turned as well. Piper stood, staring down at her phone, a shattered expression on her face.

Nick shoved back his chair and stood. "What's wrong?"

"That was the nursing home." Piper lifted shocked eyes. "My grandmother had a bad fall. She was taken to the hospital by ambulance."

Jayna watched Piper leave with Nick and bit her lip. She honestly had been trying to help. However, she couldn't help but wonder if she had just made their relationship worse.

Chapter 8

Derek

Had he just made their relationship worse? Instead of addressing their issues head-on, Derek remained closed off and emotionally stunted, ignoring the elephant in the room. He pretended nothing had happened between them and tried to joke with his twin like he used to. It fell flat, like a lead elephant-shaped balloon. Tommy had stomped back up the stairs in frustration.

Rather than spending the rest of his day off at the farmhouse, Derek jumped in his truck and drove to his best friend's house. But Nick wasn't home, and Patty's Pub didn't open until noon. Good thing he had a cooler of beer in the bed of his pickup.

He eyed the front porch of Nick's new house. Not a single chair in sight. Then he noticed the ladder beside the house and looked up. It was a one-story bungalow with a low-pitch roof.

Why not?

He set down the cooler, hoisted the ladder to the front of the house, and propped it against the eavestrough. Carefully, he balanced the cooler while climbing the ladder and stepped onto the roof. Edging himself to the peak, he sat down with the cooler precariously balanced beside him and pulled out a beer can.

Derek stretched out his legs, crossed them at the ankles, and took a long swallow of his beer. Cold beer, warm sun, great view; life was good. From the peak, he could see Main Street and the river. Nick had missed out on a great view by not building a two-story house.

Nick pulled his truck into the driveway and stepped out. He shielded his eyes and stared up. "Why are you on my roof?"

"I'm having a cold beer."

"On my roof?"

"Why not? It has the best view, and you have nowhere to sit on the porch." Derek held up a beer can. "Come on up and join me."

"It's ten-thirty in the morning."

"Yeah, so? What's your point?"

"So? You're drinking beer. It's not even noon, and you're doing it on top of my house."

"Get your chicken ass up here."

"I'm not chicken. I have common sense. There's a difference," Nick said, but he still grabbed onto the ladder rung at eye level and began to climb.

Nick reached the top and shot him a dubious glance as he carefully inched his way to the peak, sitting beside him. Derek opened the cooler and pulled out a cold can, handing it to his friend.

"So, once more. Why are you drinking on my roof?"

"Because you and I are a couple of sorry jackasses." Derek tapped his can against Nick's beer.

"Maybe you are," Nick side-eyed him.

"Nope. You definitely are too."

Nick took a long swallow.

"I hear the wedding is off for good," Derek pursed his lips, scrutinizing Nick. "Heard Piper gave you back the ring."

"You hear a lot." Nick shook his head. "We're figuring things out."

"That's what you call it? Piper is the kind of woman a man builds a life with and pops out a puppy or two."

Nick shifted, turning to stare at him. "Puppy?"

"A baby."

"What do you know about building a life with a woman?" Nick's eyebrows shot up, and he stared at Derek, his mouth slightly agape.

"I know that a woman like Piper won't wait around forever. You've got a long way to go to deserve her." He also knew that he'd never seen Nick happier than when he was with Piper or more miserable since the split.

"I think I need another beer," Nick sighed. "I need to catch up with you."

"Life can be a shit show. Take all the good that is offered before it's all gone." He crunched up the empty can and threw it onto the lawn.

"Hey." Nick stared at the empty can littering his immaculate lawn.

"I'll clean it up later." Derek pulled out two more cans from the cooler, handing one to Nick.

"So once again, why are you drinking on my roof at ten-thirty and waxing poetic?"

"Because, dumb ass, we don't always get second chances with the woman we're meant to be with. Sometimes we lose her."

Nick narrowed his eyes but didn't comment.

"This break-up, did it have anything to do with my sister? Is she the reason you and Piper are Splitsville?"

"Huh?" Nick's head snapped around.

"You'd have to be denser than I am to miss the tension between you and Kylie. I've dumped enough women to recognize the look on my sister's face when you're around. You pissed her off."

Nick downed the first beer and tossed it on the grass beside Derek's. He spoke as he stared at the second can, popping the top. "There was a time when I had a brief lapse in judgment. When Kylie was at university. But it didn't last long."

Nick brought his free hand over his face, shielding himself. "You aren't going to clobber me, are you?"

"No, Kylie can administer her own clobberings." This he knew firsthand. His little sister packed quite the punch when she was riled. "Not that you don't deserve it. Seriously, you broke the bro-code with that one."

He stared at his best friend and noticed the turmoil there.

"Nick, Kylie's moved on. She's happy."

Nick scratched at the stubble on his chin. "Yeah, I know."

"Are you using her as an excuse to end things with the hot teacher? Was it getting too real with Piper?"

Nick's head popped up. The man was probably shocked. Derek wasn't one for deep discussions, not even with his friends. But he was worried about Nick.

"It doesn't take a psych degree to understand that you would have commitment issues after everything that happened with your parents. With your dad." Nick's father had taken his own life with his service revolver exactly a year to the day that Nick's mother died from breast cancer.

Derek leaned an elbow on his bent knee. "Hell, I have plenty of issues of my own, and I was raised in a happy, stable home."

"Yeah, just why is that? Why are you so messed up?" Nick turned the tables.

"Just am," he evaded.

"Nothing's bothering you?"

"Nope. I'm fine."

Nick guffawed. "Yeah, okay! You are day drinking on my roof, but you're fine!"

"Yep."

"So, you and Tommy are just fine? You and Leighton are fine, too?"

Derek cleared his throat. "It's complicated and totally messed up. I'm the asshole who has feelings for my brother's girl. Not just feelings, but I acted on them."

Just like Nick, his unrequited feelings were obvious too. He stared straight ahead and let out a low moan. "Oh shit. Twelve o'clock."

Ophelia Meddler stood on her front lawn staring at them.

"Nick Taylor, what are you doing on your roof?" Her nasal voice was so grating.

"Enjoying the view," Nick called back.

"Is that Derek Brennan with you?" Ophelia shielded her eyes from the bright sun with her left hand as she crossed the street.

"Depends," Derek yelled. "Are you going to call my mother?"

"Maybe I will," Ophelia snapped, now standing on the sidewalk, fuming. "This is a respectable neighborhood."

"Dude, I can't believe you built a house across the street from the Meddler," he muttered out the side of his mouth, holding his hand up to cover it just in case Ophelia could read lips.

"The land was cheap."

Derek raised his eyebrows. "It was cheap because Ophelia Meddler lives across the street."

"Yeah, I didn't think this through."

"Oh, she's not going to call my mother, but she did call your grandfather." Derek let out a hoot as Earl's old station wagon came to a stop at the curb.

"Everything ok, my boy?" Earl moved to stand beside Ophelia, staring up.

Ophelia huffed, crossing her arms. "I think he's really upset over the breakup."

"I'm fine. Just doing some roof drinking with my friend," Nick moaned. "Give me another beer. You realize that I'm going to have to move."

"Yep." Derek handed him another can. "I'll help you pack."

Chapter 9

Jayna

Jayna unpacked her lunch box with enthusiasm. It was eight hours into her twelve-hour shift, and she was famished. The day began with a trauma case, which was always a sign of more to follow. And indeed, more had followed. First a car accident proceeded with a near drowning.

Her stomach growled as she pulled out her frozen dinner, glaring at the plastic-wrapped meal with disdain. Another culinary masterpiece courtesy of the microwave.

"Hey Jayna. That's been quite the shift," Greta said, breezing into the break room.

Suppressing a groan, Jayna mustered a polite, "Yep."

Was it too much to ask for a quiet break? Greta was nice, but Jayna wasn't interested in hearing about the happy couple. She ripped open the box of her frozen dinner and shoved it into the microwave. She wished for the millionth time that she possessed any real cooking skills. Takeout and frozen meals were fast losing their appeal.

Her saving grace: dessert. She'd snagged a slice of freshly baked banana bread from Blythe Landing Perks that morning. While waiting in line for her coffee, she had eavesdropped on a conversation between Ophelia and a coworker from the clerk's office.

"Did you hear that Piper and Nick broke up?" Despite whispering, Ophelia's words reverberated across the shop.

"No, but I did hear her grandmother passed away last week," the coworker had replied.

A pang of guilt had hit Jayna. She hoped hijacking Piper's makeover hadn't contributed to the breakup. The last thing she needed was to be responsible for someone else's heartache.

The microwave dinged, interrupting her thoughts. She retrieved the steaming container of pasta, which looked as unappetizing as it smelled. Sitting down at the table, she forced a smile at Greta. Her dislike for the woman was irrational, just like her feelings for Leighton. It wasn't Greta's fault that she was dating Lance, the man Jayna was interested in.

Jayna projected this super-confident woman to the world, yet internally, she battled with imposter syndrome. Women like Greta and Leighton were effortlessly kind and beautiful, attracting men with ease. Jayna didn't have trouble attracting men, but they seemed to view her differently. She was a good time until they found "the one."

But did "the one" truly exist? Could there really be that one special person out there just for her? Maybe it was easier to dismiss the idea of true love than to face the fear that she might not be lovable. If she was lovable, wouldn't her parents have stuck around?

"So, how are things going with Lance?" she asked, pushing her dark thoughts aside.

Greta sighed. "Not great, to be honest. I don't think it's going to work out between us."

"Oh, really?" Jayna sat up a little straighter. "Why not?"

"He told me he doesn't want children."

"Yeah? So?" Jayna's brows knitted in confusion.

"That's a deal-breaker for me."

"But you've only been dating a few months. Isn't it too soon to be talking about children?"

Greta shook her head firmly. "I'm too old to waste my time."

"Girl, you're only 26."

"Exactly! My sister is 28, married, and pregnant with her second child. Dating a man with no future is a waste of my time."

Jayna bit her lip to stop the smile that threatened to erupt. A man who didn't want children was a deal-sealer for her. With her own disastrous parents, she feared repeating history. No child deserved to be born to a parent who didn't want them.

Spending time at the Brennan farmhouse with Kylie had shown Jayna what a real family looked like. Marion Brennan was so involved in her children's lives. She was always meddling but in such a loving way that contrasted sharply with Jayna's own parents. She still remembered prom night, when Marion had grabbed her by the chin, reminding her to behave, and kissed Jayna's forehead to soften her firm words. It had been both wonderful and painful, a reminder of what she never had.

Jayna doubted her ability to offer more than she had received. While she was close with the Js and Kylie, forming new attachments was a struggle. However, the idea of casual dating was losing its appeal, much like her frozen pasta dinners. She was tired of being alone. Lance was starting to look like a pretty good catch, and apparently, he was about to be back on the market.

She hid her grin as she pulled a can of diet Coke from her lunch bag, popping the tab with a satisfying hiss.

Chapter 10

Derek

Popping the tab on a beer, Derek took a long swallow, grinning as Nick's truck rumbled into the driveway.

"Why are you on my roof again?" Nick called, stepping out of his pickup.

"I waited until afternoon this time," Derek hollered back.

"Barely! It's twelve-fifteen," Nick retorted, glancing at his watch as he walked toward the house.

Nick climbed the ladder with ease. "You're going to ruin my shingles."

"What do you care? You're moving." Derek held out a cold beer can as Nick settled beside him at the peak. "I hear you showed up at Piper's door with flowers and she sent you packing."

Nick choked on his beer. "Where'd you hear that?"

"Overheard Mom and Vanessa. Margie Stayner came into Vanessa's salon for a wash and set, talking all about it."

"Wash and set?" Nick's eyebrows shot up.

"Yeah, you know, the old lady helmet hairstyle that lasts a week." Derek chuckled. "Margie's daughter lives across from Leighton and Piper. She saw the whole thing. Saw Piper hand back the flowers and slam the door in your face."

"She must have pretty good eyesight," Nick muttered. "So? What's it to you?"

"It's going to take more than flowers and a lame apology to win her back."

"How do you know my apology was lame? Does Margie have

supersonic hearing too?"

Derek lifted an eyebrow. "No, I just know you well, my friend."

"Okay, yeah, it was pretty lame," Nick sighed, taking another swig. "What can I do? She's really angry. I hurt her, and she isn't going to forgive me anytime soon."

"You need a grand gesture," Derek advised. "Like Ryan Gosling did in 'The Notebook'."

"You watched 'The Notebook'?"

"Don't look so shocked. Mom and Vanessa were watching it last night. They had an amazing charcuterie board. I'd sit through a musical for mortadella and gruyere."

In addition to gossiping, his mother and sister-in-law had gushed over Ryan Gosling's character, Noah, and his grand gesture of restoring the old house where he and Allie had spent their last night together.

A police cruiser pulled up to the curb just as Ophelia Meddler stepped out of her house.

"Looks like the Meddler called the Po-Po on us," Derek chuckled.

"Hey Burke," Nick called out to the officer. "What's up?"

"Got a disturbance call." Burke climbed out of the cruiser and approached the lawn.

"Oh, yeah? Who's causing a disturbance?" Nick asked.

"Apparently, you and Derek are." Burke shrugged.

"We're just sitting on my roof enjoying the view. No disturbance here." Nick grinned.

"Nick's right, Mrs. Meddler," Burke said, turning to the woman. "Drinking on the roof isn't an offense. It might be stupid, but it's not illegal."

Ophelia threw her hands up and stalked back across the street.

"Careful, Burke. She might turn the hose on you again," Derek called down.

Ophelia stopped walking and turned. Her glare could have set him aflame. "Oh, she's calling my mother."

"Yep." Nick nodded his head in agreement.

"Did you see that video of her hosing down Burke when he refused to charge Shamus for a noise complaint?" Derek chuckled.

"Guess she doesn't like bagpipe music," Nick commented.

"Come back once your shift is over. We'll fire up the barbecue," Nick yelled down to Burke.

"Sounds good," Burke said, heading back to his cruiser. "Maybe take the drinking to the back deck."

"Yeah, okay." Nick saluted.

"Are we too old to put a flaming bag of poop on her front porch?" Derek asked.

"Yep. Hand me another beer."

Derek pulled out another cold can and handed it to Nick. "Hey, speak of the devil, there's Shamus now." He waved. "Shamus, how about some bagpipe music?"

The redheaded man gave two thumbs up and dashed back into his house.

Ophelia remained on her porch, possibly contemplating her next move. Maybe wondering just how far her garden hose would reach?

Derek raised his beer in a silent toast. "Oh, she's definitely calling my mother now."

"Yep," Nick agreed, cracking open his beer. "And I'm definitely going to have to move."

"Yep," Derek echoed.

Shamus returned, bagpipes blaring 'Scotland the Brave.'

"Are we torturing the Meddler or ourselves?" Nick asked.

"Not sure," Derek grimaced as Shamus drew closer.

"Got any ideas for this grand gesture?"

"Not a one."

"You're no help," Nick muttered.

"Oh, I'm plenty of help," Derek protested.

"You help me get into trouble, not out of it," Nick countered.

"Very true." Derek wished he could help his friend with his love life, but this was beyond him. "Just spill your guts. Women love it when you open up about your feelings and crap like that."

Nick turned, his eyes narrowing. "Was that in the movie? No way, that's from personal experience."

"Hey, it's the best I've got."

"Have you opened up to Tommy yet?"

"We're talking about you, not me." Derek squirmed. He had come to Nick's to escape Tommy, not talk about him.

"I've got stuff to do before Burke returns for the BBQ. And if you've got nothing better to do, the grass needs cutting."

Derek groaned. "Really? Manual labor? How about another beer first?"

"Nope. One more beer leads to two." Nick stood, inching toward the ladder.

"Come on, just one!"

Chapter 11

Jayna

"Come on, just one. It's only seven o'clock. You won't turn into a pumpkin until midnight." Jayna dragged Jessica into Patty's Pub.

"Ha ha," Jessica let out a forced laugh and rolled her eyes. "And it was Cinderella's carriage that turned into a pumpkin, not her."

"Whatever, I never liked fairy tales. The whole prince-saving-the-princess-with-a-kiss thing?" Jayna threw up her hands. "Never bought into that load of BS."

"Yeah, yeah," Jessica groaned. "I know you're an independent woman. You don't need a man."

Jayna scanned the busy bar for a table. Hockey playoffs dominated the numerous screens, and hockey fans occupied all the tables. She glanced back at Jessica. "Maybe you should buy into my philosophy a little more yourself."

Jessica was still torn up over that loser excuse of a man she'd dated for close to two years. The guy had been married and had managed to keep that fact hidden from Jessica and Jessica from his wife. That was the reason she and Jamie had signed Jess up for the dating app. Unfortunately, it seemed to attract even more losers.

"Jayna, I'm not like you. I just don't have that kind of confidence."

Jayna squeezed her hand. "You don't give yourself enough credit, Jess. You need to put yourself out there more."

"What I need is to get home. I have an early day tomorrow,

and the bar is packed. There is nowhere to sit."

Jayna's eyes scanned the room, finally landing on Nick and Derek seated at a table with two empty chairs. They looked to be in an intense conversation, which ignited her curiosity. She'd heard about Nick proposing to Piper last week, only to have the door slammed in his face. Gossip traveled at lightning speed in Blythe Landing, and she wasn't too proud to admit that while she didn't add to it, she certainly tuned into it.

She hadn't been shocked when news of the breakup reached her. The tension between the two had been quite obvious. But what caused Nick to propose again? And why had Piper rejected him? This called for more investigation.

"I see a couple of vacant chairs." She grabbed Jessica's hand, dragging her toward the two men.

"Hey boys," Jayna pulled out a chair and sat down.

"Oh, please join us. Sit down." Derek glared in her direction. "We were having a private discussion."

"Really, what about?" Jayna propped her chin on a fisted hand.

"What part of private didn't you understand?" Derek lifted his shoulders.

"No, it's good that they're here. I could use a woman's perspective," Nick said, smiling at both her and Jessica. "I am trying to win Piper back, and Derek had a great idea."

Jayna sputtered, "Derek had a good idea?"

Derek shot Jayna an annoyed glance before turning his attention back to Nick. "I did?"

"Yeah, the grand gesture," Nick answered. "Just what would a grand gesture be?"

"No clue," Derek shrugged.

"You seriously don't want to take romantic advice from Two-Date Brennan," Jayna leaned toward Nick, whispering loudly.

"But you'll take advice from Jayna Date-and-Dash?" Derek scoffed.

"A grand gesture. That sounds so romantic," Jessica sighed.

"But what?" Nick lifted both his hands into the air.

"You need to make it epic." Jayna liked this idea, even if Brennan had come up with it.

"I showed up on her doorstep with her favorite flowers and the ring. I proposed again, and she told me to come back when I meant it. Slammed the door in my face." Nick shook his head as he spoke. "What more can I do?"

"You need to mean it," Jayna told him, and an idea formed. "Where was the original wedding booked? I remember Piper was so excited about it."

"The Old Mill for the reception after the ceremony at the church beside the river," Nick told her.

Jayna grabbed her phone out of her purse and pulled up the internet. She googled the Old Mill, hit the contact info, and tapped the call button.

"What are you doing?" Derek asked.

She shushed him.

"May I help you?" A female voice answered, and she set her phone on the table, putting it on speaker.

"I was wondering when you have the next opening for a wedding reception?"

"We book two years in advance," the woman replied. "But we did have a last-minute cancellation for next Friday."

"We'll take it!" Jayna felt her fingers tingle. "Nick Taylor can come by tomorrow to sign the paperwork."

"Great, I have an opening at 11 a.m."

"He'll be there." Jayna swiped to end the call and snapped her fingers. "And there you have it, an epic grand gesture."

"Uh, Jayna?" Nick sat open-mouthed. "What did you just do?"

"I booked the venue for your wedding. Weren't you listening?" She giggled. "How epic is this? A surprise wedding."

"It's stupid, not epic," Derek scoffed again.

"Shut up, Derek, no one asked you." Jayna side-eyed him before returning her attention back to Nick. "Don't you see? You will recreate her perfect wedding and surprise her with it. She said to come back when you meant it. This is how you show her you mean it!"

"Oh, it's so romantic," Jessica sighed, louder this time.

"It's impossible, is what it is," Nick shook his head adamantly. "How do I plan an entire wedding in under two weeks?"

"We'll all help," Jayna said, then frowned. Had she just volunteered herself? Oh, what the hell. Piper was just about the sweetest person she'd ever met. "Jessica, Jamie, me, Derek, and I'm sure Leighton would pitch in as well."

Her frown increased. Leighton was the last person she wanted to collaborate with, but she was Piper's best friend.

"Stupid idea," Derek grumbled.

"Since when has that stopped you?" Jayna taunted and then frowned. Why had she suggested that Derek be involved? "On second thought, maybe you shouldn't help. You'll just manage to screw it up. All you know about weddings is how to pick up desperate women."

"I won't screw it up," Derek's lip curled as he snarled at her.

"Right!"

Jayna didn't know why she was baiting him. Despite not wanting his help, she hesitated to let him off the hook for helping to plan the wedding. He was Nick's best friend, and he should pitch in.

"What if she still says no?" Nick sat forward, all the color draining from his face.

"No woman would turn down such a grand romantic gesture." Jessica fanned her cheeks. "Oh, Nick, you have to do this!"

"Let's check if Leighton is still at her store and go over this with her. Time is not on my side." Nick stood and glanced at Derek. "Are you coming or staying?"

"Staying." Derek held up his full glass of whiskey.

"Later, loser!" Jayna shot him a toothy smile as she grabbed her purse and left with Nick and Jessica.

Chapter 12

Derek

Jayna left with Nick and Jessica, and Derek heaved a sigh of relief. The woman was full of herself. Her latest idea was downright ridiculous. A surprise wedding? She hadn't so much asked but told him that he was helping. This presented him with Problem #1: What did he know about weddings besides the fact that they were great places to pick up women, as Jayna had bluntly pointed out? He really hoped this didn't blow up in Nick's face, but that was a very real possibility.

Why did Jayna have to butt into their conversation tonight? He couldn't stand the woman. And if she had zero faith in his ability not to ruin the event, why was she so insistent on his participation?

Which led him to Problem #2: Jayna was also helping. Insert eye roll here. He chugged the rest of the whiskey in his glass and held it up as the server walked past, ordering another and a pound of medium wings. No way was he going to let Jayna be right. He was going to step up to the task and help Nick create an incredible wedding.

This led to Problem #3: the bar was almost empty, and he had too much to drink. He needed a ride home.

The chair across from him scraped loudly, and he glanced up as his oldest brother Ian sat down.

"Can I please have a beer, Ivy, and a pound of wings as well? But make mine mild," Ian called over his shoulder.

"Wuss," Derek taunted.

"I have a delicate stomach and nothing to prove."

"I eat hot wings because I like 'em, not to prove anything to anyone."

"Yeah, okay, Dare. Everything is a competition with you."

Derek waved to the server. "Ivy, could you make my order of wings hot, please?"

"See!" Ian threw both his hands up in the air.

"Whatever, you're still a wuss. Delicate stomach," Derek chided his brother.

"So, my wife isn't too happy with you." Ian was starting to sound more and more like their father.

"What else is new?"

"Of all the women you can date, can you please stop asking out her stylists? She is tired of hearing how you stand them up. And I'm tired of hearing her complain about you." Ian's left eyebrow shot up, all holier-than-thou, exactly like their father.

"Tell Vanessa to stop hiring hot stylists," Derek offered as the server set down his drink.

"I'll be back with your wings." Ivy set a bottle of beer in front of Ian, along with two glasses of water.

"Thanks, Ivy." Ian smiled at the woman and lifted the beer bottle to his lips, taking a long swallow. "Vanessa recommends finding a new salon. Hank's Barber Shop was a suggestion."

"The only hairstyle Hank knows is the military cut. No way am I sitting in his chair." Derek lifted the low tumbler of whiskey and took a sip.

"It would be an improvement over the next one you'll get from Vanessa. She's threatening a reverse mohawk."

"Tell Vanessa that she doesn't need to worry. I'm taking a break from dating."

"Whoa? How many whiskeys have you had?"

"A few too many."

"I'd say!" Ian reached across and grabbed Derek's keys off the table, sticking them in his pocket. "I'll be keeping these until tomorrow."

Two plates were set on the table in front of them. Derek picked up a wing and waved it at Ian's plate. "Once you're finished with your wimpy wings, could you give me a lift home, then?"

"Sure." Ian sucked the meat off the wing and pulled out a clean bone. Show-off.

Derek stuck a wing in his mouth and immediately felt the heat. Had Patty raised the Scoville scale of his hot sauce? A burning sensation spread across his lips, and his nose started to run.

"Spicy?" Ian raised an eyebrow in such an annoying, I-told-you-so way.

"Not bad." His voice was raspy, and his breath was heated. He eyed the tall glass of water in front of him and wanted to grab it so badly. He wouldn't give Ian the satisfaction. Instead, he took a swig of whiskey, which just added to the burn.

"That's why you have sweat beading on your upper lip." Ian pointed and chuckled, then went straight for the jugular. "What's up between you and Tommy?"

Derek rolled his eyes. "That's complicated."

"Do you still blame yourself for backing out on enlisting with him?" Ian was not holding back.

"If I'd been there, I could have protected him." He licked his fiery lips.

"Or we could have lost you both." Ian shook his head sadly.

"I should have been there, not him. It was my stupid idea in the first place." Derek stared directly at his brother, who was five years older. They had never seen eye to eye. Ian, always responsible, acted more like a parent than a sibling.

"Tommy loved everything about the army. He stayed in the cadets long after you quit." Ian offered him a valid excuse. However, if he hadn't quit, hadn't bailed, then Tommy wouldn't have been alone in such a hostile, unforgiving place.

Derek leaned his elbows on the table. This talk was getting serious and honest. He needed to own it. "I kissed her, Ian."

"Kissed who?"

Kissed who? Only the one woman who was off-limits. She was number one on the untouchable list and topped the 'don't even think about it' list. But he'd bunched up both lists and set them on fire. Derek destroyed not only the list but also the relationship with his twin.

It wasn't just that one time. Everything that he touched he broke. He'd busted toys, pushed boundaries, and broken promises. And Tommy had always been the one who got them out of the messes that Derek caused.

"I kissed Leighton. The night of the harvest dance, the night before Tommy was taken captive." Wow, it sounded even uglier spoken out loud than it did on constant replay in his head.

Ian's mouth opened and closed. He'd caused his brother to be at a loss for words. His brother was never at a loss for words.

Clearing his throat, Ian finally spoke. "Well, that explains it."

"Tommy spent three years locked away, hating me."

"Can't say I blame him." Ian sat back in his chair. "But I can't say that I'm surprised either. It was blatantly obvious that you had a thing for Leighton too."

Derek's brow creased. "I wouldn't say blatant."

Ian gave a head nod that somehow conveyed both acknowledgment and sarcasm simultaneously.

Derek sent his brother yet another eye roll. His younger brother Ben, who had perfected the eye roll, would be impressed. "I shouldn't have acted on it, though."

"That is true, but then you wouldn't be you," Ian stated.

"What the hell does that mean?" He stared at his brother.

"It means that you're impulsive. It's just who you are." Ian shifted in his chair and sighed, continuing in a softer, less condescending voice. "Derek, you screwed up and made a mistake. You need to apologize to Tommy."

"Yeah." The word sorry was never easy for him to say. But Ian was right, it was time to fix his latest mess. "What if he doesn't want to hear it? I have no idea what to say or how to say it."

"Amazing! I can't believe you're an actual adult now who still can't grasp the concept of a basic apology. It really isn't rocket science, Derek," Ian let out a heavy breath, his tone turning back to the lecturer. "Take responsibility for your actions. Be sincere. Tell him you screwed up, that you were wrong."

Again, Ian was right. He needed to apologize. If only saying sorry didn't leave such a bad taste in his mouth. "I'm not very good at admitting I was wrong."

"Well, that's a shocker," Ian chuckled. "Derek, the daredevil, admitting he's not infallible."

"Alright, I'll give it a shot. Thanks, Ian."

"Just remember, actions speak louder than words. Show him you're sincere through your behavior, not just your apology. In other words, don't act like your normal asshole self."

"I appreciate the advice, even if it's coming from Mr. Responsible." He shot his brother an annoyed glance. There was a smear of sauce on the side of Ian's mouth, and he almost pointed it out. Almost, but then he decided to act like his asshole self and let Ian discover it on his own.

Ian grinned. "Someone needs to be the responsible one in this family. It's clearly not going to be you."

Ian turned to look at the big screen as cheers erupted behind him. A wicked smile lifted the corners of Derek's mouth. He quickly switched their plates before Ian turned back around.

"Hurry up and finish your wings, Mr. Responsible." Derek pointed at Ian's plate. "Your not-so-responsible brother needs a ride home."

Ian grabbed a wing off his plate and shoved it into his mouth. Derek could barely hide the laugh as he watched Ian's eyes bug out.

"What the hell?" Ian grabbed the glass of water and chugged it. "Did you switch our wings?"

Derek merely lifted his eyebrows.

"You're still the same snot-nosed, annoying brat you always were."

"I'm not the one with the runny nose," Derek laughed.

"No. You're about to be the one with the bloody nose," Ian threatened.

It wouldn't be the first time a disagreement between the brothers ended with a bloody nose or a fat lip, but it would not be tonight. Derek's eyes followed Artie Kincaide, the only taxi driver in town, making his way to the door. Pulling out three twenty-dollar bills from his wallet, he tossed them on the table and grabbed his jacket off the back of the chair.

"Thanks for the advice, big bro," he called over his shoulder as he raced after Artie. "Looks like I won't be needing that ride home after all. Hey Artie, can I catch a ride with you?"

Now he faced Problem #4: Ian had his keys, and the front door of the farmhouse was locked. Banging on the door and waking his father was not an option. The farmer was always early to rise and early to bed. A hard worker, Stan expected the same from everyone around him. Derek had seen disappointment and criticism in his father's eyes too often, and he was in no mood to see it there tonight. He'd had enough of that from Ian.

The latch on the living room window had been faulty, keeping his sneaking-in-late teenage butt safe. He was pretty sure no one had fixed it. Switching on the flashlight option on his cell phone, he shone it through the window. It had been a few years since he'd last attempted it, but with a jiggle and a tug to the left, the latch gave. With a low-pitched squeak, the window slid up.

He wasn't as agile or as thin as he'd been at seventeen, but he managed to squeeze through. The hardwood floor was still hard as he landed with a loud thump. That was going to leave a mark. He pulled himself up and jumped. Someone was perched on the floor beside the couch.

"Damn, Tommy. You scared me. What the hell are you doing on the floor?"

Tommy blinked rapidly, and his Adam's apple bobbed up and down in his throat. "You startled me. Why didn't you use the front door?"

"Forgot my key, and Dad still yells."

Tommy swiped a hand across his brow, his chest visibly lifting with the heavy breaths.

"Are you okay?" Derek asked.

"I forget." Tommy sucked in air like he couldn't get enough.

His eyelids clamped shut. "Sometimes when I wake up, I forget where I am. There was a light, then the window opened."

Tommy waved his hand toward the front window.

"I'm sorry. I didn't know you would be asleep on the couch." Derek eased himself onto the floor next to his twin. "You're safe now, Tommy."

"The nightmares won't stop. Dare, it was really bad. And every night..." Tommy stuttered as the words tumbled out. "Every night, I go straight back there."

"Give it time," Derek cringed as the words left his lips. Cliché, but just what was he supposed to say? Were there any right words for the horror his twin had suffered? "Everything is going to be fine."

"Everything?" Tommy forced a laugh that held no humor. "Nothing is fine!"

Guilt surged through Derek. Tommy had lived through a nightmare, and he had only made it worse. "I am truly sorry. I never meant to..." he paused, choking on shame as he confessed his betrayal. "It was only one kiss, just that one time."

He felt Tommy stiffen beside him and move away. He didn't blame his brother, but damn, he wished that Tommy would just punch him instead of pulling away. Moving to sit on the couch, Tommy held his head between his hands. Derek eased himself off the floor and onto the edge of the coffee table.

"It was more than just one kiss to me!" The anger in Tommy's voice vibrated through Derek.

"I would take it back if I could." He would take it all back. Every stupid, selfish choice he'd ever made. Especially the one that had him bailing on his brother, leaving Tommy vulnerable and alone.

"Would you really? You always wanted her, and we both know it."

Derek opened, then shut his mouth. The denial died on his lips. Enough lies had already passed between them.

"I never thought you would act on your feelings for her. You crossed the line." Tommy shoved himself further back on the couch, adding more distance between them.

"She was my fiancée. You knew..." Tommy gritted his teeth, and the words hissed out. "You knew how much she meant to me."

Derek ran a hand through his hair. "I did, and I still kissed her. Damn, Tommy, what do you want me to say? That I thought I was in love with her too? That I was so damn jealous you had her? Everything always came so easily to you. Everyone liked you better. Our parents, our friends' parents, the teachers."

Derek leaned forward, touching Tommy's leg. "Leighton was so perfect. So pretty, so sweet, and she liked you better, too. It drove me nuts. But I am so sorry. I would take it back if I could."

Tommy jerked his leg away and stood, walking toward the front hall.

"I'm sorry, Tommy. So sorry," he pleaded, staring at his brother's back.

Tommy paused. "There was a small window in the cell. Every night I stared out that window and watched the sky turn from blue to black. All I had were my memories. They changed each night. I tried to remember only the good ones. And every good memory included you."

Turning back around, Tommy stared straight at him. "But no matter what memory I pulled up, I always ended with the vivid image of my brother kissing my girl." His nostrils flared as he continued speaking. "That last video call I had with Leighton, the last words she spoke to me, played through my mind on an endless loop. Derek kissed me, and I kissed him back."

"It was only one kiss," Derek said quietly.

Tommy sucked in a breath before exhaling loudly. "It wasn't just one kiss to me. Not to me! It was you finally acting on your feelings for her. And Leighton admitting she had feelings for you."

"She broke my heart." Tommy stepped closer, his eyes narrowing. "But you destroyed my trust and shattered what was left of my heart."

Tommy's hands formed fists at his side. "You are my brother, my twin. I have always forgiven you in the past. But Derek, this is too big to forgive."

He watched as Tommy spun back around, walking through the hall and up the stairs. A giant sob started deep in Derek's chest, working its way up his throat before coming out in a blast of hot air and even hotter tears.

What had he done?

Chapter 13

Jayna

What had she done? Volunteering to plan a wedding? Jayna was not the romantic, wedding-planning type. Why had she opened her big mouth and suggested a surprise wedding? Was it really such a good idea? The bride still had to agree to it. The fact that Derek Brennan was pitching in was even more shocking. That man did not have a romantic bone in his body. Not a single one! He was the complete opposite of a romantic.

She pulled out a chair and sat down across from the romance-phobe himself. Derek shot her a cold, scathing look, one that he seemed to save exclusively for her. Jayna could see the cruel barbs that he also saved for her forming on his lips.

This dislike was mutual. She had probably been the one who had started this feud. But she was not going to be the one to end it. Pretty boy had it coming. He was an insufferable ass who was completely without any redeemable qualities. A knuckle-dragging, club-carrying caveman.

Derek leaned back in his chair, folding his arms over that hard chest. Her eyes were drawn to the tattoo that peeked out of his short-sleeved T-shirt. The man had been gorgeous in high school, and that was only amplifying as he aged. It was a shame really that he was so damn good-looking. Such a waste on a man so hateful. Those thickly lashed eyes, an impossibly deep violet-blue, promised heaven. His dark hair just begged for fingers to run through the silky strands. Then there was his heavily muscled chest that filled out a T-shirt so well. Jeans always seemed to hang so sinfully well on his hips.

Stop checking him out, she silently scolded herself. The man was a world-class jerk. She gave her head a good shake and licked her parched lips.

Derek continued to stare at her, letting the silence stretch out between them. Damn, she hated how long he could go without speaking, forcing her to break the awkwardness. It felt like losing a staring contest, which they were also having. She hated to lose any competition. But she hated silence more.

It took her straight back to the oversized table in the ostentatiously decorated dining room, where her parents ate in silence. The only thing worse than that was when they weren't home, and she ate alone in silence. Lonely, deafening silence.

If she was going to lose this contest, then she might as well go down swinging. "When a vampire goes out in the sun, it bursts into flames. What happens when Two-Date Brennan dons a tux and stands up in a church as a groomsman? Does he implode, or spontaneously combust?"

"Ha, ha. You're hilarious." The man could talk.

"Seriously, though, does it bother you to be a part of a wedding when you so obviously don't believe in the sanctity of marriage?"

"I believe in it. I just don't want it for myself."

"Why's that?" She leaned forward and placed her chin on a propped fist.

"None of your business."

"So, you don't have a problem with it?" she pressed, enjoying the muscle that she had caused to twitch in his jaw.

He forcibly clenched his teeth together to stop it. She was getting to him!

"The only problem I have is that you're a part of it!" he spat out.

"Ouch!" She moved her hand from her chin to cover her heart.

"What about you?" He pointed that self-righteous, accusatory finger at her.

"Me?" She batted her lashes.

"Yeah, Jayna Date and Dash," he winked as he used her latest nickname.

"I don't have a problem with marriage or committed relationships. I just haven't found anyone interesting enough yet to continue dating. Unlike you, I don't like to lead my dates on." She was nothing like him and wished that people would stop comparing them.

"I don't lead my dates on," he hissed, pumping up his chest.

"Whatever helps you sleep at night."

"I sleep just fine!" The muscle in his jaw was dancing now.

"People without a conscience tend to do that."

She was pretty sure his left eye was twitching as well.

The chair beside her scraped loudly, and she jumped. Leighton sat beside her, and Nick took the chair next to Derek.

"You two bicker like an old married couple," Nick commented.

That silenced Jayna and Derek instantly.

"He'd be so lucky," Jayna retorted with an exaggerated, sarcastic laugh. Not if Brennan was the last man on earth!

"Not even if she was the last woman on earth."

Now her mouth dropped open. That was her line! He was such an ass. She hated him like she'd never hated anyone before. She hated that he could so effortlessly get under her skin. It seemed like Derek could read her mind. Not just read her mind but that he spoke her thoughts out loud like they were his thoughts, his words. Perhaps though, what she hated most was that they were so similar and suited for each other. NOT if he was the last man on earth!

Derek flashed her that bad boy grin, the one that popped that lone dimple. It gave him a lopsided appearance. Maybe he wasn't so good-looking after all.

"Let's just skip the insults and start on the wedding plans," Leighton suggested, pulling out four folders from her bag. "I made a list of everything that needs to be done and divided it up equally between us."

Jayna flipped open the folder that Leighton handed her. The

list was extensive. Her portion of the list was enormous. Just what had she agreed to? Not only did she have to work with her arch-nemesis, but she had to work!

Jessica would love this well-designed spreadsheet. Her friend was compulsively organized. A slow smile, a bit wicked, lifted her lips. She needed to show this folder to Jessica. Maybe smudge it a little bit, spoil the perfection of it. Jessica would lose her mind, worrying that Jayna would not be capable of fulfilling her duties. Oh, she'd be so worried that Nick and Piper would be let down and offer to take over.

Jayna was not too proud to admit that she sometimes manipulated her friends. Okay, more than just sometimes, she did it often. But it was always for the greater good. And this qualified. Piper was just the sweetest person she'd ever met. If anyone deserved a perfect wedding, it was that woman. It wasn't like Jessica hadn't already offered to help. Honestly, what did Jayna know about planning a wedding? Wasn't it enough that she'd come up with the idea?

Derek wasn't so subtle in hiding his annoyance at the overwhelming list. "What the hell? I do have a full-time job!"

Leighton sighed, a frown marring her exquisite features. "Maybe you can recruit Ben to help you."

"Forget that. I'm going to scratch off my name and add his."

"We could be so lucky!" Jayna shot him a blinding smile like the one he had just given her. "Nick, you seriously can't want this Neanderthal to help plan your wedding. The only thing Derek is qualified to plan is a raunchy bachelor party."

Derek held up both hands in defeat. "Okay, first true words Date and Dash has spoken all night! I did hear about this stripper bus we could hire."

"NO!" Both Nick and Leighton spoke at the same time.

Jayna shook her head. He was so predictable. And disgusting. That man was too much!

Chapter 14

Derek

That woman was too much!!

"Jayna," Derek growled as the night before replayed in his mind. His eyes landed on the thick folder Leighton had given him that sat untouched on the passenger seat. He growled again. How was it that he was helping to plan a wedding? The universe indeed had a twisted sense of humor.

It wasn't like he had anything against marriage, despite what Jayna had insinuated. He was thrilled that Nick and Piper had made up and were about to get married. He was happy to help and honored to be one of Nick's groomsmen. However, working side by side with Jayna would be pure torture.

But he'd suck it up and be on his best behavior—for Nick and Piper.

The digital clock on the dashboard flashed 4:45. He was fifteen minutes early, and Nick wasn't home yet. Shifting into park, he killed the engine and stepped out onto the Taylor driveway. He grabbed the cooler full of beer from the truck bed. Nick's fridge was not well stocked lately, given his preoccupation with winning back Piper. Derek was just thankful Piper had said yes to the second proposal. Nick would have been heartbroken if she'd turned him down again. It was yet another reason he swore to remain single. Love was way too complicated.

He glanced at the house across the street. Ophelia stood at the front window, staring out. The woman was such a busybody. No need for neighborhood watch on this street; Ophelia had it covered. He eyed the roof as he walked up the front pathway.

He knew better, but the ten-year-old boy inside him couldn't resist. Messing with The Meddler was too much fun. What the hell! Throwing caution and better judgment to the wind, he grabbed the ladder from the side of the house.

Maybe he was destined to remain the hell-raiser who caused the townsfolk to raise their eyebrows. He definitely remained the black sheep of his family, a designation he proudly wore. He'd stopped caring years ago what others thought of him. There was freedom and empowerment in not giving a damn.

However, at night, he tossed and turned, staring at the ceiling. That's when he cared that he was the unlikeable son and possibly the town joke. However, it didn't stop him from wearing it like a badge of honor the rest of the day.

What was it about this roof that made him so introspective? Perhaps it wasn't the best place to sit after all. But it sure had a great view. He cracked another cold beer.

A car pulled up to the curb and out stepped Leighton, in all her golden beauty. He downed the beer in his hand.

She walked up the pathway to the front door, sending an annoyed glance at his truck, oblivious to the fact that he sat on the roof. He hated that she felt so uncomfortable around him. And he hated that he even cared.

He threw the empty can onto the grass near where she stood. She jumped and then moved back to stare up at the roof.

"What are you doing on Nick's roof?"

"Drinking."

"On the ROOF?"

Why did everyone keep asking that? Like roof drinking was so far-fetched.

"Why not? It has the best view."

Shockingly, she set her purse down and climbed up the ladder.

"Why are you drinking on Nick's roof?" she reworded the question as she reached the top rung.

"Afraid I'm going to jump?" His left eyebrow shot up, the

belligerent one that never failed to get him in trouble.

"Are you?"

"You'd like that!" The belligerent brow rose higher.

"No, Derek, I wouldn't," she sighed. "You'd make a mess of the flower bed I just planted."

The other brow shot up now. "That's it? You're worried about some stupid flowers?"

"The roof isn't high enough to cause you much harm."

He pursed his lips and continued to push. "Would you even care if I hurt myself?"

Leighton stared at him, gave a slight head shake, and started to back down the ladder.

"You're not going to join me?"

She paused, peering up at him. "No. Drinking with you never ends well."

Damn, that stung. But it was true. He should never have touched her that night in the cornfield maze. They'd both consumed far too much alcohol. He should have kept his no-good hands to himself.

"Are you ever going to forgive me?"

Her forehead creased as she digested his out-of-character words, and her eyes met his. They were multicolored — gold, green, and hazel. So expressive. Her hair moved in the slight breeze, shades of wheat and caramel. Even her sun-kissed skin was golden. Leighton Gray was mesmerizing, and he needed to stop noticing that.

With great effort, he forced air back into his lungs. Her presence always left him breathless. Was it caused by attraction or from guilt?

"I'm sorry, Leighton. I shouldn't have kissed you that night. I... I had feelings for you, and I acted on them."

Her mouth dropped open, and he instantly wished he could take the words back. They were far too honest. Feelings were something he kept buried and never admitted to having. And even while he regretted speaking those words out loud, he wondered just how true they were. Were his feelings for her genuine, or had she simply become a habit? For so long, he believed he wanted her, angered that she chose Tommy over him. Did he really care? Or was she just another competition between him and his twin?

He was nowhere near as torn up over losing her as Tommy was.

"I kissed you back. I could have stopped you, but I didn't." Leighton glanced away as she spoke. She looked so uncomfortable, and he hated that she felt that way around him. He hated that he had cost her so much already. She didn't need to lose her dignity as well.

"Of course, you kissed me back. I'm irresistible!" He reverted to the clown, the never-serious, full-of-himself persona he'd been playacting at for so long now.

Leighton visibly relaxed and climbed up the top rung, cautiously stepping onto the roof. "Give me a beer."

He handed her a cold can as she slowly sank beside him at the peak. He continued to stare at the woman he had no business staring at.

The truth was, Leighton belonged with Tommy. They were the golden couple. The perfect son marrying the girl he'd rescued from the wrong side of the tracks. They were a bloody fairytale come true. Tommy was her knight in shining armor. The hero.

And Derek had been the fire-breathing dragon who had destroyed that innocent love out of jealousy and spite. That was the hard and unflattering truth.

This rooftop truly did bring clarity. The biggest realization was that he wasn't meant for relationships. He ruined everything he touched. He had the right idea to only casually date. The women he dated were well aware that he was a commitment-phobe. No surprises. He was done hurting people.

She popped the tab and took a tentative swallow. "It was wrong of us. I don't know if Tommy will ever forgive us."

"So, we keep apologizing until he does." Ian's words came

back to him. "How many more times do I need to apologize before you forgive me?"

"This being the first time, I'd say at least a dozen more."

"Seriously? Sorry isn't an easy word for me." It always got stuck in his throat, tangling up his tongue. It had been that way since childhood. He hated to apologize.

She took another swallow from the beer can, staring at him over the rim. "It was a stupid mistake that we both regret."

He nodded, chugging the rest of his beer before throwing it on the grass beside the other one.

"You're picking those up." She shook her head. "You really are an ass."

"Yep," he grinned, pulling another beer out of the cooler. "Oh, crap."

"What?" Her head turned, following his stare, and she repeated his words. "Oh, crap."

Ophelia Meddler was crossing the road.

"Did Nick know he was building a house across the street from the Meddler?"

"That's why he got the land so cheap." Derek waved the beer can in his hand. "Want to join us for a beer, Mrs. Meddler?"

"Don't egg her on," Leighton warned him.

"I don't think there's been a Halloween yet where I missed egging her house. Last year included." He waggled his eyebrows at Leighton and was delighted to hear her laugh.

"Derek!"

"The Meddler has it coming! She called my mother last week when I was up here drinking. I got an entire lecture on drinking too much and acting my age." He shook his head, grimacing.

"See, it helped a lot."

"Whatever." He tried to sound belligerent, but it fell short.

"Is that you, Leighton Gray?" Ophelia stood on the curb, shielding the sun with a hand raised over her brow.

"I'll be all the talk at the next business association meeting," Leighton grumbled.

"Sure will," Derek agreed. "Sucks to be you."

"Shut up and hand me another beer." She tossed the empty can onto the grass beside the others. "You're picking that one up, too."

"Yes, ma'am." Hope began to fill him. If Leighton could forgive him, maybe Tommy would, too.

Working on this wedding might not be so bad after all.

Chapter 15

Jayna

Working on this wedding wasn't so bad. Jayna was checking items off her extensive list. She'd found place settings for the reception dinner by rummaging through Jamie's dinnerware section. It would be very eclectic with the mismatched antique China and would perfectly suit the rustic setting of the Old Mill.

Next on the list were linens. She drove to the outlet mall on the outskirts of the nearest city and cleaned out the Pottery Barn of all its neutral linens and blush-toned napkins. The third item was a little more challenging: bridesmaids and dresses for them. There were three groomsmen, and it was a given that Leighton would be maid of honor. Jayna didn't know any of Piper's friends and couldn't afford to waste time. So, she recruited herself and voluntold Jessica that she would be a bridesmaid. Beside the Pottery Barn was a women's boutique that carried formal wear. She found three identical chiffon dresses in plum. Jessica and Leighton were close to her size, and the dress fit her nicely. Sold.

Item number four, decorate the venue the night before. She could only pray that Derek did indeed hand off his list to Ben because it conflicted directly with item number one on her personal list; don't spend a minute longer than necessary with the Neanderthal.

Readjusting the garment bag on her arm, Jayna pushed open the door to Notion for Lotion. The delicate chime of a bell announced her while the soothing scents immediately wrapped around her. She inhaled deeply. Rows of beautifully displayed products caught her eye—luxurious creams and fragrant oils in colored bottles, handmade soaps, and candles.

Jayna surveyed the store with a mixture of awe and irritation. She didn't want to like anything about Leighton, least of all her incredible store.

Leighton glanced up, smiling, from behind the checkout counter. "Hi, Jayna."

Jayna nodded curtly, trying to resist the enchanting ambiance of the store. She wanted to peruse the candle selection, and her fingers itched to pick up the handmade lavender soap. The calming scent called to her. Of course, this woman who was so close to perfection would own a store that smelled like heaven.

She walked toward the counter. Despite her resistance, she couldn't stop herself from picking up a jar of whipped body butter, captivated by the blue sea glass with a wooden lid.

"That body butter is a customer favorite. The scent is a blend of lemon and lavender. It's very moisturizing and invigorating."

Jayna popped the lid and sniffed. "Hmm, well, I guess I've smelled worse."

Leighton raised an eyebrow. "You're one tough customer."

"I'm not here as a customer," Jayna stepped back and unzipped the dress bag. "I found three matching bridesmaid dresses in plum, which should go well with the neutral and blush color palette. I signed myself and Jessica up as bridesmaids and you, of course, as maid of honor."

She pulled the dress out of the bag.

"Oh, Jayna, it's beautiful! The color is perfect."

Jayna couldn't help but crack a small smile at Leighton's enthusiasm, but then recalled that she didn't like the woman and stiffened. "I'm just doing what I was asked."

Leighton touched the soft fabric, running it between her fingers. "I appreciate your help, Jayna. It means a lot to me, and I know Piper will love your choice."

Jayna looked away. It was impossible to maintain her dislike for Leighton when she was being so nice. "I just want everything to be perfect. Piper deserves to have the wedding of her dreams. I borrowed vintage dinnerware from Jamie's store and picked up the table linens."

"It's wonderful you thought of the surprise wedding. Piper will be shocked and so happy. You're right she does deserve this."

Jayna reluctantly met Leighton's gaze and found a warmth in her eyes that she hadn't noticed before. "I guessed your size. I can exchange it if it doesn't fit. But we're in a time crunch. Can you try it on right now? I have exactly one hour to exchange it."

Leighton glanced around the store.

"I'll hold down the fort while you try it on."

"Thanks. Ben and Derek will be by any minute for those boxes." Leighton took the dress and pointed to stacked boxes behind the counter.

Just her luck.

"Hurry up," she grumbled, and instantly felt bad at the hurt expression on Leighton's face. "I would prefer not to run into Derek. Unless, of course, it's with my truck."

Leighton hurried into the back room. Once she was out of sight, Jayna opened the lid on the cream again. She dipped her fingertip and spread it on her hand. Silky smooth. She needed this. And a candle. And shampoo. Jamie was raving over the shampoo she'd bought here.

What the hell? The dress had cost over three hundred dollars. She'd take it out in trade. Swallowing her pride, she grabbed a basket and started filling it. In the candle section, she chose a lavender-scented one and added two more. Moving on to the shampoo aisle, she picked up a bottle, flipping the lid. Coconut, vanilla, and pineapple—it reminded her of a Piña Colada. This one was definitely going in her basket. She frequently switched up shampoo scents. The smell of freshly washed hair was one of her favorite things, especially in the emergency department, where the smells weren't always fresh.

"What do you think?"

Jayna spun around. What did she think? She didn't want to be standing beside Leighton wearing the same dress. THAT'S what she thought. The chiffon hugged the woman's curves, and the plum shade complemented her sun-kissed skin. Leighton was simply stunning, and the green-eyed monster from Jayna's teen years reared its' ugly head.

It was crazy because Jayna was not an insecure person. Not normally. Just around Leighton.

The door chimes sounded along with a low wolf whistle.

"Wow, Leighton, you look incredible," Ben said.

"Beautiful," a low, sexy voice added.

Jayna twisted around. Derek stood next to Ben in the doorway. Both men were drooling. The green-eyed monster clawed its' way to the surface. She half-expected her own clothing to tear away like the Incredible Hulk.

She forced it back down. What did she care if Derek thought Leighton was beautiful? She couldn't care less.

She was here for Piper. All she cared about was creating Piper's dream wedding.

Chapter 16

Jayna

If this wasn't Piper's dream wedding, they'd come very close. Seated at the head table, Jayna felt pride as she looked around the reception hall. The venue was truly enchanting. She fully understood why Piper had chosen it the first time for the wedding that never happened. The historic mill was built in the 1800s and possessed an innate charm with wide plank flooring, exposed beams, and weathered stone walls. The linens she'd selected, along with the antique dinnerware, complemented the setting perfectly. The gold cutlery, added last minute, was the perfect finishing touch. She'd missed her calling as a wedding planner.

Jayna had to admit that it had been kind of fun. It was probably her only chance to plan a wedding because there was no way she'd be planning one for herself.

Her gaze moved, fixating on Piper as she gracefully twirled in Nick's embrace on the dancefloor. Where did Piper find the courage to risk her heart not once, but twice? Nick had hurt her so badly, yet she'd given him a second chance.

A strange sensation tugged at Jayna as she continued to watch Nick and Piper who were so obviously deeply in love. Was it yearning?

No, impossible.

She didn't want anything like this, did she?

Yet there was a nagging doubt that set in. Was she mistaken about the possibility of finding her soulmate? Could there be that one person who would stay by her side, someone who would be there for not only the good times but the bad times as well? Possibly there could be a man out there who would make her feel less alone.

She mentally shook her head. NO! That was not something she wanted. This romantic atmosphere was clouding her judgment. Normally, she remained detached at weddings and baby showers. But this time she'd been actively involved in not only the planning, but the execution of the entire event. Execution? Was that the right word? Maybe. Marriage did seem like a life sentence.

Forcing her eyes away from the happy couple, she gazed around the beautifully decorated room before stopping at Derek. Now that man was the perfect antidote to extinguish these unwanted romantic feelings.

Leaning against the bar, Derek tugged at the bowtie, appearing thoroughly miserable. She couldn't help but feel pleasure at his obvious discomfort.

Begrudgingly, she had to admit that he looked very handsome in the black tux. He'd even gotten a haircut for the occasion.

He met her gaze, and his eyes narrowed. Jayna hadn't failed to notice that Derek purposefully became more annoying and arrogant when she was around. And she reciprocated in kind. But for this wedding, they'd declared a ceasefire. Now her tongue hurt from biting it. By the pained expression on Derek's stupid face, it was taking all his willpower to behave as well.

The DJ called for the wedding party to join the bride and groom on the dancefloor. Jayna's head snapped back to Derek. He looked equally horrified. It had been bad enough that she'd been paired with him, having to walk down the aisle on his arm. But now she'd have to dance with him? A slow dance? Why her?

She stood, reluctantly walking to the edge of the dancefloor, side-eyeing him as he came to stand beside her. He held out his hand, and she took it, none too gently.

"Let's get this over with," he said, sounding annoyed. She

didn't want to dance with him any more than he wanted to dance with her.

"Wow, always the gentleman!" She moved into his arms.

He glared down at her, yanking her closer which caused her to stumble against him. "Hey, don't get the wrong idea," he muttered.

"What does that mean?" She forced herself away from his chest.

"It means don't fall for me." He blew her a kiss.

She snorted. "No chance of that!"

"What does that mean?" He used a high-pitched voice, regurgitating her question in an attempt to imitate her. It was a pretty good imitation.

"Derek, you are safe with me. I'm the last woman who would ever fall for your charms, or rather, your lack of them."

"I'm plenty charming," he answered, turning her in a slow circle.

Surprisingly, the baboon was a great dancer. The guy could be smooth when he wanted to be. Tonight, on his best behavior, he was almost tolerable.

"Yeah, okay," she snorted again. "If you were charming, you would have complimented my dress."

He pushed her back and slowly looked her up and down. "Your boobs look great in that dress."

"That's not a compliment!"

"There isn't a true compliment that a guy can give a woman."

"That is not true." She scrunched up her nose and narrowed her eyes.

"It is true. Every compliment can be taken the wrong way," Derek defended. "Your hair looks beautiful in that updo," he changed his voice to the high-pitched imitation of a woman. "Oh, so it doesn't look good when it's down?"

She huffed.

"Does my ass look big in these jeans?" he imitated again before lowering his voice. "No, it's your ass that makes your ass look big. Not the jeans."

"Speaking of asses! You are the biggest one I have ever met."

"I'm just honest."

"No, you're just blunt. You have no filter," she snapped. "Just shut your stupid mouth before I shut it for you."

The guy was a caveman. Insufferable.

"Like to see you try," he taunted.

"Don't tempt me," she clenched her teeth. "Just behave."

"I am."

He continued to spin her around. Her back tingled where his hand rested. He pulled her closer, his breath warm against her ear. "If you shut up, then I'll shut up."

"Like that's possible." A smile formed on her lips against her will. It felt good to be in his arms. The guy smelled amazing, and his chest was as hard as it looked. The smile died on her lips as an attraction for him blossomed. No, she'd be feeling this way with anyone. It was just this romantic venue. And any ape she danced with would probably cause the same effect.

She forced her eyes away from his impossible violet-blue ones. There was a mark on his neck. "What's that red mark?" She leaned closer. "Looks like syphilis."

"Ha, ha." He rubbed the spot she pointed out, staring at the red smear on his finger. "Some nurse you are. It's lipstick."

"I feel sorry for the poor woman. She'd be feeling bad about being single at yet another wedding. But I'm quite sure five minutes in the closet with you cured her," Jayna snorted and shook her head. "Is there a wedding where you didn't hook up?"

"Again, you're way off. That's my grandmother's lipstick. She tried to kiss my cheek and missed."

"I should advise her to get her lips swabbed for syphilis."

"I thought it was chlamydia that you gave me." He imitated her snort and winked.

"In your dreams, cowboy."

"Come on, you'd be so lucky. I bet I'll be in your dreams tonight." Derek gave her that lopsided grin, and it did something strange to her stomach. Or maybe the chicken she'd had for dinner was undercooked.

"More like in my nightmares."

Derek pulled her closer again. His head lowered. What the hell? "Did you just smell my hair?" she asked him.

"No," he shoved her away. "I was just muffling a sneeze."

"You are a charmer, Derek Brennan."

Thankfully the song ended, and she moved out of his embrace, stepping off the dancefloor. The guy was a Neanderthal. Seriously, why were there so many women vying for his attention? The dark good looks were completely wasted on him.

Jayna reclaimed her seat at the head table, relieved to find her glass of wine waiting. She picked it up and took a big gulp. Her eyes followed Leighton as she walked out the door to the waterfall patio before landing on Derek. He was back leaning against the bar, tugging on his tie. His eyes were trained on the patio door, staring after Leighton.

The guy was too much. He sneezed into her hair! Who did that? The same guy who was lusting after his brother's fiancée. Did it bother him to see that Tommy had followed Leighton to the patio? Did it even cause him a moment of guilt to realize that he'd caused such a rift between the couple?

She wasn't certain what had occurred between Leighton and Derek, but she was certain something had. Tommy was angry with them both. And Leighton always appeared so uncomfortable when Derek was around her. Oh, something had happened!

She'd bet her life on it.

Did the man have no morals? Were any women off-limits? And Leighton, what had she been thinking? Jayna had been observing them for a long time. There was something there, something undeniable. Had it happened while Tommy was deployed? She narrowed her eyes, taking in the tightness in Derek's jaw as he continued to stare at the closed door.

"Have you seen Leighton?"

She jumped and turned. "Oh, Piper. Uh, yeah, she went

outside to the patio."

"I'm about to toss the bouquet. Would you mind finding her?"

"No problem."

She stood and hurried past Derek, avoiding making eye contact. The man was not worth the aggravation. And poor Tommy. He had loved Leighton so much. No wonder he appeared so torn apart.

Pushing open the door, she stepped out onto the waterfall patio and paused. Tommy and Leighton stood at the railing. Tears were coursing down Leighton's cheeks, and Tommy looked so sad as he reached to wipe them away.

She should have turned and gone back inside. It was an intimate moment between them. But her curiosity overrode manners, and she continued to eavesdrop on their conversation.

"Seems like I also need forgiveness. How did everything get so messed up?" Tommy spoke quietly, but not so quietly that she couldn't overhear. "But we are different people now. We're not those teenagers anymore. I need time and so do you."

Jayna sucked in a breath. She was witnessing a breakup. Oh, no! They belonged together. Stupid Derek! The man not only broke hearts but destroyed relationships as well.

"I understand," Leighton replied.

No, Leighton shouldn't give up so easily. *Fight for him, Leighton,* Jayna wanted to shout out loud.

Tommy turned and noticed her. Busted.

"There you are." She cleared her throat and pretended that she hadn't just overheard their heartbreaking words. "Piper is looking for you. She's about to throw the bouquet."

Leighton glanced over her shoulder. Her expression was shattered. "I'll be right there."

Jayna stepped back inside. Derek was still propped against the bar. She reached out and swatted the back of his head as she walked past.

"Ouch, what was that for?" the Neanderthal complained, rubbing the back of his head.

Chapter 17

Derek

Derek rubbed the back of his head, glaring at Jayna as she sauntered past.

Without turning around, she lifted her right arm and flipped him off.

Typical Jayna. Annoying and argumentative. Nothing he said was right, and everything he did was wrong in her eyes.

Yet, she had great-smelling hair, always a different scent. Not that he went around sniffing her, of course. The first time was purely accidental when she'd fallen off the truck and into his arms, smelling of strawberries and cream. Tonight, she smelled like a tropical vacation. And that dress—wow. The woman had curves. He frowned. Was he seriously checking her out? Impossible.

Jayna had attitude and way too much of it. And she hated him. Mutual, sure, but it still bugged him. Women didn't hate him. Well, most didn't. Just two: Jayna and Leighton. The rest found him funny, even charming. But Leighton had preferred Tommy, and Jayna outright disliked him. She'd even said it to his face, "Derek, I don't like you."

That had to be the reason he was standing at the bar, nursing a whiskey sour and checking her out. The reason why he'd pulled her closer while they danced, inhaling her sweet scent. She was a challenge, nothing more. Just like Leighton had been. His feelings for his brother's girl had been more about competition than anything deeper. He really was messed up. Luckily, he had zero interest in a relationship, so his skewed feelings didn't matter.

His eyes stayed on Jayna as she joined the women on the dance floor for the bouquet toss. Why was she participating? She was as dead set against relationships as he was. Wasn't she worried that there might be actual magic in a flying bouquet of peonies?

The balcony door opened, and Leighton hurried in, looking extremely upset. She swatted at her eyes. Had she been crying? Even with tear-streaked cheeks, she was beautiful. She wore the same dress as Jayna, but it looked completely different on her. She wasn't as curvy. When he first saw Jayna, his jaw had dropped. Leighton, on the other hand, looked classy, as always. And as untouchable as ever. After their talk on the roof, he realized he no longer wanted to touch her.

The door swung open, and Tommy stormed in, his mouth set in a hard line. He must have been on the patio with Leighton and caused her tears. Derek shook his head, letting out a heavy breath. Leighton didn't deserve Tommy's anger. It should be all directed his way. More guilt surged.

Tommy should just haul off and punch him, like back in their teens. Then they could put this all behind them, and Tommy could finally forgive him. This silent animosity was worse than a bloody nose or a fat lip. The guilt was eating Derek alive. Why hadn't he just kept his hands to himself?

"Keep apologizing," Ian had said. That's what he'd told Leighton the other day on the roof. Well, to hell with that! If Tommy wanted to hold on to his anger, so be it! Next month, he and Ben were leaving for the TL Village in Sierra Leone to help install wells for Jovanny's charity. That day couldn't come soon enough. He needed to distance himself from his twin and this small town.

A cheer erupted as Piper threw her bouquet, and it landed in Jayna's hands. Hopefully, it was pure fiction that the woman who caught the bouquet was the next to marry, because he felt sorry for the poor schmuck who'd end up as Jayna's groom.

Jayna met his gaze from across the dance floor. She mouthed

something to him. Pretty sure she'd called him an asshole. The day he left for West Africa couldn't come soon enough. He was desperate to escape, not only from his twin, but from Jayna as well. The woman was everywhere.

He let his mind drift, picturing the unmatched landscape of Sierra Leone.

Chapter 18

Derek

The landscape of Sierra Leone was unmatched. Beautiful, and brutal. Such a contradiction. It was a place Derek connected with. He was both handsome and dark. He'd overheard enough people remark that his good looks were wasted on a man so cold and closed off. A handsome exterior that hid an ugly soul. Harsh, but true. It had to be true; otherwise, his twin would have forgiven him, and the universe wouldn't be so hell-bent on teaching him lesson after lesson.

Derek shot an annoyed glance at Tommy. Like what the hell? This trip was supposed to be a reprieve from all the crap at home. Sierra Leone was his escape, a place where his ugly soul became beautiful. But escape was impossible when his conscience, in the form of his twin, had tagged along.

His eyes moved back to Tommy, who had claimed the front seat with a smug grin just begging to be wiped off his face. Sufta, the hired driver for the TL Village, had met them at the pier. Tommy had hopped into the front seat, forcing Derek to climb into the back with Ben. His scowl deepened as Sufta navigated the narrow, heavily congested roadways. The back seat proved to be a much bumpier ride. Normally, he would have been chatting Sufta's ear off, sitting shotgun while taking in the mountain-backed capital city of Freetown.

The sun beat down relentlessly, and the infamous red dirt blew in. Derek was exhausted, grumpy, and now covered in a layer of dust that clogged his sweaty pores. Sufta expertly drove through the vehicular chaos of Freetown's main street but still managed to hit every single pothole. The road was barely wide enough for two lanes of traffic, yet somehow it fit four lanes as it curved through the crumbling colonial architecture.

Tommy sat directly in front of him. Derek couldn't resist giving the back of the seat a hard kick, letting his inner shit-disturbing ten-year-old out for a moment. They crested a hill, and he sucked in his breath, knowing what was coming. It never failed to shock him.

"That's Kroo Bay." Ben leaned between the front seats, acting like a tour guide. "It was once a fishing village and is now home to over sixteen thousand residents who were displaced during the civil war."

The shanty town was built on top of garbage next to a polluted river that flowed into the ocean. During the rainy season, the river swelled and overflowed, flooding the homes that were no larger than garden sheds. This was where true poverty lived.

Everyone deserved a safe place to call home and to have access to clean water. Yet in West Africa, that wasn't the case. Many remote villages were barely surviving, their residents forced to use contaminated streams as their only water source. This was where Jovanny's water well installation charity was making a difference. Yet, the harsh reality remained; the demand here far surpassed the limited resources available. Progress was happening far too slowly.

Relief filled Derek as Sufta drove past Kroo Bay, which was quickly replaced by guilt. Soon he'd be home, living a life of luxury while the people here continued to suffer.

Sufta pulled in front of TL Village, and Derek jumped out of the jeep before it came to a complete stop. The pristine white stucco building was a sight for sore eyes after the 20-plus hour travel day. He couldn't wait to lay his head on a pillow after showering off the grime from the dusty ride.

Rushing up the steps, he pushed open the large wooden door and stepped into the welcoming lobby. It never failed to astound him just what a wonderful place Jovanny Grotto, fellow actor Nash Logan, and billionaire cameraman Sam Marek had created here. They had renovated a run-down hotel, turning it into small apartments for families who had been casualties of the decade-long civil war. The lobby, painted a soft moss green, was filled with framed photographs of the families who now called this inspired place home.

It had become a home away from home for Derek as well. Here, he could be someone different, anyone he wanted to be. Here, he wasn't the hell-raising adult or remembered as the trouble-making teen, but rather a man who was respected and did good. He was even admired here, not that he came for admiration. When Jovanny first started the well-drilling charity, he signed up out of curiosity. He had the skills and knowledge needed to get the operation off the ground. Now, he felt a strong pull to keep returning to pitch in. While they could only help one village at a time, it meant one more community that no longer had to suffer.

Despite having little to be thankful for, the people of Sierra Leone always found reasons to be grateful. It was humbling to be part of it. Working in the impoverished country made him feel good about himself in a way he never felt at home.

A middle-aged blonde woman entered the lobby, and he rushed towards her. "Heidi!" He scooped her up and twirled her around. "Miss me?"

"Put me down. And no, I didn't," the Swedish doctor demanded, but the grin tugging at the corners of her lips negated the firm words. "You are annoying. Always up to no good, flashing that hard-to-resist smile, using it to get yourself out of trouble. But I have your number, Derek Brennan."

"So why don't you ever call me?"

A blush reddened her cheeks. "You are still an incorrigible flirt."

"And she's spoken for," Wils, Heidi's partner, said as he walked down the stairs.

"That's never stopped him before," Tommy muttered as he

and Ben carried in the luggage.

Derek turned, frowning. This was not going to be the escape it normally was for him. Why did Tommy have to tag along to the one place that had become Derek's calling in life?

Chapter 19

Jayna

Nursing had never been Jayna's calling in life, yet it had become her passion. During her final year of high school, she felt completely lost. Her friends had their futures mapped out, while Jayna had no clue. Jamie wanted to pursue carpentry, which held no interest for Jayna. Jessica was taking a psychology course which didn't resonate with her either. But Kylie's decision to apply to Toronto University for a Bachelor of Science in Nursing sparked something within her. The allure of living in such an exciting city, coupled with Kylie's fun-loving nature, had Jayna applying as well. Plus, it was a far cry from the business degree her parents urged her to pursue.

After earning her nursing degree, Jayna remained in Toronto, working in the bustling ER of the city hospital. The fast-paced environment provided an exhilarating rush but also took a toll, leaving her mentally and physically drained.

Returning to Blythe Landing had been a wise decision. She missed her best friends, who had all moved back, and she missed the close-knit community. However, the Blythe Landing Emergency Department was much slower paced. And dating? Well, that was slow-paced too. There just weren't as many men in the small town as compared to Toronto.

Jayna glanced at the time displayed in the lower right-hand corner of the computer monitor. This shift was dragging painfully slow. They'd seen fifteen patients all day. Fifteen! The Toronto ER saw fifteen every half hour. She couldn't wait for her shift to be done. Tonight, she had a date. It was not just any date, but a double date. The new X-ray tech was gorgeous, and he had a friend who she'd set Leighton up with.

Leighton had been less than receptive to the idea, but Jayna insisted. She felt a deep compulsion to make up for her past bad behavior. Witnessing Leighton's heartbreak at Piper and Nick's wedding had left Jayna feeling guilty and ashamed. She'd misjudged Leighton like the rest of the town. Leighton's upbringing was far from easy, thanks to parents who were the town joke. They were the complete opposite of Jayna's—poor and unrespectable. However, there was a shared common thread of dysfunction and neglect.

Jayna was determined to make it right with Leighton. The best way to get over a broken heart was to get back on the horse. She just prayed that Leighton didn't bail.

She sent a text: <See you at Patty's tonight at 8>

"Jayna, you have a patient in exam room 3," Michelle, the charge nurse, said, shooting a disapproving look at Jayna's cell phone.

Jayna shoved the phone behind her computer monitor and stood, grabbing the chart off the wall. Overdose, 22-year-old female. Sadly, even in a small town, drugs and overdoses were becoming epidemic.

"Hi, I'm Jayna, your nurse." She identified herself and pulled the privacy curtain behind her.

The young woman sat on the exam bed, tightening her arms around her legs, refusing to meet Jayna's eyes. The makeup was thick on her cheek, covering a bruise.

"I see that you ingested quite a few OxyContin today," Jayna stepped further into the room and glanced at the chart. "Talia, is it?"

"Yes, and it was an accident. I'm fine." Talia swiped at her lips, smearing the activated charcoal drink the triage nurse had given her.

"Are you sure, Talia?"

Talia's eyes darted. She reminded Jayna of a distrustful, wounded animal. Life had clearly been unkind to her. And why wouldn't she try any means possible to escape? Unfortunately, the sterile hospital room was not comforting.

"I need to get an IV started," Jayna pulled over the nursing cart and sat on the edge of the bed, smiling kindly.

Talia held out her arm, and Jayna tied an elastic band above a vein.

"I'm more than just an addict," Talia said softly while Jayna swiped an alcohol swab across the vein. "I wasn't always this way."

Jayna glanced up and met her eyes for the first time. Big brown doe eyes. Frightened and so very sad.

"It's not too late to make this right," Jayna told her softly.

Talia sighed, blinking back tears. "Oh, I've tried. The past year has been a living hell. I wish I was stronger."

Jayna reached for the tissue box off the cart, handing it to Talia.

Talia wiped at her tears. "I am a mother of a beautiful four-year-old boy. I once had a nice home for us. It wasn't big, but it was clean and safe. I had a good job and a nice car. Now I have nothing. I lost my job, my car, my home," she choked on a sob, "my son."

Setting a comforting hand on Talia's arm, Jayna blinked back tears herself.

"And now I've lost all hope as well. I've lost everything," Talia repeated. "I've ruined my life. I have lost absolutely everything I have ever cared about. I have nothing left."

"It's never too late," Jayna said again, with more conviction this time.

"I only have the clothes on my back. The bank repossessed my car, we were evicted, and my parents took my son. The storage unit auctioned off my belongings. I was living in shelters, and I thought I had met a great guy," she pointed at the bruising on her cheek. "But again, I was wrong."

"You can't just give up," Jayna persisted. "You have too much to live for."

Talia shook her head. "I have tried. I worked hard to become clean. It didn't make a difference. Everyone still sees me as a drug addict. My mom refuses to let me see my son. No one will give me a job. Without a job, I can't get an apartment. Without an apartment, I have no chance of getting my son back. And without my son, I have no hope."

"That was before you met me, Talia." Jayna leaned forward and squeezed the woman's hand. "I have enough hope for both of us until you can find your own."

Jayna wasn't quite sure why she had made that promise to Talia. Something about the woman deeply touched her. She wanted to help her, just as she wanted to help Leighton get over the break-up with Tommy.

Unfortunately, the blind double date did not go well. But it was only her first attempt. Sorting through her closet, she filled a duffle bag with clothing. She had way too many clothes, and some of the items still had price tags attached. With the bag filled, she headed to the shelter where Talia was staying.

The shelter was bare bones and depressing. How did anyone thrive living in a place where hope came to shrivel up and die? More was needed than just a duffle bag filled with clothing and toiletries. She found Talia watching an episode of 'Friends' in the common room. "Pivot", Ross was saying. Pivot. That's exactly what was needed. This woman needed to pivot her entire life, and Jayna would be there to help.

Chapter 20

Derek

Derek just needed to pivot. This was bigger than just the shared animosity between two brothers. He needed to remember exactly why he had returned to Sierra Leone. He was here to help the incredible people who were struggling to survive in such a harsh and challenging land.

But Tommy? He had no idea what Tommy's motivation was in tagging along. Was it to continue making Derek's life a living hell? No, Tommy was not that nefarious. He was the perfect son, after all.

Whatever his brother's motivation was, it didn't concern him. He would keep himself busy. There was so much work to be done. Water well installation was hard, tiring work. It was actually back-breaking under the intense African sun. He'd work hard, go to bed early, rise even earlier, and repeat. Tommy could do whatever Tommy was here to do. Their paths didn't need to cross.

It was working. Three days in and he'd barely seen his brother. Then Tommy had to go and be wonderful Tommy and come up with an incredible idea. Rejoice! All hail the amazing Tommy. The guy was here all of five minutes and was already the hero.

It didn't matter that this was Derek's third trip here. That he was the one with the engineering degree and the skill to actually make a difference. Oh no, Tommy just came up with a great plan. Everyone was raving over it, and now Derek had even more work to do.

However, he grudgingly had to admit that it was pretty good. The idea was to build a workshop for one of the villagers, Mariama. Currently, she was making African black soap to sell at the local market. With a well in the village, she no longer walked 2 km each way to the stream for water which meant she now had time to dedicate to soap making. But she was forced to use a heavy black cauldron over an open fire pit. It was unsafe and time-consuming.

Tommy had spoken with Leighton about ordering modern equipment that would streamline the production of this soap. Leighton planned to carry the soap in her store, and the TL Village Mercantile would stock it as well. Both stores had a successful online business, which meant Mariama's soap would be sold worldwide. And she'd need to employ more villagers to help keep up with the demand.

Mariama needed a workshop with solar panels installed on the roof to provide a power source for the modern equipment. And that's where Derek came in. He'd drawn up plans and was now drilling a metal track into the cement pad that had been poured the day before. He straightened, stretching out his back, and wiped the sweat from his forehead.

Unscrewing the cap on his water bottle, he took a long swallow and took in the scenery all around. Makeni Village was made up of clay huts with straw-thatched roofs. A tropical rainforest lay behind the huts, and the once barren field was now planted. With clean water and stocked pantries, the villagers already appeared healthier.

Pens were being built to house goats and chickens. Ben put his fancy agricultural degree to good use, planting the fields with sustainable crops. Soon, this entire village would be sustainable as well.

"Son of a … Derek!" Ben howled and hobbled on one foot.

Derek set down the water bottle and ran toward his youngest brother, who was leaning on Tommy's shoulder.

"What's wrong?" He reached his brothers just as Heidi did. The doctor was here with the medical van, checking up on the villagers.

"You left a piece of wood with a nail sticking out is what's wrong," Ben yelled and pointed at his right shoe where blood was pooling, and a nail stuck out the top.

"Really, Derek, how could you be so careless?" Tommy chastised him.

"Damn, Benji. I'm sorry." Derek swiped at his brow again. How had he been so careless?

"It could have been one of the kids," Heidi scolded him as well. She bent down to examine Ben's foot, touching the blood on top of his shoe where a nail protruded. She lifted her finger and frowned as she sniffed the red splotch on it. Heidi lifted Ben's foot higher and yanked off the piece of wood under his shoe. Duct tape had been holding it in place.

Heidi stood and grabbed the ball cap off Ben's head, hitting him with it. Then she smeared the red 'blood' from her finger across his cheek and swatted Tommy as well.

"Ketchup! Damn fools. The entire Brennan clan is a bunch of jokers." Heidi sputtered and stomped back to the medical van.

Derek stared at the ketchup smear on Ben's cheek and then down at the nail that Ben had quite obviously stuck through the top of his shoe. His little brother was an ass who thought he was freaking hilarious. "Ketchup? Seriously, Ben? I have a ton of work to get done. And you're wasting my time being a jackass."

Ben doubled over laughing, as did Tommy. Derek was happy that they were both enjoying themselves so much while he was breaking his back in the scorching sun, working on Tommy's project, no less.

"You two don't want to start a prank war with me," he warned. "It won't end well for either of you."

"Whoa, shaking in my boots," Ben taunted. "Bring it, big bro."

Derek narrowed his eyes and shook his head. They were not worth it. The kids here did not need to witness a Brennan brother scuffle. It was never pretty. It also was immature. Oh, but it would feel so good.

He turned and stomped back toward the workshop build. "Why don't you take the higher road?" his mother used to ask him. Today he would, because in Sierra Leone he was not a hothead daredevil.

"Need a hand?"

He spun around. Tommy was following him. Didn't his brother realize that he was taking the higher road? Following him was not a good idea.

"From you?" he scoffed.

Tommy glanced over his shoulder at the empty space behind him. "No, the guy standing behind me."

"He'd be more helpful," Derek sneered.

"He probably would be more help. But it looks like I'm the only one offering."

"Nah, I'm good. You'll mess it up and make more work for me," Derek told his brother, his voice smug and dismissive.

"Pretty sure I can manage to hold up the wall while you nail it in place without MESSING IT UP," Tommy emphasized the last three words.

"Knock yourself out." Derek didn't want to accept his brother's help, but it would make the build go faster with an extra pair of hands.

"I'd rather knock you out," Tommy muttered, and Derek pretended not to hear.

Tommy bent and picked up one end of the framed wall. "Wow, it's hot here."

Derek glared at him. He was not going to make small talk with his twin. Tommy could help, but it would be in silence.

They lifted the frame onto the foundation, attaching it to the metal plate.

"So, I was thinking that I've been kind of a jerk," Tommy said nonchalantly.

Derek snorted. "Just kind of?"

"Are you going to make me say it?"

"Yep." Derek paused from hammering.

"I am sorry that I wouldn't accept your apology."

"Damn straight you should be. You know how hard that word is for me to say." Derek straightened and stared directly at him. "While you're admitting your shortcomings, you should also acknowledge that you were too hard on her."

Tommy's brow furrowed.

"Leighton," Derek clarified. "You should never have blamed her. You should have come home and decked me. I deserved your anger. Not her."

Tommy stared at him. Was he considering punching him in the face? It would probably make them both feel better. He watched Tommy ball his hand into a fist, but he kept it at his side.

"I was so sick of hearing about the stupid wedding," Derek continued. "Once again, it was all about Tommy. Tommy this, Tommy that. And I was acting stupid and selfish."

"So, your normal self, in other words," Tommy spat out.

Derek sent him an annoyed glance and then shrugged his shoulders. Tommy was right. "Pretty much. Still no excuse, but I had been pounding back whiskey that night. Then frigging Ben goes and suggests a game of manhunt like we were all still ten..."

Clearing his throat, he kept confessing. "I ran into her. Literally. And I kissed her."

He could see his brother's face growing red, and it wasn't from the intense heat. "It's just like my bike. You hated that I saved enough to buy it."

"Not that stupid bike again," Derek moaned. When they were twelve, they shared a paper route. Of course, Tommy saved every dime he earned. But Derek spent it as fast as he made it. When Tommy saved enough, he bought this bike, and Derek had been so envious of it. But he really hadn't meant to ruin it. He truly thought he could make the jump with it. Instead, he'd cracked the frame.

"I didn't mean to wreck it," he told Tommy.

"Yeah, I still don't believe you."

Derek closed his eyes, exhaling. "Seeing we're on this whole spill-your-guts thing, I will admit that I was jealous. Jealous of the stupid bike and jealous of Leighton. I was jealous of how much time you spent with her. I was jealous that she liked you better than me."

Tommy blinked. He had not been expecting the truth from Derek. "Why? You could have any girl you wanted in high school."

Derek sat on the pile of lumber, taking a long swallow from his water bottle. "Those girls didn't really want me. They just wanted the bad boy. I was a challenge for them. Or maybe the guy to piss off Daddy. I was a good time, not their forever guy."

He held out the water bottle to Tommy, and he took it, taking a drink.

"I was not boyfriend material like you were. I was never the guy they dreamed of spending forever with, just their right now. You were the forever guy, though. And I was so jealous of the way Leighton looked at you. You could do no wrong in her eyes."

Tommy stared at him, his brow furrowing as he digested what were probably the first honest words Derek had spoken in a very long time.

"Maybe you should punch me, and then we can move past it. Add in a second punch for the bike."

"I should," Tommy agreed. "But you need help to build this workshop. I won't be much help with an injured hand. You have a really hard head."

"Just as hard as yours." Derek stood. "This workshop isn't going to build itself."

He grabbed a hammer out of the toolbox and tossed it in the air. Tommy caught it.

"You know that I have carpentry skills. They may be rusty, but I can still out-build you any day."

"Really?" Derek narrowed his eyes. "Care to place a wager on it?"

"A wager?"

"Each of us builds a side wall. Let's see who finishes first. The loser has to give Heidi a foot rub. Walk up to her and pull off her shoe. Just start rubbing her foot."

"Deal!" Tommy nodded. Apparently, they hadn't outgrown their competitive nature.

Derek spread out the cut lumber on the ground. Tommy was cranking his head, spying. He'd allow that, because he truly did have the edge. He was the one who had designed the blueprints and did this for a living.

He hammered the first nail, then the second. He could hear Tommy hammering away too. Now he was stealing glances over his shoulder. What the hell! Tommy was really moving. Damn, he was not going to lose. The doctor absolutely terrified him.

"Done!" He heard Tommy yell.

What the bloody hell!

"Hurry up, looks like the doctor is packing up shop," Tommy taunted. "Bet she'll really appreciate that foot rub you're about to give her."

Derek groaned and hammered in the last nail into his frame. "Seriously? You're going to hold me to it?"

"A bet's a bet!" Tommy said, a little too smugly. "Hey Benji, get your butt over here. You don't want to miss this."

"You're such an ass," Derek grumbled and started to walk toward the medical van. He strolled to the back of the van, where Heidi sat on the tailgate, writing in a notebook. He shook his head. Damn, Tommy. Stupid bet. He stooped down on one knee in front of her and pulled off her shoe.

"What do you think you're doing?" she yelled.

Derek took hold of her bare foot and started rubbing. She swatted him across the head repeatedly with her notebook. He let go of her foot, falling backward. She stood and continued to hit him. Damn, she had good aim. He crab-crawled away.

"Get him, Heidi," Ben yelled.

Both his brothers were jackasses. He really hoped they were enjoying themselves. Tommy's face was lit up with laughter like it once had before Kandahar and before Derek had betrayed him. His brother was transforming, as was this village.

He stared at the workshop. Ben was helping Tommy erect the wall he'd just built. It was going to mean so much to the community. There was going to be a new business in town, and it was going to be life changing.

Chapter 21

Jayna

There was a new business in town, and it was spectacular. Jovanny Grotta, along with his movie star friend, Nash Logan, and billionaire cameraman, Sam Marek, had opened this store that was filled with treasures from West Africa. Tourists were flocking to the town, hoping to spot a celebrity, but stayed for the enchanting store. Jayna welcomed the competition. The more foot traffic on the sidewalk, the better. Plus, all proceeds from TL Village Mercantile went to charities established by the actors in Sierra Leone.

This unique approach supported the people of the impoverished country by purchasing their handmade items to be sold through larger, more far-reaching stores. People who struggled to sell their goods locally now were selling globally. The online store was apparently thriving, as was the second physical store in Los Angeles.

Jayna pushed open the door of TL Village Mercantile, her neck cranking from left to right. Everywhere she looked was a visual pleasure. Hand-painted murals of the Sierra Leone landscape covered the walls, making her feel like she had left Canada and been transported to an African market. Handwoven baskets were stacked by the front door. She picked one up and proceeded to fill it with jewel-toned fabric for a beach cover-up, a large straw hat, and a matching straw bag—exactly what she needed for the upcoming trip to Mexico.

She stood in line to pay. Picking up a brochure for Joe's Sunflower Farm charity, which raised money for water well installations, she flipped through it. And there, in full color on the second page, was the ape-man himself.

In the full-page photograph, a shirtless Derek leaned on a shovel, beads of sweat glistening on his forehead and his hard chest. Behind him, a stream of crystal-clear water gushed from the new well as local villagers filled bright, colorful containers, their smiles wide and eyes shining with gratitude.

Jayna brought the brochure closer, studying Derek's face. His usually cool, detached demeanor was replaced by something she had rarely seen—a genuine smile tugging at the corners of his lips. It was undeniable, even to her. This man, whom she found insufferable in so many ways, was making a significant, positive impact. Maybe under that hard chest, there was a heart after all.

She sighed, her fingers tracing the edge of the photo. Jayna couldn't help but begrudgingly admit it: Derek Brennan was doing a wonderful thing and looked very sexy while doing it.

She'd heard that he was back from another trip to Sierra Leone. How had it gone with Tommy tagging along? Were the brothers finally able to put their differences aside? However, only Derek and Ben had returned. Tommy had stayed to continue working with the TL Village charities. Jessica was there as well, offering her counselling services to some traumatized women.

Jayna stepped out of TL Village Mercantile just as Jamie came out of her store. "Hey Jamie, I got some great things for our trip."

"Wonderful," Jamie smiled and peeked in the bag. "Wow, I love the hat."

"Me too. I want to slip into Leighton's and grab some of that black soap you were raving about." She wanted to check up on Leighton as well. How was the woman faring with the news that Tommy had remained in Sierra Leone?

They jaywalked across the road, setting the chimes off as they pushed open the heavy black door.

"It always smells so incredible in here." Jayna inhaled deeply and then pointed a finger at Leighton. "You've been holding out on me."

"I have?" Leighton turned from the teak cabinet she was stocking.

"You have this amazing new soap and I have to hear about it from Jamie." She pursed her lips in a dramatic pout. "I thought we were besties?"

Leighton grabbed two bars and gave one to each of them. "I thought we were friends too until you set me up on the blind date from hell."

"You too?" Jamie gave Jayna a light punch in the arm. "Jayna, you need to take down your shingle. You suck as a matchmaker."

"I do not!"

"You can't even find yourself a suitable date," Jamie countered.

"That's because I don't want a suitable date. I like my men slightly disreputable."

"How much do we owe you for the soap?" Jamie pulled her wallet out of a vintage Dior bag. Jayna eyed it up. When they were done here, she needed to go check out Jamie's store.

"It's on the house."

Jayna pulled out her wallet as well. "Nope, we are paying. This soap is supporting families in Sierra Leone. I'm going to pay double."

Leighton moved behind the counter. "Okay, then."

"Jamie is paying double too," Jayna volunteered.

"Great, I'll send an e-transfer to Sam Marek. He can see that Mariama gets the extra money."

"We didn't just come in for the soap," Jayna said, handing over two twenties. "We are planning our fall girls' trip. Mexico is the winner this year, and with Jessica off having her own adventure, we are short a J. You have blonde hair, so we just need to change your name. Maybe Jade or Jewel."

"Oh no! I couldn't possibly go. I have the store to run." Leighton took the money and set it in the cash register.

Siobhan Winston, Burke's mother, came out from the back room. Leighton had hired the woman about a month ago. "She can get away. Mary Beth and I can manage the store for a week or two."

Leighton shot her new employee a scathing look. "And the cat. I have no one to watch Tuesday."

"Shamus can check in on Tuesday. He works in your gardens every day," Siobhan said matter-of-factly.

Leighton opened and closed her mouth, not able to come up with another excuse. "Mexico is a place I've always wanted to visit."

Chapter 22

Jayna

Mexico was a place on Jayna's bucket list. Watch the sunset over the Yucatan Peninsula—check. And it didn't just set; it cast a jaw-dropping golden glow over the lush landscape. The crystal-clear waters of the cenote below mirrored the vibrant colors of the sky. Beside her, Leighton and Jamie sighed.

The air was thick with the scent of tropical flowers and the echoing calls of exotic birds. The three women carefully navigated the rocky path to the cenote's edge. Jayna dipped her toe into the water, shivering at its' coolness—no surprise, as it was fed by groundwater. Without hesitation, she jumped in.

Swimming in the caves was another bucket list item. Convincing Jamie and Leighton took a bit longer, but soon they were all exploring the underwater cave together. Majestic stalactites hung from the ceilings like ancient chandeliers, making Jayna feel part of something timeless and magical.

When they emerged, the sky had turned a deep shade of purple, and they rushed to catch their bus. That night, they dined at an authentic Mexican restaurant, yet another bucket list item. The charming little place had a thatched roof with tables set under the stars and served the most delicious chicken mole.

The next morning was perfection. Early sunlight bathed the resort, casting long shadows over the manicured gardens and sparkling pool. The aroma of her coffee mingled with the sweet scent of the frangipani that bloomed next to the shaded terrace. Jayna inhaled deeply.

A week was never long enough on vacation. There was something about being close to the ocean, the sound of the crashing waves, and the feel of warm sand beneath her feet that brought a peace she couldn't find anywhere else.

Taking a sip of her coffee, she glanced up as Leighton stepped onto the terrace and sat in the empty seat across from her.

"Wow, that's quite the breakfast spread," Leighton said, setting her plate of fresh fruit on the table. "Jamie's still out cold?"

"She's a lightweight. That last margarita did her in," Jayna smiled, then grimaced at her own plate filled with bacon and fried eggs, not a piece of fruit in sight.

"I'm so grateful that you included me on this trip." Leighton's expression grew more serious. "It's exactly what I needed."

Jayna leaned back in her chair and nodded. "I have never seen you so relaxed."

"The past four years have been a whirlwind. It's been non-stop stress, grief, guilt, relief, sadness," Leighton squeezed her eyes shut. "So many emotions tangled up in one big, messy knot. It turned into such a train wreck. One which I had no idea how to fix. I still don't."

Jayna knew it wasn't her business. However, Leighton had become an honorary J, which meant her life was now an open book. The Js butted their noses into each other's business. "So, what exactly happened there? Was it over Derek?"

Leighton's mouth dropped open, and she stuttered. "Oh... um...nothing that I'm proud of."

"No judgment here, Leighton. I am far from being a pillar of the community," Jayna encouraged her to continue. She didn't ask because she was being nosy, although she was, but she felt that Leighton needed to get it off her chest. Holding onto secrets was unhealthy.

"The night of the harvest dance, before Tommy went missing in action," Leighton paused momentarily before continuing. "I had way too much to drink. And we started to play that stupid game of manhunt, running through the corn maze like we were all still a bunch of kids."

Groaning, Leighton looked upward and shook her head. "I ran into Derek. I literally ran into him. And I still don't know how it happened or why it happened. But he kissed me, and I kissed him back. I can try to blame it on the alcohol. Yet that's no excuse. That night I had a video call with Tommy and confessed. Told him all about the kiss."

Leighton squeezed her eyes shut again. "The expression on Tommy's face will forever be ingrained in my mind. He looked so hurt, so angry, and disappointed. For the first time, he looked at me like the rest of the town once had. He looked at me like I was no good, just like my mother."

Instant shame filled Jayna. She attended the harvest dance that night as well. She'd been the one plying Leighton with alcohol because she wanted to see the woman who was so perfect come a little undone. She'd dragged her into the corn maze when Ben had suggested the game of manhunt. But she'd never wanted to ruin Leighton, merely take away the shine.

"I guess, though, it's always been there," Leighton continued. "I was curious. Tommy was wonderful and safe. And Derek, he was so different. Dark, dangerous, mysterious. I felt like I had to be perfect for Tommy. It was exhausting sometimes."

Jayna leaned forward and grabbed Leighton's hand, squeezing. "I get that, Leighton. I can understand that you would feel guilty about it. But wow, you and Tommy were so young. He was your one and only boyfriend. I still remember Tommy at the age of 10, telling anyone who would listen that he would marry you one day."

"He did do that," Leighton smiled at the memory.

"Leighton, you shouldn't be so hard on yourself. You made a mistake and owned it. You apologized; now it's all on Tommy to forgive you or not. We have no control over other people."

"You're right. I know you are, but I still have deep feelings for Tommy." She paused, brow wrinkling. "Can I tell you a secret?"

"Of course."

"Tommy was always good looking, but now there is more of

a ... I don't know, a more dangerous edge to him. This new Tommy makes my knees weak in a way the old Tommy never did."

Jayna nodded, encouraging her.

"But the new Tommy no longer feels the same way about me." Leighton wiped a tear.

Jayna leaned forward and squeezed the woman's hand.

"It's time to move on. Time to move past the Brennan brothers." Leighton cleared her throat. "So, why did you and Derek never date? You're so much alike."

Jayna shot Leighton a skeptical look.

"What? It's not like he's hard to look at."

"No," Jayna said, shaking her head. "He's just hard to take! He's a total ass." She shifted in her chair and stared directly at Leighton. "Are you saying that I'm an ass, too?"

"No, of course not," Leighton said quickly, holding up her right hand. "That's not what I meant. It's just that you're both rebels."

"That we are," Jayna agreed. "But we also hate each other."

"It's a fine line between love and hate," Leighton murmured, picking at the fruit on her plate.

"Well, I do love to hate him," Jayna admitted.

Leighton shifted uncomfortably before meeting Jayna's gaze. "And you hated me too."

Jayna raised an eyebrow and was filled with even more shame. "Not hated. I was jealous."

Leighton set her fork down and blinked. "Jealous of me? Why?"

Jayna leaned back in her chair, thinking back to that time. "I didn't always hate Derek. In high school, I had it bad for him. When he asked me out, I just couldn't believe it. My crush noticed me. Then he crushed me."

"Oh, Jayna, I'm sorry."

"Yeah, well, I should have known better. Why would he treat me any differently than the other girls he dated? I wasn't stupid. I saw the way he used and discarded them. But I thought he would be different with me. Until I was just like all the others."

"So, why would you be jealous of me?" Leighton asked softly.

"Because you were the one girl he was truly obsessed with. I noticed the way he couldn't keep his eyes off you."

"You must realize that I was just another challenge for him. Yet another competition between the two brothers. It wasn't any deeper than that. Derek admitted it to me before Nick's wedding. He even apologized."

"Wow, the ape-man said sorry?"

"He did," Leighton said with a small laugh. "No one was more shocked than I was. And that night at the wedding, Tommy and I had a long overdue talk. It's truly over between us."

Jayna shook her head. "Relationships are complicated and require way too much work. Especially if you add in trying to figure out the Brennan twins."

Leighton laughed, a genuine, warm sound that made Jayna smile in return. "Tell me about it. But enough about Derek and Tommy. What about you? Anyone new?"

Jayna rolled her eyes. "Nope. Only a string of bad dates. Maybe I'm destined to remain single."

"Or maybe," Leighton said, reaching across the table to squeeze Jayna's hand, "you just haven't found the right person who can handle your fire."

"My fire or my ire?" Jayna laughed and her eyes moved upward as she continued speaking. "There is this one guy, though. He's absolutely dreamy. A paramedic who doesn't know I'm alive. It's just like high school all over," she chuckled.

"Doesn't know you're alive? Impossible!" Leighton exclaimed.

"I've watched everyone around me find 'the one'—Kylie and Piper—and I kept telling myself I was fine, just doing my own thing. But lately, I've been thinking… maybe they're onto something. I don't need a relationship, but what if I want one? And Lance, the paramedic, I could see myself wanting more with him. He has substance."

"So, what's stopping you?"

"He doesn't see me as a woman to settle down with. He just sees Jayna Date and Dash."

"So, prove to him that he's wrong," Leighton said with conviction.

Jayna laughed, but it was hollow. "It's easy to say that, but in this town? I'm the punch line of almost every joke. People don't see me as someone who could settle down or be serious about life. I've become this... this caricature, and I hate it. I hate that everyone assumes I'm happy with being the 'fun girl,' the one who's always up for a good time but never for something real."

Leighton sighed, her eyes searching Jayna's face. "You're allowed to want more, Jayna. And you're allowed to tell people it hurts when they reduce you to a joke. If it bothers you this much, why do you let them keep doing it?"

Jayna leaned back, staring down at her coffee cup. "Because it's easier to laugh it off. If I let them know it hurts, they'll just pity me. I don't want anyone's pity. I just..." She hesitated and blew out her cheeks. "I don't know if I'm even capable of settling down. Maybe they're right."

Leighton frowned. "No. They're not right. And neither are you. You're capable of anything. You've just been hiding behind that laughter because you're scared to let anyone in. And I get it. But if you want something real, you need to go after it."

Jayna closed her eyes, feeling the weight of Leighton's words settle over her. "I think what I need is to take a break from dating, serious or casual. I need to spend some time working on me."

It dawned on her as she spoke the words just how true they were. It wouldn't be wise to start a relationship until she'd dealt with all the issues that had stopped her from pursuing one in the first place.

Jayna shrugged. "A problem for another day. Today, I'm happy to be here with you and Jamie. This trip is exactly what I needed."

As they finished breakfast, the sun climbed higher in the sky, promising another day of adventure and possibility. The past and all its complications could be set aside.

Part 2

9 months later

Chapter 23

Jayna

The past and all its complications kept coming back to haunt and humiliate her. The conversation Jayna had with Lance last week kept replaying. Every embarrassing word. Why had she put herself out there like that?

Tired of waiting for him to make a move, she took charge and asked him out first. She squeezed her eyes shut as the memory resurfaced. "I'm sorry, Jayna, while I'm flattered, I'm not into casual dating," he had said gently. Clearly, the rumors about her were still circulating.

Over the past year, she had done a lot of soul-searching, tackling her trust issues and commitment struggles head-on. She had matured and had grown tired of the endless cycle of casual flings. She was finally ready for something real, something lasting. And she wanted that with Lance.

However, her transformation must not have been obvious, because neither the town's gossips nor Lance had taken notice.

"I am attracted to you, it's just that." Lance had continued and she interrupted him before he finished the sentence.

With a bright smile that hid the hurt, she blinked away the sudden tears that had formed in her eyes and brushed him off. "No worries, have a great day." Didn't he see how well suited they were for each other? Why didn't he see her as a woman who was worthy of his time?

As Jayna pulled open the door to Patty's Pub the scent of spicy wings and stale beer greeted her. Nothing had changed here in the past nine months that she'd been avoiding this place in attempt to improve her image. She hadn't been on a date in over nine months either. Not that any of it had helped. Would she ever live down her reputation?

Her gaze swept across the room, landing in the far corner where Lance sat with a couple of other paramedics. She stepped back, reaching for the door. Too late—his eyes locked onto hers.

Swallowing hard, she felt her cheeks heat up. What the hell? She was Jayna Sutton. Jayna Sutton didn't blush or back down. She never cowered or ran away.

Lance was staring across the bar at her with pity. Pity? No one pitied her. She sucked in a deep breath and looked away. Derek Brennan sat at the bar, and she quickly walked toward him, pulling out a stool.

Just why was she planting her butt on the stool next to the neanderthal? Over the past year, she'd also managed to avoid any encounters with Derek. That was quite the feat in a town so small! Yet here she was, purposely sitting next to him. Maybe she hadn't matured quite that much after all.

Had it actually been close to a year since they sat in this bar together helping Nick plan the surprise wedding? Time had certainly flown by. The surprise wedding had ended with a surprise pregnancy. Nick and Piper had welcomed a beautiful baby boy last month. The thought made Jayna smile, and her eyes drifted toward Lance again. Her smile slid. An entire year of flirting and laughing at the paramedic's unfunny jokes all in vain. He still didn't see her.

"What's got you scowling into your drink?" She turned her attention on the ape.

Derek swirled the amber whiskey in the lowball glass before lifting it and chugging it back. He grimaced before turning to look at her. "I'm not scowling."

"Yeah, okay! Can you get him another glass of get over himself? Add in a straw so he can suck it up!" Jayna placed an order with the bartender. "And I'll have a margarita, please."

"Make it extra salty, just like she is," Derek chuckled low.

"Oh, good one!" Jayna scoffed.

Derek's phone dinged, and he glanced down at it, scowl deepening.

"Your latest girlfriend unhappy with you?"

"No, her father."

"That's classic," she giggled. "What did you do to get her father pissed off?"

"I didn't ask her last name before I asked her out," he said through clenched teeth. "She turned out to be the daughter of the developer I am working for. A very well-connected developer."

"What the hell were you thinking? Not even you could be that stupid!" She wasn't sure why she was surprised. While she had evolved the ape-man hadn't. Derek was still a commitment-phobe.

He lifted his palms upward. "I didn't know who she was."

"What are you planning to do about it?"

"No clue." He shrugged and pointed to Lance's table. "So, what's happening with Lance Romance? Is he still dating that other nurse?"

"No, they broke up a while ago."

He sat up straight, staring directly at her. "Why are you here, making my life a living hell, when you could be at his table ruining his life?"

"Shut up, Derek!" She made a face at him then smiled at the bartender when he set down her drink.

"Oh, did I touch a nerve?"

With a twist of the lime, she removed the salt from the rim of the sombrero shaped glass and let it drop into her drink. Taking a sip, she narrowed her eyes at Derek. "If you must know, he isn't into casual dating and thinks that's all I'm interested in."

"And he'd be right. You're not interested in a relationship."

"Who said that?" Jayna's forehead furrowed.

"You did." He pointed that annoying sanctimonious index finger at her.

"Well, maybe I've changed my mind!"

"Or maybe he's just a challenge. A man who is finally immune to your charms."

"Seriously, Brennan. I'm not in the mood for your crap tonight."

"Yet, you sat down. Uninvited. Next to me!" His phone dinged, and he swiped to read the incoming text message, groaning as he did.

Jayna leaned over his shoulder, not bothering to hide the fact that she was reading the text on his phone.

<My daughter called and said you're ignoring her. I will have both your legs broken if you hurt her>

"Is this guy for real?"

Derek stuck the phone in his back pocket and took a long swallow of whiskey. "He's legit. Rumored to have mafia ties. Lots of friends in high places and even more friends in low places."

She let out a whistle. "So, is this threat real?"

"Yep."

Jayna's eyes flitted to the table in the corner. Lance was watching her. Interesting.

"You should show the boy toy that you can do relationships." Derek's eyes followed her gaze. "Get some poor schmuck to date you for a while. Make Lance Romance jealous."

Her gaze shifted back to Derek. She stared at him long and hard. "For once, Brennan, you've actually had a great idea."

She stood and grabbed his hand, yanking hard until he stood as well.

"What's happening?" he asked.

"We're dating, schmuck, make it look good!"

"Whoa, I wasn't offering to be the schmuck!" He pulled his hand free.

"Too bad." She grabbed his hand again, steering him toward the dance floor. "I need a fake boyfriend and you need a fake girlfriend to keep you out of a full-body cast."

"Hooking up with another chick is not going to help me."

Derek wrapped his arms around her waist, and she looped hers around his neck.

"Oh, we are not hooking up!" Jayna scrunched up her nose. "This is pure show. You tell the mob boss that your old girlfriend reappeared and is pregnant. You're going to try to make it work for the baby's sake. Get married."

"Whoa!" He pulled back, blinking rapidly. Oh, she was really enjoying the look of panic on his stupid face. "I go from being a fake boyfriend to a fake fiancé?"

"Unless you have a better idea to keep yourself out of traction?"

"This is the stupidest idea I've ever heard, and I'm the king of stupid ideas," he moaned.

"And when has the fact that an idea is stupid ever stopped you from going through with it?"

He shook his head rapidly back and forth. "No one will believe that we're a couple."

"Why not?" She frowned.

"Because you're you and I'm me. We're basically the same person. Anti-relationship people." He looked at her like she had just lost her mind. And maybe she had. Was she actually proposing that they date?

Her eyes found Lance again. He was definitely watching her with Derek. It might be a really stupid idea, but it may just work. She had nothing to lose, and Derek—well, he could lose his ability to walk unassisted.

"We're perfect for each other!" Jayna exclaimed, her eyes growing large.

"No, we are not!" he said, enunciating each word. "I hate you and you hate me."

"Love and hate are a fine, blurry line," she quipped.

"No one will buy it." Derek's eyes narrowed.

"I've always had bad taste in men. So, dating you should be an easy sell." She flashed him a saccharine smile.

His lip curled up. "Are you saying that I'm not boyfriend material?"

She snorted. "Yeah! You're definitely not boyfriend material. If you were this great guy, then Daddy Warbucks wouldn't be threatening bodily harm."

"That is true," he acknowledged.

"Besides, we only need Vito Corleone and Lance to buy it."

Chapter 24

Derek

"We only need Vito Corleone and Lance to buy it," Jayna had said. Derek was more than a little impressed that she could name the main character in The Godfather.

Following her back to their barstools, Derek's eyes narrowed. She couldn't be serious about dating. Fake or otherwise. The phone in his back pocket vibrated, and he pulled it out. Mario Flavia's name flashed, and he swiped to answer, cringing as he did.

"Mario."

"Derek, my boy, we need to talk." The gruff voice crackled through the phone. "Have you been avoiding my calls along with my daughter's?"

"Uh, no. Just have a lot going on." He stepped outside of the bar. What the hell had he been thinking when he asked Francesa Flavia out? She was a dead ringer for Penelope Cruz, that's what he'd thought.

"You have such a promising career in front of you. I have big plans for you, my boy." Again, he used that term of endearment, yet it was far from endearing in the tone he used. The threat was loud and clear. The earlier threat to break his legs may have been a bluff, but the threat to end his career was not.

"So, care to tell me why my daughter has called crying?"

There was a long, tense silence. The last thing Derek wanted was to go along with Jayna's fake dating scheme. But hearing the anger in Mario's voice had him quickly reconsidering. The man was seriously pissed.

While he was fairly certain that Mario wouldn't go through with the threat of bodily harm, he knew that Mario could seriously derail his career with a single phone call.

So, he just went and blurted out Jayna's hare-brained idea. "My ex just showed up. She's pregnant. Looks like I'm going to be a father. No one is more shocked than I am."

That part was true. He was totally shocked that he was agreeing to Jayna's proposal.

"We owe it to the baby to attempt to make it work," he continued to blubber. Would the guy even buy it?

There was another long pause.

"I agree. A child needs their father in their lives," Mario conceded. Though he was a cutthroat businessman, he was also a devoted family man. It was evident by the lengths he would go to ensure his daughter's happiness.

"Our gala is in a couple of weeks. Make sure to bring this woman with you. I want to meet her." More like demanding to meet her to prove that she actually existed.

"Of course." Derek disconnected the call and frowned at the cell phone in his hand! Mario had bought it. Now he just had to sell it.

Stepping back into the pub, his eyes settled on Jayna. He just needed to fake date the one woman he couldn't stand.

No problem.

No problem! Yeah, right! Trusting Jayna with his career felt like a huge risk. His career meant everything to him, more than anyone knew. Unlike Tommy who had excelled effortlessly, Derek struggled with his grades until his final year of high school. Determined to shed his reputation as an underachiever, he worked hard, earning the grades needed for university. His effort paid off. Not only did he receive an Engineering degree, but he graduated with distinction, proving that even a "failure" like him could turn things around.

Derek walked up behind Jayna, wrapping his arms around her waist. Leaning down, he whispered in her ear, "Looks like we're doing this. Hope you have a classy dress because you and I have my work gala to attend in two weeks."

She stiffened for a moment and then beamed up at him. "Black or red?"

"Definitely black."

A vivid picture of her wearing a sexy little black dress flashed through his mind. He quickly shoved it away. This was annoying, pain-in-the-ass Jayna Sutton. He was not going to start daydreaming about her.

A smile lifted the corners of her full lips. His eyes settled there. Her lips looked natural, not artificially plumped and were a glossed in a pretty shade of raspberry. Did they taste like raspberries? He was curious, so that must explain what he said next. It was yet another stupid idea. However, he was the king of stupid ideas. So, he just blurted it out, "If we are dating, then we should kiss."

Chapter 25

Jayna

"We should kiss," Derek had said.

He'd been taunting her, and Lance had been watching intently. So, she stood, grabbed a handful of his T-shirt, and planted a kiss on that stupid, smirking mouth of his. She left him standing there more shocked than she was. Had she just kissed Derek Brennan?

Now, three days later, she stood in her kitchen, still shocked that she had locked lips with the Neanderthal. She was even more shocked that he had agreed to her plan. Was she happy that he had, or absolutely dumbfounded? She was fake dating Derek Brennan—the man she despised. And she had no one to blame but herself.

Forcing her attention back on the tray of nachos, she finished dumping the grated cheese and placed the sheet pan into the oven. Her eyes moved around the old craftsman home she had bought. The kitchen was possibly her favorite room.

She had renovated it because it was dated and badly laid out. But the renovation had complimented the house, not modernized it. She'd wanted white, cream, and golden wood tones. Apparently, shabby chic was her decorating style. A blend of vintage and cottage elements in soft, romantic colors and textures created an elegant, yet worn and welcoming look.

The kitchen was a chef's dream and a baker's fantasy, not that she knew how to cook or bake, for that matter. One day she'd take up cooking. Pigs, of course, would be flying past the window over the sink because she didn't have a domestic bone in her body. But this gorgeous kitchen did inspire her to sign up for a couple of cooking classes. Nah, she'd just sign up for that ready-made meal delivery service.

The cabinets were painted off-white, and the butcher block countertop was stained in a honey shade. The white oversized farmhouse sink was big enough to bathe in, and the decorative copper hood vent added to the warmth she'd been going for. But the island, now that was a wow factor. It had been sourced from Jamie's store. A large antique dresser with intricate carvings that had been stripped, repainted in rich cream milk paint, and distressed. It was topped with an expensive slab of marble in rich hues that picked up the cream of the cabinets and the honey oak of the butcher block.

She could have afforded a larger, brand-new house. It would have barely put a dent in her trust fund. But she wanted a home her nursing salary could afford. The minute she'd set foot inside this house, she knew it was home. Using the tainted trust fund money would have tainted it as well.

The cozy cottage was a far cry from the expensive opulence of the house she'd grown up in. It was truly the first place she'd felt at home. That was possibly the reason she'd changed her mind about sharing her life with someone. It wouldn't be the worst thing in the world. And it would be a lot less lonely.

However, she was still dead set against having children. In the end, everyone became their parents with their own children, subconsciously picking up traits that were taught to them. Behavioral patterns, no matter how undesirable, tended to be repeated. She wouldn't take that risk with a child. The fact that Lance did not want children might be the most appealing thing about the man. It didn't hurt that he was also easy to look at.

When the timer dinged, she opened the state-of-the-art oven and pulled out the pan of nachos. Her big splurge in the kitchen had been on the appliances, not that the six-burner stove ever got used. The microwave was the star of the show, and the oven was used for warming. Nachos were her only specialty.

Carefully, she transferred the contents of the sheet pan onto a large serving platter. She popped a cheese-covered tortilla chip into her mouth and picked up the platter, walking into the living room.

While the kitchen was her favorite room, the warm and welcoming living room was a close second. The walls were painted in a rich cream, and the windows were covered in white linen. Soft pastel color blankets were draped on the white couch. Blue glass vases and a mint-green antique lamp completed the look. The fireplace was the focal point of the room. The natural texture and earthy tones of the stone complemented the shabby chic aesthetic perfectly. A crackling fire added to the ambiance, and once encased in the overstuffed cushion of her sofa, she never wanted to leave.

Setting the platter on the distressed wooden coffee table, she fluffed the pillow on the floral print armchair. She added another piece of wood to the fire and replaced the wrought iron fire screen with the intricate scrollwork. Taking another nacho, she stuffed it in her mouth and headed back to the kitchen as Jamie came in through the back door. Seven p.m. on the dot. The woman had never been late a single day in her life.

"Hey Jamie, how was your day?"

"Great, I'm starving though." Jamie slipped off her jacket and hung it on the back of one of the mismatched kitchen chairs.

"Nachos are in the living room. I just need to whip up the margaritas." Jayna stepped behind the island and began to twist the cut-up limes over the stainless-steel juicer. She poured the juice into a blender.

"Why are you holding out on me?" Jamie pulled out a bar stool from under the island and sat down.

Jayna glanced up. "I'm not holding out on you."

"I have to hear it from Ophelia that you're dating Derek. I'd say that's holding out."

"Ophelia knows? Wow, she doesn't miss a trick." Jayna hid a grin as she turned to fill a large glass with ice from the fridge dispenser.

"So, it's true then?"

"Never said that," Jayna answered evasively as she dumped the ice into the blender.

"You also never said it wasn't true." Jamie persisted. "Come on, I know you've had a thing for him since high school."

Jayna scoffed. "A thing that lasted all of five minutes."

"So, you're not dating then?"

"You're psychic, you tell me." She measured double the amount of Triple Sec to that of the lime juice. 3-2-1. She had the recipe memorized. Three parts tequila, two parts triple sec, one part lime juice, and a dash of agave syrup to add a little sweetness.

"You know that I can't read people who are close to me," Jamie huffed. "But I do know when my best friend is bullshitting me. So, spill! What's going on?"

Jayna twisted off the cap of the tequila bottle and measured out three parts, then a fourth part. Jamie would need to sleep over. After they polished off this blender of margaritas, she'd be in no shape to drive.

"Nothing to spill."

"Not buying it. What is going..."

Jayna switched on the blender at high speed and drowned out the rest of Jamie's question.

Jamie reached across the counter and hit the kill switch on the blender. "WHAT. IS. GOING. ON?"

Her finger tapped the pulse button, and the blender swirled noisily again. She shot Jamie a smug smile.

Jamie's hand shot out and yanked the plug out of the socket, her smile even more smug.

Jayna shook her head and took her time sliding a lime wedge around the rim of the two margarita glasses before dipping them in a bowl of salt. "Seriously, Jamie, you missed your calling. You should become a P.I. With your psychic abilities and that built-in bullshit detector, you'd be amazing at the job."

Lifting the blender off the base, she filled both glasses, sliding one over in front of Jamie.

Jamie took a sip and scrunched up her nose. "Little heavy on the tequila."

Jayna picked up her glass and wandered into the living room, plopping on the overstuffed sofa in front of the fireplace.

"Okay, okay. We're dating," she finally admitted when Jamie sat across from her, staring non-stop.

"I knew it!"

Jayna took a long swallow and forced herself not to grimace. This was one strong margarita.

"So, what's it like finally dating him?" Jamie sighed over the rim. "It must be so exciting! Does your heart race every time he touches you?"

This time, she did grimace. "More like he's completely annoying and opinionated and full of himself. I don't know about my heart racing, but my fist does clench when I'm around him. Stopping myself from punching him in his stupid face is challenging."

Last night, they strolled hand in hand down the sidewalk. They found a table for two at Frank's Ice Cream Shoppe, and shared a banana split. It had been his dumb idea. He wanted a couple of selfies to share on his social media accounts. He'd shrugged out of his jacket and wrapped his arm around her shoulders as he held up his phone and snapped a couple of pics.

"Can you put the gun show away?" she'd snapped as he flexed for the next picture. "Yes, we all know that you work out. Yes, you're good-looking. Yes, you have biceps and a sexy tattoo."

"Thanks for noticing." He flashed her that dimple-popping grin.

"Wasn't noticing!"

"You were just checking me out!"

"Was not," she huffed. "I was merely pointing out that you're a show-off."

"A show-off who you think is hot." He waggled his brows.

"A show-off who I think is a conceited ape."

"You think I'm good-looking," he said in a sing-song voice.

She'd shoveled a big scoop of ice cream into her mouth to

stop the smile that threatened to erupt. It was going to be a painfully long two weeks. Two weeks? Exactly how long did they have to pretend date for this to work? With a frown, she stared into the fire, realizing they needed to go on more dates.

Jamie cleared her throat and pulled her back to the present. Her best friend's brows furrowed in confusion.

"We're pretend dating, okay," she blurted out. Jamie was like a bloodhound. This was a conversation she'd hoped to avoid. She wasn't very proud to admit that she and Derek were pulling a con.

"Pretend dating? Why?"

She took another long swallow. Maybe this drink wasn't strong enough, after all. Jamie was going to ask tough questions and demand honest answers. The rule for margarita night: no bullshit allowed. You spilled your guts over the salty rims, and no judgment would be served.

"Because of Lance Roman, the paramedic. He thinks I'm a serial dater, and he's not interested in a casual relationship."

"But you are a serial dater," Jamie blurted out and then softened her voice. "Sorry, but you are, Jayna. You continually insist that you're not interested in a relationship."

"Maybe I changed my mind, okay?" she rebuffed. "But apparently, my reputation has come back to haunt me."

Jamie pursed her lips and looked upward. "Then why are you pretending to date Derek?"

"To prove to Lance that I can do a committed relationship."

"And Derek? Why would he go along with this?"

"So, he doesn't get his legs broken."

The furrow between Jamie's brows deepened. "Did you threaten to break his legs if he didn't go along with your plan?"

"No, not me." Jayna laughed. "It was the father of one of his 'two-dates max.' Apparently, the man is well-connected with mob ties. Derek needs to start asking the last name of his potential one-night stands."

"What about the pregnancy rumor? I heard you were pregnant, and that's why you two are together."

"No, of course not!" Jayna rolled her eyes. "That's just what he told the mob Dad. He said we had to get back together because I'm pregnant. So not true!"

"Wow, Jayna." Jamie took another sip. "You never take the easy road."

"Never!"

Jamie stared into the crackling fire, a look of concern crossing her face. "I have a bad feeling."

"It will be fine, Jamie."

"You once had real feelings for Derek. I don't want to see you get hurt."

"I was fifteen!"

"And he broke your heart."

Jayna let out a heavy breath. "It's only make-believe. I know it, and he does too."

"Just be careful. I really am getting a bad feeling." Jamie turned those intense, all-seeing icy-blue eyes directly on her, and she shivered.

Jamie was wrong, though. There was no way she'd be hurt by Derek. Sure, in high school, she'd been over the moon for him. All the girls had. Derek had been so devastating, with thick dark hair, carelessly styled, a deep olive complexion, and those intense violet-blue eyes that were always storm-filled. He had been dangerous and callous, and she'd been drawn to him even with the knowledge that getting close to one so volatile would end badly.

And she'd been right.

He'd been her first kiss and her first heartbreak. Her only heartbreak because she'd never let anyone get that close again. So maybe it was serendipitous that the one to turn her into a serial dater would be the one to help her open her heart again. As a bonus, she could make his life a living hell while doing it.

Chapter 26

Derek

His life had become a living hell. Fake dating Jayna Sutton? What had he been thinking?

He hadn't been.

Desperation had clouded his judgment as he tried to save his career. He'd been desperate enough to suggest they post pictures from their staged date the other day. Naturally, his brother Ben had stumbled upon them and wasted no time sharing the posts with everyone.

Derek stepped into Patty's Pub, silently praying that not everyone inside had seen the photos. His gaze landed on Ben sitting at a table with his best friend, Connor. Ah, little Benji. At the very least, Ben owed him a beer or two for poking his nose where it didn't belong.

"Did you card him, Ivy?" Derek asked the server as she set a pitcher of beer on Ben's table. Dipping a couple of fingers into Ben's water glass, he swiped them behind his brother's ear. "He's just a baby. Still wet behind the ears."

"I'll show you wet behind the ears," Ben grumbled, shoving Derek's hand away.

"Oh, bring it, lil bro," Derek chuckled as he pulled out a chair, sitting uninvited. "Hey, Connor."

"Hey, Derek," Connor replied. "I hear that you're dating Jayna Sutton."

Derek shifted in the chair, narrowing his eyes at Ben. "Wonder where you heard that?"

"Two-date Brennan and Jayna Date-and-Dash dating is the

talk of the town," Ben grinned. "Heard she's knocked up for real this time."

Derek sent Ben a shut-your-mouth glare before helping himself to the pitcher of beer, pouring a tall glass. A loud, distinctive laugh came from the corner of the bar. Only one person belonged to that obnoxious laugh: Jayna. He hid the groan with a long swallow of beer. Just his luck.

Connor turned and stared in her direction. "You are so damn lucky."

Apparently, his definition of luck was vastly different. His gaze trailed after Connor's, landing on Jayna and another woman engaged in a game of pool with two fresh-faced paramedic recruits. A long table, known as the first responders' corner, sat adjacent to the pool table. It had become the gathering spot for the fire department, police service, paramedics, and ER staff after a long day shift. A few nurses sat there with a couple of paramedics including Lance.

"She's so beautiful," Connor gushed, his eyes still trained on Jayna. "And a great pool player."

More like a pool shark. Those two young paramedics were about to have their asses handed to them. Derek squinted, attempting to see Jayna through Connor's eyes. Tonight, she wore tight blue jeans, a vintage Black Sabbath t-shirt, and her hair was loose in tumbling waves.

Admittedly, she did look beautiful along with having great taste in bands. He watched as Jayna lifted the tumbler of whiskey, downing it before letting out a loud whoop. Nope, her annoying personality overrode her hotness.

"She can drink most men under the table," Connor gushed. "She's nothing like the women I date. They prefer wimpy, fruity drinks, and not a single one appreciates a good dirty joke. But Jayna? She tells the best dirty jokes. She's something else."

"Oh, she's something else alright," Derek agreed. Just what that something was, he wasn't sure. She was rough around the edges, but she had cleaned up real nice for Nick's wedding. She could be classy when she wanted. She just chose not to be.

Derek's eyes traveled to the table of her co-workers. Lance sat at the far end, a deep scowl on his face. His eyes were trained on Greta, who was completely ignoring the man. If Jayna wanted to win Lance's attention, she had a long way to go. If she wanted the man to believe she was done with casual dating, why the hell was she flirting with those paramedics who looked as young as Ben?

Jayna let out another annoying as hell hoot when she made the winning shot and high-fived the woman with her. Her eyes met his from across the room, and she flashed him an instant smile. He smiled back and then frowned. What was that feeling that just zapped through him? Excitement? No, impossible.

She strolled in his direction. "Hey boyfriend, love of my life," she snorted at the last part. "Shove over and make room for your girlfriend."

Dragging a chair from the table beside them, she squeezed in next to him. "Hi, Ben. Hey Connor. Don't you boys look handsome tonight."

Connor visibly blushed under her attention.

"Done hustling for the night?" His tone sounded sulky, and he had no idea why. Despite his better judgment, he leaned close, his mouth inches from her ear. He couldn't help but notice that her hair smelled like lavender. She'd switched her shampoo again. The woman couldn't make up her mind to save her life. What if she decided to bail on this fake dating scheme?

"What's with flirting with those two baby paramedics?"

Her head turned, and she stared directly into his eyes. Her pink glossed lips were mere inches from his. "Jealous?"

"Nope!" He lowered his voice to prevent Ben and Connor from overhearing. "If the plan is to show Lance Romance that you're in a committed relationship, then you shouldn't be acting like a trollop."

She leaned back, her lips pursing. "Trollop? Is that even a

word anyone under the age of eighty uses? And I was not flirting. I was merely being myself."

"Which is a big flirt."

"You are so jealous." A laugh escaped those shiny, full lips.

He forced his eyes off her lips. "I am not. Just saying that if you're my girlfriend, then you should be acting like it."

"You're jealous," she repeated, blowing him a kiss.

"Hi Jayna, I thought that was you." A brunette woman stopped next to their table.

"Maisie, how are you?" An icy coolness entered Jayna's voice.

"Great, I guess you heard that I'm engaged." Maisie's perfectly manicured nails were thrust out and the large diamond ring glinted in the light.

"No, I hadn't," Jayna shrugged indifferently, which caused a deep frown to mar Maisie's heavily contoured face.

"Oh, well, I am. And I just signed myself and my fiancé Wentworth up for the karaoke contest tonight." Maisie pointed to a table where a preppy-looking man sat.

"Well, congratulations, and good luck." Jayna's smile looked forced.

"We don't need luck. We have it in the bag," Maisie bragged. "Is it true that you two are dating?"

"Who would lie about a thing like that?" Derek chimed in. Jayna gave him a sharp kick.

"Have a great night, and I hope we can count on all of your votes." Maisie gave a little wave as she walked away.

"She is still full of herself," Jayna muttered.

"Thought she was a friend?" Derek leaned down and rubbed his shin.

"More like a frenemy," Jayna's eyes were trained on Maisie as she walked up on stage with her fiancé. "She insults me in the sweetest of voices and I compliment her with thinly veiled sarcasm."

Derek couldn't hold in the laugh.

"What's so funny?"

"That you think your sarcasm is thinly veiled," he told her.

Her nose crunched up, and the left corner of her lip lifted. "Whatever!"

Jayna shook her head and frowned as Maisie began to belt out a very bad rendition of 'Summer Nights.' "Of course, she'd pick that song." She shoved back her chair and stood. "I'll be back."

"Don't hurry," he called after her and was awarded with the flip of her middle finger.

He continued to watch her walk toward the bar. The woman was too much. He should have stayed home. Pretending to be Jayna's boyfriend would require much better acting skills than he possessed. He turned back to the stage, cringing as Maisie attempted to hit a high note. Why did any couple think that was a good song choice for karaoke? Why did any couple think karaoke was a good choice?

A shot glass landed in front of him, and he glanced up. Jayna set a glass in front of Ben and Connor as well before sitting down in the chair beside him.

"Bottoms up, boys."

"What is it?" Derek stared at the clear liquid in the shot glass and the plate of lemon wedges.

"Tequila."

"I don't drink Tequila." He shoved the glass back in her direction.

"It will make you a better singer." Jayna used her right index finger to push the glass back in front of him.

"Why would I want to be a better singer?" He pushed the tequila toward her again.

"Because I just signed us up for the karaoke contest." She waggled her brows at him and moved the glass in front of him once more.

"I don't sing karaoke." He pushed the shot glass to the center of the table, out of her reach.

"You do now." Jayna leaned across the table and picked up the glass.

"No way. Not happening!"

"No problem." Jayna placed the shot glass next to hers. "I just hope I don't have a problem being available for your work thing next weekend."

The threat was loud and clear. Damn her. He needed her to honor their agreement more than she needed him to. All she had to lose was a chance at winning the paramedic's attention, but his career and ability to walk unassisted were at risk. The woman who couldn't even decide which shampoo scent she liked could very well decide that Lance was not worth the trouble.

She moved the glass back in his direction. "Come on Dare, don't be a wuss."

Wuss? That was his word, one he used to describe his uptight older brother. No one called him a wuss. Ever!

"I am not a wuss. I just happen to think karaoke is lame. And I don't do lame."

"You also don't do relationships," Ben chimed in. "But look at you now."

He shot his youngest brother another shut-your-mouth-before-I-shut-it-for-you look. "Why don't you take my place, Ben?"

"No, I'm good." Ben grinned.

"That is debatable," he fired back before turning his attention to Jayna. "I am not drinking that poison. And you've got it wrong. It's vodka that makes you a better singer, not tequila."

"True, but tequila makes you invincible," Jayna smirked. "You're not chicken, are you?"

"Chicken?" No one ever called him chicken either. "Never. Tequila tastes like ass and karaoke makes you look and sound like an ass."

"Good thing you're already an ass, then. You have nothing to worry about." Jayna let out another loud snort and grabbed his left arm, twisting it over.

His breath hitched as her head dropped and her tongue traced a tantalizing path along his wrist. What the hell? Confusion, along with arousal, warred in his mind as he watched her sprinkle salt on the moistened area of his wrist.

"Tequila is so much fun to drink. It is the most sensual of all the shots," her voice was low and gravelly, sending shock waves through his body.

With a swift motion, she licked off the salt before tossing her head back and downing the contents of the shot glass with practiced ease. Connor's loud exclamation broke through the haze he found himself in. Derek couldn't tear his gaze away from Jayna.

Jayna made a show of slowly sucking the lemon wedge, staring into his eyes. He swallowed hard.

"Hot damn," Connor exclaimed.

Hot damn was right. But this was merely a physical reaction, nothing more. Any woman with her looks and confidence would have caused his body to react in the same way.

Her triumphant grin brought him back to earth. Jayna wasn't just any woman. She was annoying and abrasive. Her eyes were still locked on his, the silent challenge issued. If she wanted to play games, then she was about to learn that she had just met her match.

He reached over and grabbed Jayna's wrist. He copied what she'd done to him, but added in a little bite and smiled against her wrist as he felt her jump. He dumped salt on her wrist, but instead of licking it off, he just left it there and downed the shot glass in front of him. It took all his willpower to restrain himself from grimacing. He picked up the lemon wedge and tossed it at his brother's head.

The DJ called their name, and he stood grabbing Jayna's hand.

"Let's do this." As the words left his lips, he cringed. He was in a fabricated relationship, fueled by tequila, and now coerced into karaoke. Three things that had been taboo just last week. But he hated losing more. Dare Brennan never backed down from a challenge. He could only hope Jayna hadn't picked another lame song from Grease.

They stepped up on stage. "Just what are we singing?" he hissed.

"In Spite of Ourselves." She took two microphones from the

DJ.

"The John Prine song?" he didn't bother to hide the surprise in his voice.

Jayna handed him the microphone, a smirk playing on her lips as he begrudgingly took it.

"I hate you," he mouthed.

"Right back at you," she whispered, a mischievous glint in her eyes.

She damn well knew that he hated karaoke. This wasn't about beating Maisie. Oh no, this was payback, pure and simple. As the opening chords of the song filled the air, his apprehension mounted. He really should have stayed home. Karaoke sucked. As did humiliating himself in front of a bar full of people. He turned his attention to the monitor. Great, his part was first. He closed his eyes for a moment, forcing his nerves to settle, and began to sing the opening lines. Ben and Connor let out wolf whistles. His brother was really asking for it.

Yet as he continued singing, a smile formed. He turned in Jayna's direction as he sang the next lyric in a loud, clear voice. He substituted her name into the lyrics. "Jayna likes to get it on like a bunny." This song was hilarious.

He noticed the shock on her face. She had not expected that he would have a good voice and he couldn't help but feel more than a little satisfaction. Squaring her shoulders, she stepped forward, lifting the microphone. Her voice was soft and sultry as she effortlessly hit the notes.

She ran a finger seductively down his arm as she sang about him sniffing her undies and not being too sharp. Oh, game on.

He reached out and wrapped his arm around her waist, pulling her close for the chorus. Their voices blended perfectly, and the crowd cheered loudly. His smile increased as she looked up at him.

With each verse, he grew more comfortable. They improvised, adding their own humorous twists to the lyrics, much to the delight of the crowd. Jayna leaned her back against him, rubbing her body up and down. When did she become so sexy? Wow, she was really turning it on. He sucked in a deep breath, forcing his hormones to settle down. She was trying to get him worked up on purpose.

As they reached the final chorus, he realized that he wasn't hating this. Even though he did indeed hate karaoke, and this woman gyrating all over him, their connection in this moment was undeniably powerful. They finished the song to thunderous applause, singing the final lyric about spiting their noses right off their faces. Derek couldn't help but wonder if that might be a real risk because in this moment he was really into Jayna.

Maybe it was the adrenaline rush from the cheers of the crowd, or the tequila shooter that made him do it. Whatever the reason, he dipped Jayna backward and kissed her. Not just kissed her, but really kissed her. Kissed her senseless. He kissed her like he didn't want to stop.

Chapter 27

Jayna

He'd kissed her like he didn't want to stop. What the hell had that been?

She gave her head a good, firm shake and forced herself to focus on the two black dresses hanging on the closet door. Both dresses were black, yet each gave a completely different vibe. One was sexy and the other more classic. She felt torn.

While she wanted to knock Derek's socks off, she didn't want to WANT to knock Derek's socks off. And she didn't want him to think she was trying to knock his socks off. What did it matter what she wore?

She reached for the demure dress, but her hand hesitated. This conflicted feeling had been with her all week, ever since the karaoke contest that they had won!

Karaoke had seemed like a good idea when she signed them up. The number one reason: she couldn't miss the chance to defeat Maisie Whyte. Number two: no way was she missing an opportunity to annoy the hell out of Derek. He despised karaoke. And number three; the reason she was fake dating Derek; to get Lance Roman's attention.

She hadn't been able to gain the paramedic's attention all night. Begrudgingly, she had to admit Derek may have been right. Lance would have gotten the wrong impression earlier when she'd been 'hustling' the two paramedic students. 'Hustle,' was Derek's word. She had not been hustling them. It was not her fault that men naturally assumed she couldn't play pool because she was a woman. They had been proven wrong.

She had been guilty of assumptions herself. Just because Derek hated karaoke, she'd believed he must not be a good singer. She'd been proven wrong as well. The man had a deep, low, completely in tune sexy voice. And he'd worked the crowd right beside her.

Wow, what a kiss at the end! Her toes had curled. What exactly had prompted that?

He'd helped her gain Lance's attention and secure the win against Maisie. But the kiss hadn't been necessary, unless he'd wanted to kiss her. No. He was up to something.

Derek Brennan always did what he wanted. The only reason she'd been able to coerce him into karaoke was by threatening to pull the plug on their arrangement. Derek's limbs and career were on the line. He had significantly more at stake than she did. Sure, she wanted Lance like she'd never wanted a man before. But she'd survive if it never happened. Derek's career might not be so lucky.

Was the kiss his way to get back at her? Or was it his way to take control of the situation? Maybe he was trying to get her to fall for him.

Oh, he wouldn't stoop that low, would he?

Of course he would. What an ass!

"Hold them both up. I can't see," Jessica's voice interrupted from behind.

Turning, she stared at the computer monitor on the desk and held up the classy black dress in front of her. "This one or..." She lowered the first dress and then held up the black dress that would drop jaws and socks.

"Oh, that one," Jessica's sigh vibrated through the speakers. "Definitely the second one."

How she wished her friend was sitting on her bed. With Jessica still in Sierra Leone, video calls were the next best thing.

"Who is the date with tonight? You never go to this much trouble."

Jayna turned her back and cringed. Obviously, Jessica had not spoken with Jamie recently. Perhaps Jamie could be trusted with secrets.

She spun back around. "Um, it's with Derek Brennan."

"Derek Brennan?" Jess's eyes grew large, her voice echoing.

Normally, Jessica was her conscience and Jamie was her confidant. These two women kept her grounded. Jamie had a built-in bull shit detector and Jessica had no patience for bull shit. It was impossible to lie to either woman.

"You have a date with Derek? There has to be static in the line. No way, that's what you said. I must have heard wrong!"

"Nope. You heard right." She set the dresses on the bed and pulled out the desk chair, sitting down. "But it's not what you think."

"I don't know what to think. I'm shocked, dumbfounded, close to speechless."

"Speechless? You really must be shocked," she joked. Jessica always had lots to say about everything. And she prayed that when she told Jess about what she was doing with Derek, her friend didn't have an entire lecture for her. "We're not really dating."

Jessica blinked. "Not really dating? What does that mean?"

"Fake dating."

"Fake dating? What the hell is fake dating?"

"We are just pretending to date. Exactly like it sounds."

"I know what fake means! What I am asking is why would you be FAKE dating him?"

"Because I want to date Lance Roman like I have never wanted to date a man before. I mean, I want to SERIOUSLY date him."

"Well, you should have said that in the first place. Now I completely understand. NOT!" Jessica threw both her hands up in the air. "If you want to date Lance, then why are you fake dating Brennan?"

"Because," she began again, speaking slowly. "Lance thinks that I'm a trollop who can't be in a serious relationship. He isn't interested in casual dating."

Jayna frowned. Trollop was the old-fashioned term Derek had used. "And if Lance sees me seriously dating another man, then he will see me in a different light."

Jessica leaned closer, her face growing large on the screen. "You need to keep explaining. I am not following."

Jayna blew out a long breath. "It's not that complicated. We date for a few weeks, then have a bad breakup. One that Lance will have to console me over."

Jessica blinked again. "Okay. I get it for you. But why would Derek agree? What's in it for him?"

"He gets to retain use of both his legs." At Jess's continued look of confusion, she elaborated. "Derek went out with his boss's daughter without realizing who she was. He was his normal sleazy self."

Jayna leaned back in the chair. "It's safe to say that his boss was far from pleased. And this boss is well connected with questionable people on his payroll. Derek is pretending that we got back together because I'm pregnant."

"You're not pregnant, are you?"

"No, of course not." Why did everyone keep asking her that question?

Jessica rapidly shook her head back and forth, her voice laced with sarcasm. "Well, it sounds like a really solid plan. I can't see how it can go wrong."

"It's working, Jess. Tonight, I'm attending a work function with Derek, so we can sell our relationship to his boss. Last week we were at Patty's and sang karaoke together. Lance was paying attention."

"Whoa, back up. Derek sang karaoke with you?"

"Yeah, he's pretty good. And a great kisser."

"Kisser? You kissed him? Thought it was fake?"

"It is only fake. He kissed me." Her brows furrowed. "Honestly, I'm still trying to figure that out. I think he may be messing with me."

"No, not Dare Brennan!" Jessica laughed, but then her face turned serious. "You don't need Derek to win over Lance. It's a lie and lies never end well."

"Well, Ms. I-Never-Tell-A-Lie," she chirped back. The nickname was accurate. Jessica was honest to a fault. Jayna leaned back in her chair, preparing for the lecture that was about to come. "How would you propose I win over Lance?"

"You just need to smooth the rough edges."

"Rough edges?" Jayna sat forward again.

"You are intimidating," Jess told her softly.

"Intimidating?" she repeated Jessica's words again. Wow, it wouldn't hurt her friend to be a little less honest sometimes.

"I'm not trying to insult you, Jayna. But..."

"But," she repeated yet again. "Buts are always followed by an insult. That word is only used to soften the blow."

"True," Jess giggled. "BUT," she emphasized. "You are intimidating, Jayna. You have so much confidence. And you're gorgeous."

"That is true on both accounts," she agreed, pumping up her chest.

"You also have a smart mouth, and you take pleasure in showing up men."

"What? How?"

"At playing pool, cards, drinking, telling dirty jokes." Jessica raised a finger for each item she listed.

"Okay, okay. It's just so much fun to beat them at their own game."

"Men don't like that."

"My perfect guy would," Jayna said wistfully and immediately frowned.

"If Lance was your perfect guy, then none of this would be necessary," Jessica spoke softly again.

"Ah, BUT," Jayna's mouth twisted into a sad smile. "There is no such thing as the perfect guy. Just close enough."

"That, my friend, is just about the saddest thing I've ever heard." Jessica shook her head, then sucked in a breath. Her hand raised, and she pointed. "Your window. I saw a face!"

"What?" Her back tensed and she spun around, staring at the

bedroom window. No one was there.

She turned back around, her scalp tingling, goosebumps covering her arms. This wasn't the first time she had the sensation of being watched. "No one is there, Jess."

"I swear I saw a face," Jessica let out a nervous chuckle. "Guess it was just a shadow or the monitor playing tricks on my eyes."

"Okay, I better finish getting ready. You're sure about the second dress?"

"It's a showstopper," Jess told her, and then her face grew serious again. "Please be careful."

"I will." She hit the disconnect and sat for a moment, staring at the window. Had Jess's warning been about Derek, or the possibility that someone was watching her? She stood and walked to the window, pulling the curtains shut.

Be careful. She swallowed hard and rushed to shower before Derek showed up at her front door.

Chapter 28

Derek

Derek swallowed hard. Jayna stood with a towel wrapped around her head and a second around her midsection.

"Do you always open the door without clothes?" he grumbled. The intense frown on his face was more about the immediate, unwanted attraction that surged through him than about caring how she answered her front door. "I could have been a degenerate stalker."

"Could have been?" she snorted, holding open the door for him to enter. "You're early."

"I'm right on time." He glanced at his wristwatch. "Seven on the dot."

Jayna looked over her shoulder at the oversized clock on the wall above the console table. "Shit. You should get used to the fact that I am never on time."

He didn't want to get used to any of it. Of course, the most annoying woman on the planet would also be chronically late. He prided himself on being punctual and had zero tolerance for tardiness. What the hell? Tardiness? He sounded like his father or his uptight older brother.

"Wow, Derek, who knew you owned a tie, let alone knew how to tie one?" She reached out and grabbed the lapel on his tux jacket. "Is this made out of boyfriend material? Because you look halfway presentable."

"No, it is not! And I can look presentable." This woman!!

"Make yourself at home," she laughed and waved toward the living room just off the front hall. "I'll hurry, I promise."

"Be sure you do. I, unlike you, am never late," he snarled and wandered into the inviting room.

He sat on the overstuffed sofa, more like sank into it. This was a cozy home. He liked the stone fireplace and the neutral décor. It was layers of texture with soft creams and whites along with wood tones mixed in. It was soothing and shocking. Jayna was 'Ritchie Rich' rich, and this understated small home was not what he'd expected. He'd pictured her in a McMansion with ultra-modern designer furniture and priceless artwork, not a home that felt like a warm hug.

Fifteen minutes later, Jayna appeared in front of him, and he swallowed hard again. The gown she wore was floor length. The black silk looked fluid, flowing down her body, accentuating every curve. His eyes slowly descended, taking in every inch of the strapless gown, starting at the plunging sweetheart neckline that barely contained her ample cleavage. He paused at her impossibly small waist that flared into curvaceous hips. There was a slit on the right side that stopped mid-thigh, exposing a leg that was endlessly long.

Jayna was breathtaking. He almost told her that she was worth the wait. Worth making him late. But he caught himself, a frown replacing the instant smile that had formed.

"What, don't you like the dress?" The smile left her pink glossed lips.

"No, it will do. You look fine," he cleared his throat. What wasn't fine was the way his body instantly responded to her. His heart had picked up a beat, and his palms grew damp. Had that been his breath catching?

She gave an entirely new meaning to the term 'little black dress'. It was sexy as hell and yet still managed to be classy. Every man at the gala would be gobsmacked when he walked in with her on his arm. Gobsmacked? Another phrase he never used. This whole fake-dating Jayna was starting to mess with his mind and vocabulary.

The stupid smile returned when he entered Casa Loma's iconic ballroom. Every head turned in their direction.

"Oh wow," Jayna exclaimed beside him. "It's breathtaking."

The exact word he had used to describe her. She twirled in a slow circle, staring up at the stained-glass dome ceiling of the conservatory, and he couldn't pull his eyes off her.

"I've never been here," she smiled directly at him and damn if his breath didn't catch again.

His smile grew. She was right. The 1914 castle was a landmark in Toronto for a reason. This room was particularly beautiful, with the stained-glass ceiling and the marble floor. Suddenly, all the worry and hesitation evaporated. Apparently, she could be classy when she wanted to be. He had so much riding on Jayna not acting like Jayna. Never had he given anyone so much power over his life before. Jayna was the last person he'd ever trust. But tonight, she was different.

Thankfully.

Tonight was important. Not only was Mario Flavia in attendance but so were many other influential investors along with the owner of the large construction firm he worked for. His career was on the line. If Mario didn't buy his relationship with Jayna, then he could kiss it all goodbye.

Reputation had never been something he'd concerned himself over. If his work was done well, it shouldn't matter how he spent his days off. He didn't understand why his marital status should have any bearing on his career. But obviously, it did.

While he didn't care if people called him a hound dog or a daredevil, he did care about his career. He loved his job. One careless mistake, like dating the wrong girl, could cost him it all. Which found him at the mercy of Jayna Sutton. She would either help him get back in the good graces of his employers or she could sink him completely.

The minute word had gotten around the firm that he was in a committed relationship, he was suddenly being taken seriously. Sure, it bothered him to lie. But it also bothered him that a person's marital status should have any bearing on their career. Old-fashioned values still prevailed in the modern world. Antiquated as it was, he'd play the game.

He splayed his hand across the small of Jayna's back, not failing to notice that the dress felt just as silky as it looked. "You owe me. Behave tonight," he whispered in her ear.

She really did owe him after last weekend. Karaoke! Like, what the hell? His brother was still ribbing him over it. In fact, Ben had videotaped it on his cell phone, uploading the video to all his socials, tagging Derek in them. When he walked into the office Monday morning, two of his co-workers had stood clapping loudly. The karaoke video was streaming on all the monitors. And while he wanted to skin Ben alive, it did help sell his relationship with Jayna.

Mario demanded that he and Jayna sit with him. Jayna made it through the entire dinner without a single snort, her laughter instead soft and magical. She had all the men at the table eating out of her hand. While she outshone every woman in the room, she remained personable enough to avoid being hated.

"I must say, I'm shocked," Daniel, the CEO of the company, said. "Never thought I'd see the day that you would settle down. You used to swear on your life that you'd remain single."

"Aren't I just the luckiest girl ever." Jayna shot him a sweet smile and reached over, squeezing his hand. "Guess your life is now over."

He hid the grimace. "No, honey, it's just beginning." He could turn on the syrupy sweet as well. He looped his arm across her shoulder and pulled her in close. Her hair smelled like apples. Jayna really couldn't make up her mind.

Chapter 29

Jayna

Jayna really couldn't make up her mind. Was this date heaven or hell? It was truly a heavenly setting, and she was sitting beside the devil himself. So maybe it was purgatory.

She had to admit, fake dating the man she loathed could have been worse. It could have been better, too. Derek was, and apparently, always would be, a total jerk. Although he could turn on the charm when it suited him, it just never suited him very often and never where she was concerned.

It wasn't that she wanted him to charm her. No way, no how. But would it have killed him to tell her she looked good tonight? This was a killer dress, a splurge from Saks Fifth Avenue when she'd been in New York. It was indeed a showstopper and was supposed to knock his socks off. He'd barely said a word about it. Just a grunt and a frown. The man was an ape. Maybe he didn't wear socks.

This work gala he'd brought her to was incredible, though. She'd never been to Casa Loma and the 19th century castle did not disappoint. The function being held in the conservatory, which was simply breathtaking. The dome ceiling was made of stained glass, and it was jaw-dropping. And as the evening wore on, Derek relaxed beside her and became less of an ape.

She could tell that he'd been worried she'd embarrass him or expose him for the fraud he was. But a deal was a deal. She still couldn't believe he joined her on stage last week.

Mario wasn't quite as terrifying as Derek had made him out

to be. However, he was scrutinizing them. She put in extra effort to charm the man and hold back the normal insults she directed Derek's way. And as if they'd entered a bizarre new world, the dinner conversation puzzled her.

"Who decorated your house?" Derek leaned close, asking quietly.

She blinked. "My house?"

"Yeah, I like it."

"You like it?" She repeated his words.

"What's the name of the decorator you used?"

"The name of the decorator?" She repeated his question.

"It's not a difficult question," he continued, speaking slower this time. "What. Is. The. Name. Of. Your. Decorator?"

"I didn't use one. I did it myself." She blinked again. Why did he care? "I scoured Jamie's store for unique furniture and then bought the rest out of the Wayfair catalog."

"Really?"

"Really. Why? Are you in need of a makeover to your bedroom at your parents' house?"

Now he blinked, frowning. "No, smart ass. I just so happen to be building my own house. I'm still living at home to save money. And my mom is a great cook."

"Oh." That she wasn't expecting. Not the fact that he'd eventually move out of his parents' house, but that he was building a home. She'd pictured him living in a condo. All sleek lines, black leather and mirrors on the ceilings. A true bachelor pad. Nothing homey like what she'd created.

The man kept surprising her. A good singer. A great kisser. Her eyes landed on his full lips again, and she gave herself a firm head shake. It was just this romantic setting, and the ape did look so handsome in a tux. Maybe it really was made out of boyfriend material. He'd even splurged on a haircut for the event. She couldn't help but wonder where he'd gone. She'd heard he was banned from his sister-in-law's salon after dating and dumping all her single stylists. He certainly had not received such an amazing cut from Hank's Barbershop.

"Can I get you another drink?"

"Uh, no thanks." Seriously, who was this charming man?

She reached over and pinched his arm.

"Ouch. What was that for?"

"Just wanted to make sure you're real. I thought for a moment that I was dreaming."

"Aren't you supposed to pinch yourself?" he asked, brow furrowing.

"Why would I pinch myself? That would hurt."

"You are one of a kind, Jayna," he chuckled, low and deep. A sexy sound that vibrated up her spine.

He stood and held out his hand. "Let's dance."

"Wow, such a gentleman."

He twirled her before pulling her into his arms. Leaning down, he whispered in her ear, "I'll adamantly deny it if you tell anyone."

His breath was hot against her earlobe. The intimacy of it sent shock waves through her entire body. She had to remind herself that this was indeed the ape-man, Derek Brennan. He was not a man to fantasize about, but one to be cautious of.

But Derek was a great dancer. Which was something else to add to the list of his growing attributes.

His left hand gently pressed against the small of her back, while the other hand intertwined their fingers. Hell had officially frozen over because she liked the way their hands fit together so perfectly. When Derek was pretending to be a boyfriend, he was attentive and sweet.

Pretending was the keyword. Fake date. Fake boyfriend. Fake feelings.

He was just putting on a show to save his career. But as he continued to twirl her around the dance floor, she started to believe it herself. He pulled her closer and stared down into her eyes like she was someone he cared about.

Fake. It wasn't real.

None of it. Not his feelings or the nice guy act. Derek Two-Date Brennan didn't catch feelings, and he definitely was not a nice guy.

It was FAKE.

Yet as that one song blended into another, she allowed herself to be held close, sinking into his hard chest. She gave herself permission to believe the lie, too.

Just for this one night, she could dream and fall and believe it. A shiver raced up her spine. Falling for Derek Brennan would be emotional suicide. It would destroy her as it had in high school.

She stiffened and pushed backward. His eyes narrowed questioningly.

"I need to use the ladies' room," she managed to find her voice.

This man was pretending. He was and always would be heartbreak wrapped up in a far too handsome package.

Fool her once, shame on him.

Fool her twice, shame on her.

She was Jayna frigging Sutton. She did not fall for men with agendas. Besides, she had an agenda of her own; win over the very handsome and stable Lance Roman.

Now that man was the real deal. He was the man to settle down with and build a life. It was time.

Lance wasn't playacting to save his smarmy butt. He wasn't the kiss-and-bail type or breaker of hearts like the man in front of her. She just needed to recite all the reasons she disliked Derek, and that was one big-ass list. Derek Brennan was not the man of her dreams. He was more like her worst nightmare.

Chapter 30

Derek

This was his worst nightmare come true; he was catching feelings. But the more time Derek spent with Jayna, the more he liked her.

He liked her.

The realization hit him like a hard blow to the head.

And he didn't just like her, he REALLY liked her.

Jayna was beautiful, accomplished, funny, and honest. She was a no-bullshit, call-it-like-it-is woman.

'I'm falling for her', he thought as he pored over the blueprints on Monday morning. And those words filled him with terror.

Derek Brennan did not fall for women, especially pain-in-the-ass women like Jayna Sutton.

He needed to remember all the reasons he couldn't stand her. That was one very long list. Yet as he stared down at the blueprints, his mind refused to focus. He was having difficulty making sense of these plans that would turn a farm field into a mini village, and it was impossible to recall the 'reason Jayna sucks' list. Somehow, all he could think about was how appealing he found her.

He also couldn't stop from wondering what she was doing at this very moment.

Was she working? Maybe she'd brought his grandfather and Nick's grandfather specialty coffee again. That had been so considerate of her. It had made the two old men's day, if not their entire week.

Whoa. He couldn't care in the least what Jayna was up to.

It was nothing more than this whole fake dating thing that was messing with his head.

He searched his memory for the how and the when. How and when had he stopped loathing her and fallen in love?

Whoa, again. Like a big whoa. Back up. In love?

Derek 'Dare' Brennan didn't do third dates, or dinner with parents and most definitely DID NOT FALL IN LOVE!!

Never.

Not once.

Oh, he may have had a crush on Leighton for almost a decade, but the L-word had never crossed his mind or his lips.

So, when exactly had he crossed the line that he swore he'd never cross? More importantly, how did he cross back over it? He had no intention of staying there.

Or maybe this wasn't love. It wasn't like he was experienced. He never stuck around long enough to find out. It was just that her annoying traits had stopped being annoying. It used to bother him that Jayna didn't care what anyone thought, speaking her mind, popular or not. Now, instead of finding her abrasive, he found her refreshing.

He was the same way.

And there it was, the reason and problem, all in one. She was exactly like him. Jayna was not dating material, definitely not wife material.

WHOA!! Time for all this introspection to come to a screeching halt! Wife material? That breakfast bagel must have been bad. He had food poisoning, which was causing him to become delusional.

The answer that he needed was simple. It was time to put an end to this fake dating immediately.

This brought him to Tuesday evening.

"Wow, Derek. It's incredible." Jayna twirled, staring up at the vaulted ceiling with the exposed wooden beams.

His eyes were fixated on her. They weren't narrowed with disdain. Was that longing they were filled with? What the hell happened to the plan? Call her over and end it. It was a simple plan. It was easy to execute. He ended relationships all the time.

But there she stood, twirling in tight blue jeans and a snug t-shirt, bringing back images of her in that sexy black dress. That dress was still haunting his dreams and waking hours.

Why had he invited her to tour his almost-finished house?

Because he wanted her help decorating it. Yeah, that was the reason.

"It is really beautiful, Derek."

"Thanks," he answered. Why did her praise fill him with so much pride?

"I love the fireplace." She brushed a hand over the stonework. "What do you plan to do for a mantle?"

"That's why you're here. I liked the live edge mantle on yours. Where did you find it?"

"Jamie's store. She has some incredible salvaged wood. Let's get the dimensions and we can check out her storage room."

He nodded. Yes, that was the only reason she was here. To help. Today would not be the right time to end it. She may not be so interested in helping if he dumped her.

"And the flooring, Derek, it's so incredible." She stared down at the wide plank flooring.

"Sedona," he told her the name. "It's white oak."

She flashed him a smile. "Jamie has the perfect area rug. She just got it in. It's a vintage Persian carpet."

He frowned back. "I didn't spend an insane amount of money on this hardwood to cover it up."

"Oh, Derek," she laughed and shook her head. "That's why I am here. It's not that you're covering it up, it's about defining the living spaces."

Her hand swept the open concept space. The large room flowed into a well-laid-out kitchen. "The area rug will go in front of the fireplace, and the couch will sit on the edge of it. It will bring in warmth."

"Okay," he nodded.

"Let's go shopping at Yesterday and Tomorrow. See what we can score from Jamie and then we can go to Patty's for dinner and pour over the Wayfair catalog for the rest. You're buying."

"Yes, boss," he saluted her.

"Oh, grab those rubber boots," she indicated to the pair sitting by the front door.

"Rubber boots? Why?"

"You'll see," she winked and stepped out his front door.

Derek followed Jayna to Yesterday and Tomorrow and stepped out of his truck, shutting the door. "Jamie trusts you with a key?"

"I'm a silent partner." Jayna stood at the door of Jamie's workshop, which was located behind the store.

"Silent?" His left brow shot up. "Why do I find that hard to believe?"

"Okay, more like an enthusiastic investor." She pushed open the door and hit the light switch.

He'd heard that she'd put up the money when Jamie had been turned down by the bank. It had been a decent thing to do, and a smart investment. Yesterday and Tomorrow was a flourishing business.

He stepped into the workshop that had once been an auto repair shop. Now it was converted into a woodworking shop and massive storage unit. Old furniture was stacked along the back wall, waiting to make it to one of the work bays to be stripped, refinished, and reimagined. Jamie was truly talented. He brushed a hand across a long harvest table that sat in the center of the first bay, in the process of being stripped of white paint and brought to its original wood finish.

New furniture wasn't built this solid. The table was beautiful and well made with intricately carved legs. "Has she sold this table yet?"

"No, I don't think so," Jayna stopped to look at it. "Are you thinking that it would look great in your dining room?"

"I am," he nodded. "But what about chairs?"

"Those we can find on Wayfair," Jayna waved towards the back wall. "Over here are the mantels."

He followed her to the stacked pile of reclaimed beams and wooden fireplace surrounds.

"This one looks long enough," she pointed to a large wooden beam. Reaching into a crate, she pulled out two matching wooden corbels. "With these corbels attached underneath, it will look stunning against the stonework of your fireplace."

He agreed.

"And this," she moved to a stacked pile of old windows. There was an arched frame missing the glass. "If you had a mirror cut to fit, it would look incredible on the mantel."

He also agreed.

"Now for the area rug," Jayna walked to a corner where rolled rugs were piled. "Jamie salvaged this old Persian rug the other day. It's 9 x 12, and I think it is soft cream with greens and rust tones."

She pulled out a rug that was covered in cobwebs and about fifty years of embedded dirt. "It will be the perfect finishing touch in your living room and will enhance those gorgeous oak floors."

"Uh, no. That filthy carpet is not touching my new floors. It belongs in the dump, and it should be put there by someone wearing a hazmat suit." He frowned. "Seriously, stop touching it. You're going to pick up a skin infection."

"Don't be such a wuss," she told him as she dragged the carpet towards the car wash bay that had been left intact.

Again, there she went, calling him a wuss. What was wrong with this woman? He was not a wuss. He just had common sense. Could she truly believe this rug was salvageable?

She unrolled the carpet, and it was even dirtier than he'd originally thought.

"Patience, young grasshopper. Not everything is as it seems."

Had she just quoted one of his favorite movies?

She unhooked the hose from the power washer that was mounted to the wall. Hitting the water button, she turned the water spray on the carpet and dark brown water immediately pooled. Now he understood the rubber boots.

"Wax on, wax off," she swept the pressure washer across the carpet.

She was quoting Karate Kid.

"Here, give it a try." She released the trigger on the sprayer and handed it over to him. "Jessica and I fight over this job. It's somehow relaxing and so satisfying."

He took the nozzle from her and pressed the trigger, blasting the dirty carpet.

Jayna flipped the switch to the shampoo setting and damn if she wasn't right. The tension started to leave his shoulders as he slowly swept the foamy spray over the now soaked carpet.

"Okay, now for the really fun part." She brought over a rotary floor buffer, setting it on the carpet. Holding out her hand, she took the hose from him. "Get that shampoo worked in."

"It's a floor buffer."

"Yeah, it works great."

He switched the machine on, slowly moving it across the carpet. The spinning disk immersed the shampoo deep into the carpet fibers.

Jayna stepped onto the carpet with a squeegee mop, pushing the excess water and shampoo toward the drain on the floor. "Can you grab the power washer again? Use the water setting. Give it another rinse."

Damn, if the carpet hadn't become clean after they repeated the steps twice over. The pattern and colors were becoming visible. It was a beautiful rug, although it was now sopping wet.

"Help me roll it," Jayna leaned down at the far end.

He moved to the other side, rolling the carpet.

Jayna hit the play button on an old-style MP3 player and Van Halen's "Jump" blasted through the speakers.

"Thought you liked country?"

"I do. But this kind of work calls for head-banging, stomp-your-feet kind of music." Jayna grinned and jumped up on the rolled carpet. Water squirted out from the edges.

"Come on, Brennan, you might as well jump," she laughed.

He shook his head and climbed on top of the rolled carpet. Jayna jumped again, and he lost his balance. She reached to steady him but lost her footing as well. They both tumbled off, falling into the soapy carpet water on the floor.

No one besides Jayna could have talked him into this. He stared down at his wet jeans and then at her soaked t-shirt. Oh, man. He really wished he hadn't looked. He wished her snort was still annoying. But no, it was adorable as hell. She looked damn good in soapy carpet water.

He raised to his knees and held out his hand to help Jayna up. She grasped it and yanked, pulling him back down. He slipped and fell on top of her. She laughed and snorted again. Bracing himself up on his elbows, he laughed as well. She blinked away the water that beaded on her long lashes that didn't look false. He couldn't help but notice, staring at her up close, that she was a true natural beauty. Most of the women he dated used a lot of make-up along with false lashes and had their lips surgically plumped.

Jayna's eyes opened wide and met his, the laughter dying on both of their lips. She had the bluest eyes, like a perfect summer sky. Her eyes were mesmerizing, hypnotizing him.

Beneath his soaked t-shirt he could feel her hands braced against his chest. She wasn't pulling him closer, nor was she pushing him away. Did she want him to kiss her? Did he want to kiss her?

There was something building between them. Something real and undeniable. But they were fake dating. This was not real.

Then why did it suddenly feel anything but fake? His eyes moved down to her full, soft lips. He'd just have to drop his head. It wasn't like they hadn't kissed before. He hesitated and she blinked again.

"Derek." He really liked the way his name sounded when she spoke it aloud in that breathless voice.

He sucked in a breath. This kiss would be different. This kiss would mean something. He wasn't ready for that. He pulled back.

"Derek?" Confusion or was it disappointment flashed through her gorgeous eyes.

His head started to drop again, and sudden panic filled him. Could she see how much he was affected in this moment. Could she see that he was falling for her?

NO! Hell no! He did not fall for women. They fell for him. That's the way he liked it. One sided. He lifted his head again and pulled a Derek. His eyes traveled down to her wet t-shirt, and he waggled his brows. "Didn't know that there was going to be a wet t-shirt contest!"

"Ugh!" She shoved up with her hands that were still braced on his chest. "You are such a pig!"

"Thought I was an ape?"

"You're both!" She shoved harder. "Get off me, you big buffoon."

He grinned. This was better. Pissed off Jayna he could handle.

Why had he agreed to meet back at Patty's after running home to change? They should have just called it a night. It was a dumb idea. Had he almost kissed her? Now that would have been a stupid idea! One of his worst, ever. Falling for Jayna was the last thing he needed. But that wasn't a problem because it wasn't going to happen!

He didn't need Jayna to help him decorate his home. He could just ask his mom for help. His mom had good taste. Time to leave. So why then, was he still sitting here staring at the door, waiting for Jayna?

They'd made plans to eat dinner and peruse the Wayfair catalog. But the plan he should be following was to end this charade of a relationship. Mario had backed off now that his daughter was hot and heavy with another co-worker. Derek was off the hook.

Absent-mindedly, he twirled the amber-colored whiskey in the low tumbler, his eyes trained on the door. He didn't mean to smile when she walked through it and rushed toward him.

The chair across from him scraped along the concrete floor and she sat down. She had taken a quick shower, and he caught a whiff of her freshly shampooed hair. Grapefruit this time. Her shower must be lined with over a dozen bottles of shampoo.

She set a large tablet on the table and hung her purse off the back of her chair.

"I thought you were bringing the catalog?"

"It's online," Jayna replied. "Did you order yet?"

"Just drinks."

Ivy appeared with another whiskey for him and a frosty margarita for her.

"Thanks," she smiled up at the server. "My favorite."

"Any news on that missing nurse?" Ivy asked Jayna as she set the glasses on the table.

Jayna's smile slid. "No, nothing. It is so out of character for Greta. She has simply vanished. No one has heard from her."

"I don't have a good feeling about this." Ivy pursed her lips. "Has anyone asked Jamie to help?"

Derek scoffed, and both women glanced at him. Psychics, mediums, tarot card readers; it was all a big scam. Not that he disliked Jamie nor was he calling her a fraud. Admittedly, she did have great intuition. But psychic abilities? Not very likely. Besides, this missing nurse had probably met some guy and took off on an adventure.

No one knew Greta well enough to say this was out of character for her. Nick and Burke had discussed the case the other night while playing poker. Greta had not shown up for work. Her family had not heard from her and filed a missing person report. Her car was gone, and her clothing still hung in her closet. No signs of foul play were found. It was a mystery that he doubted Jamie could solve with a crystal ball.

"I'll have two pounds of wings, please Ivy," Derek placed his order, changing the subject.

"Oh, I could do wings," Jayna said. "We'll do my special order. Wing roulette."

"Wing roulette?" he questioned.

Ivy chuckled. "I don't know if he's up to the challenge, Jayna, my girl."

"I'm up for any challenge," Derek defended. "Just to clarify, what's the challenge?"

"It's actually Jayna's creation," Ivy stuck her notepad into the pocket of her apron. "I keep telling Patty he needs to add it to the menu. It's a mixture of mild, medium, hot, and suicide wings, all in the same basket. You never know which wing you'll get until it's too late."

"Give us four pounds, Ivy," Jayna told the woman. "We'll see how well Dare Brennan fares."

He shook his head, and another smile lifted his lips. Jayna was one of a kind. Just when he thought he had her figured out, she went and did something unpredictable. She was unlike any woman he'd ever dated.

Fake dated, he corrected himself. This was not real. But damn, if he ever did decide to date for real, he'd want a woman exactly like her. That thought caused the smile to dissolve. He didn't want to be in a relationship with any woman.

But wing roulette, now that was cool. Jayna was a cool chick.

So, why did Jayna have to go and turn into every other woman in this town and suddenly want a serious relationship? She was fake dating him to win over the paramedic, he reminded himself. She was manipulative, just like so many women he's dated. Maybe she wasn't cool, after all.

And why the paramedic? Why weren't her sights set on him instead, like the other women in town? He was a good catch. He had a great job that paid well. He had just built a beautiful house. And he was damn good-looking.

"Why do you hate me so much?"

Jayna looked just as surprised by his question as he was. Why had he just blurted that out?

Her face hardened for a moment. "You really don't remember?" Her voice hardened as well.

He closed his eyes as the memory from long ago took hold. That time in high school when he'd been stupid enough to think that asking out the best friend of his little sister was a good idea. However, Jayna, at fifteen, had turned into a knockout. And he'd been a typical seventeen-year-old, whose hormones had overridden common sense.

"I tell you that I'm a virgin and then you panic. You acted like I just told you that I had a contagious disease."

He had panicked. He had no intention of being the guy who took her virginity. He never wanted to be that guy. It held too much responsibility. He should never have touched her in the first place.

"Yeah, I wasn't a nice guy back then."

"Just back then?" She held his stare for a long moment, which was thankfully broken when Ivy set down the basket of wings.

"Water under the bridge," she told him and picked up a wing. She shoved it in her mouth and sucked off all the meat, pulling out a clean bone.

Wing lovers everywhere would be impressed. If Connor had been sitting with them, the young man would be a puddle on the floor. It took all of Derek's willpower not to moan at the sight. Jayna was not playing fair.

"That was a mild one," Jayna told him. "Your turn."

This woman was an enigma. She called him out for being a jerk, then just as quickly let him off the hook. She truly was one of a kind. Lance would be one lucky guy. That was once the paramedic finally got his head out of his ass and figured out how great a catch Jayna was.

Then, Derek could go back to life as normal. And he'd have a nicely decorated house. Reaching into the basket, he chose a wing and shoved it into his mouth.

Chapter 31

Jayna

Between mouthfuls of wings and wiping off her sticky fingers, Jayna swiped through the online catalog. They picked out a large sectional, a coffee table, and matching end tables, along with chairs for the harvest table. It was an understatement to say that the house Derek was building had surprised her. She hadn't expected to love it so much.

It was beautiful and homey. Her eyes had immediately traveled to the cathedral ceilings and exposed wood beams. The foyer led to an open concept space with wide plank oak flooring. It was devoid of furniture, but she had an immediate vision of how to furnish it. A floor-to-ceiling stone fireplace called for a very unique mantle. To define the living room, a large vintage area rug and an overstuffed sectional would be needed. She'd immediately pictured the Persian carpet that Jamie had bought at an estate sale.

An antique chandelier, which she was sure could be found in Jamie's storage room, would hang from the wooden beam next to the large kitchen island, establishing the dining area. They had found a large harvest table at Jamie's, too, that would fit the space perfectly.

The kitchen was a chef's dream, expertly laid out with soft green cupboards, thinly veined marble, and a white shiplap backsplash. French doors led to a back deck that overlooked the valley below. The house was spectacular, but the view was jaw-dropping. He had chosen a piece of land that sat high and kept watch on his parents' farm below. He hadn't just built a house;

he'd built a home.

She hadn't expected to enjoy spending time with him, either. He had been a great date at his work function. Attentive and charming. He'd been a complete gentleman. They'd had so much fun earlier, shampooing the carpet. But what had that been, when they stumbled off the rolled carpet? Derek had stared deeply into her eyes. He looked like he was about to kiss her, and for a moment, that's all she wanted him to do as well. Then he pushed back and reverted to the jerk with the leering look and the wet t-shirt comment. And now, he went and ruined it again, opening his big, stupid mouth.

Why was she mad at him?

It had only been one of the most humiliating moments of her entire life. Because of him! And he sat there like he had no memory of it. Maybe he didn't.

Being a self-absorbed asshole was a daily occurrence for Derek.

That one night, so long ago, had cost her so much. She'd lost herself for a while after it. Her self-worth had taken a hard hit, and she'd searched for it in all the wrong places. Like she could find it in a man's approval. That had just devalued her more. Finally, she took control and stopped letting men use her. She used them instead.

"Sorry about that. I wasn't a nice guy back then." Was that all he had to say about that night?

The way he'd turned her down had been so cruel. But he'd been right to do it. He just shouldn't have done it so carelessly.

She leaned back in her chair, staring at him. Was she being too hard on him? He'd been a teenager as well, trying to navigate those confusing, difficult years.

People make mistakes all the time. No one was perfect. However, for him to sit there and question why she was angry with him, like he had no clue, made her angry all over again. It made her want to make him pay, make him squirm.

"So, just what happened between you, Tommy, and Leighton?"

His jaw immediately clenched, and he shifted in his chair. Mission accomplished.

"Nothing."

"Right," she snorted.

She'd been there during their teen years. She'd witnessed his obsession with Leighton. That's what had broken her heart the most. It hadn't been the replacement girl he'd shown up with the following weekend. No, that girl had meant nothing to him. But the way his eyes followed Leighton everywhere, the expression on his face when Leighton kissed Tommy—that had nearly destroyed her. She had offered Derek her heart, her virginity, and he had brushed it away like it was nothing. He preferred to pine over a girl he could never have rather than start a relationship with one who was pining over him.

Knowing Leighton's side, Jayna was curious what Derek's version would be. Would he even admit to it? Maybe he had conveniently forgotten about it as well.

He looked her straight in the eye. "I kissed Leighton at the harvest dance the night before Tommy went missing. Took what wasn't mine to take."

He simply stated it and continued to hold her stare. Her mouth dropped open, but words escaped her. She hadn't expected such honesty from him.

"There is no name you can call me that I haven't already called myself." Something flashed through his eyes. If she hadn't been staring so intently, she would have missed it. It had been a combination of shame and blame.

Her eyes narrowed. While he was being honest, she might as well keep pushing. "Do you still have feelings for Leighton?"

He smiled, a sad half-smile. "No, I don't think my feelings were ever deeper than just an injured ego that she'd chosen Tommy over me."

Well, now, that was a very honest answer that didn't put him in the best light. Did the man even possess a heart?

"I'm really not a good guy, Jayna," he continued, reading her mind again. "This bad boy, player act, isn't an act. It's who I am."

He leaned his elbows on the table, closing off the distance between them. "I'm the guy who betrayed his brother. His twin, no less."

His voice was low and intense and sent a shiver up her spine.

"I betrayed Tommy. More than once. It started when I didn't enlist too. When I sent him off to that hellhole all alone."

He leaned even closer. She could smell whiskey and barbeque sauce on his breath. "Then I kissed his girl like I didn't know she was his entire world. What did I care? I'm the reckless one. The one who doesn't concern himself with consequences or feelings."

Another shiver raced up her spine. "Why did you do it then, Derek?"

He cleared his throat, holding her stare. "I was jealous. She chose him over me. Just like everyone else always did. Our parents, our teachers, even our siblings. Tommy is just more likable. And it was easier not to try. Doesn't matter what I do, I always seem to disappoint everyone. Why raise their expectations?"

She sucked in a breath. There he went, surprising her again. He was hurting and pretending that he wasn't hurting. She knew exactly how he felt. It was the way she felt. Not good enough.

NOT enough.

Then he sat back, the bad boy grin replacing the sad smile. The moment was over.

"Your turn." He slid the basket of wings in front of her.

She licked her lips and released the heaviness of emotion that had built in her chest. Forcing a smile, she picked up a wing and shoved it in her mouth.

Suicide sauce. Whoa. Hot.

At least she had something to blame the tears in her eyes on.

"Suicide," she said as she sucked the meat off the bone and dropped the bone onto the plate. Sweat beaded on her upper lip, but she didn't reach for the water.

"Your turn." She pushed the basket back to him.

"Just how do we know who wins?" he asked, picking up a wing.

"Whoever wusses out first and reaches for the water."

"Oh, that won't be me. I never wuss out."

She laughed, her eyes moving to the next table. Yet another shiver raced up her spine. Duncan, the busboy, was clearing off the table. He was staring directly at her with such intensity as he filled the white plastic bucket with dirty dishes. Goosebumps formed.

Duncan was harmless. She knew that. Someone should tell it to the tingle in her scalp, though. She was being silly. It was all the talk about Greta missing, along with the feeling that she was being watched. Jessica's claim that she saw a face in Jayna's bedroom window had unsettled her.

Without a second thought, she grabbed the front of Derek's shirt and pulled him toward her, planting her lips against his. She felt his shock before he gave in to it. He leaned closer and his lips lifted for a moment before crashing down against her mouth in a toe-curling kiss.

This wasn't the first kiss they'd shared. However, it was different. She'd instigated it, but he quickly took control. And wow, Derek could kiss. But he'd had a lot of practice. He'd definitely kissed more girls than she'd kissed boys. He was exceptionally good at it. He was so good that if she hadn't been seated, her knees would have buckled.

He pulled her closer, his hand moving to the back of her head, fingers threading through her hair. His lips pressed harder, and hers spread open.

This was a great kiss. Maybe one of the best she'd ever received. It was the kind of kiss that made a person forget their name. And it came from Dare Brennan. She lifted her hands and pulled her fingers through his hair, too. Then she realized that she was pulling her fingers through his hair as the kiss intensified. She was not only kissing Derek but enjoying it. Hell no!

She shoved backward.

"What was that for?" He blinked rapidly and then glanced all around. "I don't see Lance Romance?"

She ran a thumb over her lips, which felt swollen, and tried to will her heart back into a regular rhythm.

Forcing a smile, she answered as casually as she could while feeling so breathless. "Just because you're irresistible." She poured on the sarcasm and shoved back her chair.

No way could she remain, letting him see just how undone she was. It was all too much. The last two weeks spent with him. Their conversation tonight. His admission about feeling unworthy. His house. Greta missing. Duncan leering. Her racing heart. It was just too much.

"Later Brennan." She dropped a twenty on the table. If she paid her share, then this was not a date. Shaking off the ill ease and the mounting unwanted attraction from the kiss, she quickly left. She needed to start remembering that they were not really dating.

Chapter 32

Derek

Derek reminded himself they were not really dating as he stared at the door Jayna had just shut behind her.

"Damn," he muttered, touching his tingling lips. Hot damn, Jayna could kiss.

He stood, pulling out a couple more twenties and set them on top of Jayna's money. He signaled Ivy and quickly ran out the door.

Why, though? Why the hell was he chasing after her? This was all pretend. Jayna certainly wasn't going to be the woman who would finally take him off the market.

"Jayna!" he yelled, still chasing after her.

She had opened the door of her truck and paused, back stiffening. She turned around. The dim lighting of the parking lot cast her face in shadows.

"What, Dare?"

"What was that kiss about?"

Her forehead creased. "Nothing. Not a damn thing."

"It felt like a lot more than nothing."

"This is all pretend," she told him, waving her hand dismissively.

"Is it really? Because that didn't feel like pretend to me. And the paramedic was nowhere to be seen."

"Wow," she laughed caustically. "You really are something. Your ego is massive! If you must know, it was the busboy. Duncan makes me nervous. He's always staring at me. I wanted him to believe I had a boyfriend."

Now it was his turn to look confused. "Oh, okay."

"You didn't honestly think I was kissing you for another reason?"

"Uh, no." He narrowed his eyes. What was this woman doing to him? She was messing with his head. No one messed with his head.

He stepped closer to her, his hand resting on the top of the truck door, just above her head. "But you're wrong, Jayna. There is more between us than just nothing. And there is way more going on here than just pretend."

She looked up at him, her forehead creasing. He should take a step back, instead he moved closer. Her hands had raised and were now braced against his chest. He dropped his head, pausing, waiting for her to shove him away. She wet her lips, and that flick of her tongue nearly destroyed him.

With the lightest of touches, he brushed a kiss across her lips. Their lips had just barely touched but it was one of the most exhilarating kisses he'd ever experienced. What the hell was wrong with him when a chaste kiss nearly dropped him to his knees?

He needed to stop this before it was too late. But her lips were making it impossible for his mind to listen to reason. His head dropped again, and she sighed against his mouth. A low, primal groan escaped him, and he stole her next breath as his lips crashed against hers. He kissed her like he'd wanted to kiss her while they lay in the soapy carpet water. Kissed her until he felt her breath catch and her body slacken against his. His fingers threaded through her hair, and he pulled her closer, deepening the kiss.

How could a simple kiss be so all consuming and soul shattering? He had never kissed a woman like this before. This was not about desire or want, this was about surrender. He wasn't sure who was surrendering, though. Was it him, or was it her? Did it even matter? There was this need he felt to possess her and claim her and give in to her.

Her hands moved up his chest, across his shoulders to his

neck. Another moan escaped her lips and with that sound sanity returned to him. He pulled his head up, breaking the kiss. She blinked rapidly, staring at him with a mixture of confusion and shock crossing her beautiful face. His heart felt like it was going to burst out of his chest. Her fingers lifted to her swollen lips. He was playing with fire here, and if he continued, he was definitely going to get burnt.

He stepped back and forced a low chuckle and an indifferent grin before he turned and walked away. Thankfully, she couldn't see his face anymore because his laughter didn't match the conflicted expression he wore. This was becoming far more complicated than just 'fake dating.' This was why he had hesitated back in Jamie's workshop—he knew that if he kissed her while feeling this confused, walking away would be much harder. Not only did he like spending time with her, but he really liked kissing her. And that was problematic. He didn't want to like her period. His life had been much less complicated when he hated her.

It was time to end things!

Chapter 33

Jayna

It was time to end things. Whatever this confusing situation with Derek had become, it needed to stop. Jayna had spent the entire night tossing and turning, the kiss they shared in the parking lot replaying endlessly in her dreams. Was it a dream or a nightmare? The one thing she knew with all certainty was that she was catching feelings for Derek Brennan. And that was dangerous.

She needed to call it quits. If only there was a pill for this, like the DayQuil she took when she had a cold. There had to be something to overcome these unwanted emotions. Maybe there was a vaccine.

As she drove past Patty's, she noticed both Lance's Prius and Derek's pickup parked outside. The time was now. She signaled and pulled in. Sucking in a deep breath, she let it out on a slow exhale before stepping out of her truck. She walked straight to the door before she lost her nerve.

Her eyes adjusted from the bright sunshine as she entered the dark interior of the bar. Lance, along with two other paramedics, sat in the far corner. Her gaze flickered to the bar where Derek was seated. He wasn't alone.

Lacey Bellamy sat on the bar stool beside him. Her hand rested on his shoulder, and she leaned close to him. Derek tilted his head, listening intently to whatever she was telling him. He threw his head back and laughed.

A flash of anger surged through Jayna. Why, though? It hadn't been real between them. Just when had Derek come to mean something to her? He did matter, she realized. In the past few weeks that they had been 'fake dating,' their relationship had become real to her. But obviously it hadn't for him. Derek met her eyes and didn't acknowledge her. He turned away and leaned in close to Lacey, whispering in her ear.

The woman was even more flawless than she'd been in high school. It came as no surprise that she'd become a successful model. Lacey was tall, rail-thin, but still had an amazing figure. With her dainty features, the camera loved her. And if the rumors were true, she was also recently divorced and apparently on the prowl.

Why did it have to be Lacey?

Lacey had been the one he dated right after he'd broken Jayna's heart in high school. That following weekend, at the bonfire, would forever be ingrained in her mind. There had been that one vacant look when he'd met her eyes across the fire pit. That had hurt more than his rejection. He'd looked right past her like she hadn't been the girl he kissed the weekend before.

She shouldn't be surprised. Derek was just being Derek. The player. She released a slow breath, letting the anger go with it. Her eyes shifted towards Lance, who glanced between Derek and her. Lance's eyes locked with hers, and she saw compassion and concern in his.

Now, this was just the perfect scenario. Lance would believe that Derek's flirtation had hurt her. She brushed away the tears that should have been fake yet were all too real. This was the opportunity she had been waiting for. It was the perfect scenario to end things with Derek and make Lance believe she was the spurned party instead of the party girl he once thought she was.

On unsteady legs, she walked toward Derek. Hurt filled her voice as she spoke, and it required absolutely no playacting. She felt it. "Seriously, Brennan?"

He looked up, giving her a half smile. "Hey, Jayna."

"What's going on here?" she demanded, hands on her hips.

"Nothing."

"Doesn't look like nothing," she exclaimed and brushed away more tears that fell. "Looks very intimate to me. It's high school all over again."

"High school?" His brows furrowed.

No way he didn't remember. Or maybe he didn't. Maybe she was giving him too much credit. Maybe he was that callous.

"At least in high school, you had the guts to dump me before you took up with Lacey. Now, I don't even get that?"

The V between his brows deepened. "We're just talking. Just catching up."

"Just breaking my heart all over again." More tears escaped. "Derek, I don't think you even begin to understand how badly you hurt me in high school. Seeing you with Lacey destroyed my confidence. The least you could have done was not so blatantly flaunt your relationship with her. It was cruel."

She finally said all the things her younger self couldn't before. "I cared so much for you. I offered you my heart, and you didn't want it. You walked away. Without a backward glance."

Roughly, she wiped away the river of tears pouring down her cheeks. Derek stood, but she held up a palm, stopping him. Lance was walking in her direction, concern written all over his face. Standing between the two men, she felt torn.

The expression on Derek's face looked strained. Why though? Shouldn't his expression be one of relief now that she'd finally let him off the hook? He was finally free to take up with the stunning Lacey.

Lance moved toward her. Relief should have filled her. Her plan may just have worked. She had Lance's full attention.

Eyes on the prize, she reminded herself. Lance Roman was the reason for all of this. He was the man she could settle down with. So, why had she gone and fallen for her fake boyfriend? It wasn't part of the plan. Yet, once again, Derek brought her back to reality.

His feelings for her had not been real. He'd been pretending all along. Now, what did she do?

A good place to start would be by giving her head a firm shake. In front of her stood a man who could offer her a real and stable relationship.

She'd be stupid not to seize this opportunity. It's exactly what she'd wanted.

Blinking away the remaining tears that pooled in her eyes, she moved toward Lance. "I can't believe he's done this to me. Again!"

Lance held out his arm to her. "Why don't we go somewhere else and talk?"

She sniffled and nodded, taking hold of his extended arm.

"Jayna!"

She heard Derek call after her, but she didn't turn around. There was no point.

Her plan had worked. This was exactly what she had wanted.

Chapter 34

Derek

This was exactly what Derek wanted. The whole fake dating fiasco with Jayna was finally over. So why did it feel like the last thing he wanted? Why did he feel like that chicken-shit teenager all over again?

In high school, he'd quickly learned that good looks and a bad-boy attitude could get him far with the girls. They practically threw themselves at him. Who was he to turn them down? So, when Jayna started chasing him, he relented. Sure, she was his little sister's friend, which had given him a moment of pause. However, Jayna had seemed so sure of herself. She was the stereotypical beautiful, popular rich girl. Jayna was a girl who had never been told no. He had believed she was spoiled and didn't see beyond that.

But something happened in the back seat of his jeep. When she told him that he'd be her first, he panicked. Seeing vulnerability in her eyes, he didn't want to be responsible for adding to it.

Yet he had added to her vulnerability. More than a decade later, she still clung to the pain of his rejection. The break-up scene was too convincing to be anything but genuine. He had seen Jayna when she pretended, and she wasn't that good of an actress. The tears streaming down her cheeks had reminded him of fifteen-year-old Jayna, and of seventeen-year-old couldn't-give-a-crap Derek.

Their relationship had started out as fake, but over the course of a few weeks, it had changed. There was something between them. She saw him like no one had seen him before.

That scared the hell out of him.

He didn't want to be seen.

She might be the first woman who could make him feel.

He didn't want to feel.

That fear had caused him to revert to that immature teen who had carelessly broken her heart. When Lacey had pulled up the barstool beside him and then Jayna walked in, he'd panicked again. He turned into that guy who had no concept of how to deal with his emotions or those of others. He'd leaned into Lacey, knowing full well that Jayna would react.

But what he hadn't counted on was how he would feel watching the tears pour down Jayna's cheeks. Or how deeply it would sting to watch her leave with Lance. He was the world's biggest jerk. Correction, he was the world's biggest chicken-shit jerk.

His cell phone rang, and he swiped to answer. "Hey, Grandma Rose, what's up?"

"Oh, Derek. It's those two men again," his grandmother huffed. "I swear your grandfather is going to be the death of me."

"What have Pops and Earl done now?"

"Oh, they think they're still young instead of the foolish old men they really are," she continued her tirade. "Bought one of those silly double bicycles and installed a motor on it. Crashed into a car."

"What? Are they alright?"

"Oh, I think so. Just scraped up. It was a parked car they hit."

"A parked car?"

"Earl said the motor gunned on them, and they hit the back of the neighbor's Mini Cooper. Luckily, the only scratches are on them. I am confiscating every tool from both of their garages."

"So, what can I do?"

"Can you take them to the ER to get checked out? They both need a few stitches. And they definitely need a psych exam."

He chuckled. "Be right there, Grandma. Try not to inflict any more harm on them."

"I won't make any promises."

Guiding his grandfather and Nick's grandfather into exam rooms 3 and 4, he helped them onto the cots leaving the privacy curtain open. Both men were fortunate to escape the accident with only minor injuries.

"Tell me again why you installed a motor on a tandem bike?" Derek asked.

"Seemed like a good idea at the time," Norm shrugged, smiling, then winced. He had a long cut down his cheek where he hit the back windshield of the Mini Cooper.

"Okay, which one of you ordered the sponge bath, and who ordered the catheter?" Jayna stepped into the exam room, and Derek's head spun around. Just his luck.

"We both ordered the sponge bath," Earl said.

"Derek ordered the catheter," Norm chuckled. "And an enema as well. The boy has a stick stuck up his butt. Maybe that would help."

He shook his head at his grandfather, then met Jayna's intense stare. Almost a week had passed since the fake break-up, and damn, she looked good. How was it possible for scrubs to look sexy? But on Jayna, the scrubs looked incredibly sexy.

Jayna let out a derisive snort. She was probably imagining all kinds of uncomfortable medical procedures she'd like to perform on him. For a fake break-up, she was acting like it had been real. She looked pissed.

"Let's clean up these cuts." Jayna stepped closer to the cot where Norm sat, swinging his legs. "What were you two thinking?"

"That they're still eighteen and invincible," Derek chimed in, earning glares from both men and Jayna.

"Look who's talking," Earl pointed at Derek. "Dare Brennan. No dare too dangerous or too stupid."

He let out a sigh. Would he ever live down his reputation? "We are not talking about me."

"No, God forbid Derek Brennan opened up." Jayna narrowed her eyes and pursed her lips. "I need to get some suture tape for that laceration on your cheek, Norm. I'll be right back." She was pissed!

"How did you ever let that girl go?" Norm asked, far too loudly. Jayna and the entire emergency department would have overheard.

He let out a long sigh. Of course, news of the 'break-up scene' had made it to the gossip tree of Blythe Landing.

"Dumbest thing ever," Earl added.

It hadn't been real. Someone just needed to tell that to his heart because seeing Jayna again had set it to beating erratically. Maybe while they were here in the ER, he should get checked for arrhythmia.

"It was never real between us," Derek admitted to the two men.

Chapter 35

Jayna

Jayna knew it had never been real. But hearing Derek say it out loud stung. When she'd been assigned to the two men, the last person she expected to find with them was Derek. With their knack for finding trouble, Norm and Earl were frequent flyers to the ER. Usually, it was Rose or Norm's son who brought them in.

Coming face to face with Derek in the exam room had hit her hard. After making such a fool of herself, she wanted to be prepared for their first encounter. Had he realized that her tears were genuine, that her heartbreak was real? Or did he think that, like the fake relationship she had suggested a month earlier, their breakup was just another act?

However, she had achieved her initial goal. Lance had asked her out yesterday, and tonight was their first official date. Sitting at a cozy table for two at Patty's Pub should have had her feeling elated. This was exactly what she'd wanted.

This first date with Lance should have been perfect. And it almost was.

Almost.

Lance was incredibly handsome, with warm hazel-brown eyes and a strong, chiseled jaw. His dark blonde hair was cut in a stylish fade that he touched up frequently. He was perfectly groomed, from his hair to his collared shirt, free of any holes.

He was also smart, toned, tanned, and he smelled amazing —just the right amount of cologne. The man even chewed with his mouth closed, pulled out her chair, and was a great conversationalist.

On paper, he was perfect.

Yet she felt no tingles. Perhaps, though, tingles were overrated. Or maybe, sometimes, tingles took longer to develop. That could be it. She was accustomed to instant chemistry. Patience was needed.

Jayna knew that chemistry alone was not enough for a successful, long-term relationship. But damn, chemistry was so much fun.

In the past, she'd had chemistry with so many men and look where that got her. Nowhere. Case in point, she'd even had chemistry with Derek Brennan. Chemistry was truly deceptive if she could feel it with a man she hated. Or a man that she'd once hated because after spending so much time with him, she wasn't sure that was true anymore. After lifting the curtain on his entire bad-boy act, the man had proven to have way more depth than she'd given him credit for. And wow, could he kiss!

Whoa, Jayna, get your head back in the game, she silently reprimanded herself. Lance was the prize she'd worked so hard for. And she'd won. He was a great catch. Leaning over, she lightly brushed her lips across his. He startled, but then deepened the kiss.

Wait for it.

Come on, tingles.

She wiggled her toes.

Nothing.

She pressed her lips harder against his, and he reciprocated. His lips were soft, firm, and tingle-free.

As the kiss ended, she leaned back in her chair. It had been a decent kiss. He didn't slobber. It wasn't overly wet or too dry, and he had fresh, minty breath. The kiss was nice. But the Bunsen burner didn't light.

Maybe it just needed more fuel.

"Hey Ivy, can I have another margarita, please? Do you want another cranberry and vodka?" she asked Lance, trying not to cringe as she said it. Who the hell other than twenty-something university girls ordered cranberry and vodka? Lance was going to get kicked out of the boys' club if he wasn't careful.

And speaking of the boys' club, in walked Derek Brennan, the head of it. He wore stonewashed jeans and a stony face. The bad boy looked like he was in a bad mood tonight as his eyes flicked over her. But damn, he made a tattered T-shirt look good.

Head in the game, Jayna girl.

Lance Roman was the man for her.

Derek Brennan was the man for no one. That was a fact she needed to remember.

Derek broke her heart once and once was more than enough. He was her past, and Lance was her present. Lance was her wonderful, incredible future.

But hell, if her past wasn't heading straight toward her present.

No way!

Turn the hell around, Brennan, her eyes shot a silent warning in his direction.

Derek's grin only increased, and damn if it didn't cause the Bunsen burner to light.

"Evening," he said. His voice was low and gravelly, scraping her insides in the most delicious way. And it just wasn't fair. She was sitting with Mr. Right, trying hard to feel something, anything. And up walks Mr. Completely Wrong, and all the feels start up.

"I'm Derek," he held out his hand to Lance, who glanced up, confusion showing before he accepted the hand.

"Lance Roman. Nice to meet you."

"No hard feelings that you stole my girl." Derek winked.

Oh no, he didn't! She shot another death stare his way.

"I didn't steal her." Lance's eyes narrowed. "She broke up with you."

"True. Can't say that I blame her. I'm not the relationship kind of guy," Derek stated. He didn't appear overly fazed by her continued penetrating glare. "Just know, you have a great girl."

Derek shifted his stare straight at her, and she gulped. "If I was cut out for relationships, I'd be putting up a fight to win her back."

Lance cleared his throat. "Well, I guess it's good you're not. I'm not the fighting kind of guy."

Of course, he wouldn't be. Lance was too much of a gentleman. The guy truly was perfect.

"I won't interrupt you any longer. Enjoy your date." Derek shot her a blinding smile, popping that lopsided dimple. The flame on the Bunsen burner shot straight up.

Derek is not the man for me. She repeated the new mantra. If she repeated it enough times, hopefully it would become true.

"I see there is some fresh talent at the bar," Derek pointed to the three pretty women seated on bar stools, all stealing glances in his direction. "Think I'll stroll over and make one or two of their nights."

He was so not the man for her! What an ego! The guy was completely full of himself.

"I'm sure they will love to have their night ruined." The snarky words escaped her lips. Why did she let him get to her?

"Oh, baby, it will be the night of their lives."

She made a gagging sound, which she quickly muffled behind a loud cough as Lance shot a disapproving glance her way.

Jess's words came back: Smooth the rough edges. Lance wanted a woman with class. And she could be classy. Her mother had sent her to debutante school. She had manners coming out of her yin-yang. She had been born with the proverbial golden spoon in her mouth. It was the very mouth that was often foul and smart.

My perfect guy wouldn't care; he'd love me for who I am. She dismissed the thought as quickly as it went through her mind.

She could do this. Her eyes narrowed, watching Derek as he pulled out a bar stool next to the pretty redhead. His hand was on her lower back as he leaned in close, listening to the pointless chatter that was probably coming out of her far-too-glossy, full lips. No way those lips were not hyaluronic acid injected, or maybe the plastic surgeon had used fat taken from her ass to plump up her lips. When Derek kissed Red, he'd be kissing her ass. The thought made her snort and caused Lance to send her another shocked look.

She let out another cough. "I hope I'm not coming down with a cold."

Jealous. You're jealous. That internal voice ranted. She forcefully looked away from the redhead twit, who was trying too hard to be sexy. She forced her eyes away from Derek, who was enjoying every second of the woman's attention. How was she jealous of Derek Brennan? What the hell?

Pathetic. You're pathetic. That internal voice again. She needed to change to a rational, more reasonable internal dialogue—one that wouldn't sabotage the good thing she had going now. She had a chance at a healthy relationship with a man who wanted the same. It was time to stop wasting time with men where there was no future.

She needed to stop being that person who always wanted what she couldn't have. She had to stop being that person who changed her mind about what she wanted the minute she got it. That was messed up. It was self-sabotage.

Get over it. Get over him. Lance is a great guy. This was the voice she needed to listen to. This was the voice of reason. Lance Romance was the guy for her.

Damn it. Now Derek had her calling him Lance Romance.

Damn that man to hell!

It was time to grow up. Time to make smart decisions. It was time to start adulting. Lance Romance it was. Her forehead creased.

"Is something wrong, Jayna?" Lance asked.

"No, everything is perfect," she smiled. Or close enough. She wasn't missing anything by letting Derek go.

Chapter 36

Jayna

"Have I missed anything?" Jayna dragged a chair from the front porch to the center of the lawn where Piper, Leighton, and Jamie sat.

"What kept you this time?" Jamie asked.

"I stopped by to see Talia," she answered, squeezing in her chair beside Piper and Leighton. Nathaniel sat on Leighton's knee, and Jayna reached out to touch his soft curls. Piper and Nick's son was a beautiful baby.

"How is she doing?" Piper took a hard lemonade from the cooler beside her and handed it to Jayna.

"Thanks," Jayna accepted it with a smile. "She is doing so well. Amazing, in fact."

Talia was excelling at her barista job. The woman had put on weight and was regaining her self-confidence. Working and attending addiction counseling was doing wonders for her. Add in hope, and the sky was the limit.

"Talia's mother has agreed to a visit with her son on her next day off. She is so excited."

"That is such a wonderful thing you did for her," Leighton squeezed her knee.

"I think I have benefited just as much, if not more, from helping Talia." It had been one of the most rewarding things she'd ever done. The obscene amount of money sitting untouched in her bank account accruing interest had never been put to better use. Jayna had been paying for the two-bedroom apartment and the counseling sessions for Talia out of that account. It was a sight to behold, watching the woman transform from one who had given up to one now filled with purpose.

Her thoughts drifted to the week before. "Do you think he'll like this color?" Talia had asked, her eyes narrowing as she looked around the room.

"He will love it," Jayna answered, smoothing out the spiderman comforter on the bed. Talia had said her son loved spiderman and Jayna had purchased bedding and pictures for the wall along with toys for the large toy box she'd also bought.

"Jayna, I can't even begin to express how grateful I am for everything you've done for me. You have changed my life." Talia's big brown eyes had shone with happy tears and hope. There was actual confidence starting to emerge. Hope was such an amazing thing when it surfaced.

Somehow, over the course of less than a year, Talia had become a very close friend. No, that wasn't quite accurate. Talia was more like a little sister and Jayna felt so protective of her. She couldn't wait to meet this little boy who had been so inspirational in helping Talia crawl out of the deep, dark hole of addiction.

"Oh look, Shamus just came out." Jamie pointed as the redhead stepped out on his front porch.

For the past few Sunday afternoons, Shamus had taken to playing his bagpipes while his hound dogs howled back up. And every Sunday afternoon, Ophelia complained equally as loud. Shamus's concerts always ended with the police showing up. It had become a bit of a sideshow that the neighbors enjoyed watching.

"I just saw the curtain move at Ophelia's." Piper sat up straighter.

"When you're done hogging the baby, hand him over." Jayna grinned at Leighton, reaching beneath her to pat the puppy's head. Albert, the lab mix Tommy had found in the ditch as a teenager had passed away, leaving a huge void. She'd gone with Leighton to pick out a puppy to surprise Tommy with.

Jayna was thrilled that she'd formed such a wonderful friendship with Leighton over the past year. She was even more thrilled to see Leighton and Tommy reunited. They were meant to be together.

"It'll be a while. I had to wrestle him out of Tommy's arms." Leighton held the baby tighter.

"The boys are here?" She didn't mean to crank her head around, but her neck had a mind of its own.

"Derek isn't here, if that's what you're asking?" Jamie chuckled.

"It isn't. It would totally ruin my entire day to see that jerk."

"Yeah, okay!" Jamie rolled her eyes. "So, how are things with Lance?"

"Just dandy!" She grabbed the popcorn bowl off Jamie's knee, shoveling a handful into her mouth.

"Oh, no!" Jamie let out a long sigh.

"What does, oh no, mean?" Jayna spoke around the mouthful of popcorn, turning a questioning stare in Jamie's direction.

"What does 'just dandy' mean? I sense a big BUT to follow," Jamie held her stare.

"Lance is great," she answered and smiled brightly.

"But?" Jamie drew out the word.

"There's no but," Jayna raised her voice.

"I hear a but," Jamie persisted.

"You're the butt," Jayna blew out her cheeks. "He is perfect, Jamie."

"Just not perfect for you?" Jamie refused to give up.

"I never said that!"

"You never didn't say that."

"Jamie, that sentence doesn't make sense."

"Neither do you and Lance," Jamie shot back.

"What about you and Derek? There seemed to be something going on between the two of you for a hot minute," Piper questioned.

Jayna exhaled loudly. "We have nothing besides a really bad judgment call in high school and, well, a stupid hot minute last month." She used Piper's turn of phrase. "It was over before it even began."

It was all pretend, just like Derek had told Norm and Earl.

The sound of loud bagpipe music drifted across the street, along with the bang of Ophelia's front door.

"Can we make requests?" Jayna slapped her knee and then groaned. "Damn it, speak of the devil."

Derek pulled his truck up at the curb, blocking their view. She really needed to stop saying his name out loud, or even thinking about him.

"Derek!" It was a chorus of annoyed voices.

He stared over the hood. "What?"

"Move that truck!" Leighton yelled.

He glanced over his shoulder, noticing the Shamus and Ophelia show ramping up. Jumping back in his truck, he moved it further down the street.

In jean cutoffs and a chest-hugging T-shirt, he strolled up the sidewalk. His hair was still damp from a recent shower. Wow! Just wow. Jayna tossed more popcorn into her mouth.

"Ladies and Jayna," he spoke in that low, rumbly voice. "See, I'm just in time for the show."

He used that old line that he hadn't used in a long time. Was he letting her know that they had reverted to their less-than-friendly, strictly platonic friendship?

"Now little Nathaniel will have company," Jayna huffed out.

Derek turned in her direction, a confused eyebrow arched.

"You know, because you both have the same maturity level," she explained her lame joke. She was losing her edge. A good burn never needed an explanation.

"Ouch," he moved a hand over his heart. Reaching down, he scooped Nathaniel out of Leighton's arms.

Watching Derek bring the baby up for a soft kiss and then cradle him so gently in his arms did twisty things to Jayna's insides.

What the hell was that?

He laid down on the grass, holding the 3-month-old above his head, making cooing sounds, and she lost feeling in her legs. Who knew the ape could be so good with babies?

Not her.

Not that it made a difference.

She didn't want kids. She didn't want Derek. She had Lance Romance.

Stop calling him that, she reprimanded herself. Damn, Derek Brennan with that lopsided grin and those muscles and that chest. He had a way with babies that was causing her ovaries to jump to attention. Was that her biological clock she could hear ticking?

No, that was just very loud, very obnoxious bagpipe music mixed with equally loud and equally obnoxious yelling from Ophelia.

Derek brought the baby down and kissed his cheek and lifted him back up when the puppy ran over. "Hey doggie, with the really stupid name."

Sitting up, he snuggled the baby into the crook of his arm and scratched behind the dog's ears. He was good with puppies and babies. Was the universe out to get her? Her heart expanded along with her pulsing ovaries. This was just not fair.

"Norbert is not a stupid name." Tommy appeared behind Leighton and leaned down, pressing a kiss on her forehead. It was such a sweet, intimate gesture that stole Jayna's breath. The couple had overcome so much to be together. Maybe this entire forever love theory had some merit after all. For certain people, that was. But was it really not for her?

Could Lance be the person she shared this with? Watching Tommy and Leighton had her wishing. Seeing Piper and Nick with Nathaniel made it seem possible.

Her eyes drifted back to Derek on the grass with the baby and puppy. It made her want things she'd never wanted before. It made her want those things with him.

Derek lifted the baby in the air again, and her heart stuttered dangerously. He was so good with Nathaniel. He'd make a great dad one day.

The thought skidded through her brain, screeching to a halt. He didn't want children any more than she did.

As he lowered the baby, Nathaniel vomited all over Derek's chin, barely missing his open mouth.

Jayna let out a loud snort.

"Hey, not cool, little man." Derek sat up again. He didn't seem overly upset. "You are your father's son. Can't hold your liquid either."

"Hey, I resemble that remark," Nick laughed heartily. "That's my boy!"

"Oh, Derek. I'm so sorry," Piper jumped out of her chair, taking the baby from him.

He shrugged and pulled up his T-shirt, wiping off his chin. Exposing those tight abs and tanned belly speckled with just the perfect amount of hair. Her eyes moved up as he wiped his chin. He had full lips that were normally pulled into a grumpy frown and usually directed straight at her.

But that frown was badass.

And when that frown lifted into a smile, holy hell. Melt. Sizzle.

Back up.

Stop checking him out, another silent reprimand. She needed to stop right now before the drool started to drip off her lips.

"Yeah, Lance is so the guy for you," Jamie had moved over to Piper's abandoned chair and leaned over to whisper in her ear.

"Shut up." Jayna tossed more popcorn in her mouth, chewing vigorously.

A police cruiser pulled up and Burke Winston stepped out. He shook his head in annoyance, staring at Ophelia screaming on the sidewalk in front of Shamus' house. The cop sent a wave in their direction before walking toward the disturbance.

It took less than five minutes to talk Ophelia off the ledge and Shamus into packing up his bagpipes. Burke strolled back across the street and Nick grabbed another lawn chair for his friend.

"I heard a body was found." Nick held out a can of Pepsi to

Burke.

Burke nodded, and his eyes fastened on Jayna. "It will be released to the media in the morning, so I may as well tell you all now. The body has been identified as Greta Cochrane."

Jayna sucked in a breath.

Derek stood. "Do you have any suspects?" His eyes moved from the cop to Jayna.

"If you're asking if Lance Roman is a suspect, I can only say that he is a person of interest."

Chapter 37

Derek

A person of interest? The man Jayna was dating was now a person of interest in a murder investigation.

It wasn't Derek's business. Not his concern. She was no longer his 'fake' girlfriend, who he needed to pretend to care about.

Pretend?!

He had stopped pretending the minute he first kissed her. Maybe it had started when she dragged him up on stage, picking out that hilarious song for karaoke. Or was it that night he'd picked her up for the gala? That dress! She'd been so beautiful. Or had it been when she toured his house, taking him to Jamie's storeroom, cleaning the carpet that his feet now rested on? It could have started while playing wing roulette and choosing this very couch he was sitting on. Or that mind blowing kiss in the parking lot.

Derek heaved a sigh and stared down at the carpet. Jayna had been right. A reproduction carpet could never come close to the aged beauty of the real deal. And the salvaged mantle above his fireplace was also incredible. It highlighted the stone detail of the fireplace. These found pieces, along with the well-chosen furniture, turned the sterile new house into a home.

Blowing out a frustrated breath, he ran his fingers through his hair. He kept going back to the fact that she was dating the paramedic. And that it bothered him! Only because the guy was implicated in a murder! No way was he going to admit that it bothered him for any other reason.

That would be admitting too much.

He preferred to keep all his feelings and emotions buried deep. It had worked well for him so far. At least up until now.

Now he sat on the softer-than-soft couch, staring at the mantle that was missing family photos and other cherished memories. He wished he'd gone for a cold slab of marble instead. And he wished he had never asked Jayna for help because her imprint was all over his home. She was everywhere, in his home and in his thoughts. He was jealous and was that regret he was feeling? Did he miss her?

All of this was only temporary. It would pass. He needed to resume his normal life. Tugging his phone out of his back pocket, he swiped to open the contact list. The redhead from the other night had added her number to it. Nevaeh. Heaven spelled backwards; she'd whispered in his ear.

His finger paused over the text icon and then moved to delete contact instead.

"Knock, knock."

He turned around. His mother and grandmother, Harry, stood in the foyer.

"We came to check out the new bachelor pad," Harry stated.

"This does not look like a bachelor pad," his mother commented.

"Yeah, thanks to Jayna. She helped me decorate it." The minute the words left his mouth, he wished he could take them back.

"Oh, really?" Harry raised an eyebrow. "Are we talking about the same Jayna who dumped you?"

"I'd hardly say she dumped me."

"Not what we heard," Harry persisted. Of course, news of their breakup would have traveled at lightning speed around town.

"It was never real. We were only fake dating." Again, words he didn't mean to say aloud were flying out of his mouth.

"What does that mean?" his mother questioned as she sat beside him on the couch.

"Fake dating? Is that some new slang you kids are using for

hooking up?" Harry sat on his opposite side.

Hooking up? What did his grandmother know about 'hooking up'?

"No, Mom, I think what Derek means is that they were never really dating." His mother turned her attention back to him. "Why pretend to date?"

"Let's just say that I dated the wrong girl with a father who wasn't happy that I didn't want to keep dating her. This father just happened to be a big investor in the company I work for. He was threatening not only bodily harm, but my job as well. And Jayna posed as my pregnant girlfriend to get me out of hot water."

"Was the pregnancy fake too?" his mother asked.

"Yeah!"

"A mother could hope," she shrugged.

"So, you dated a bunny boiler with an overprotective father, and that's why you were fake dating Jayna?" Harry pointed her finger at him as she spoke.

"A bunny boiler?" His mother leaned across him, staring at her mother.

"Like in Fatal Attraction," Harry clarified.

"Why did you let Jayna break up with you?" Mom asked.

"Because he's a dumbass," Harry offered.

His head snapped back in her direction. These two women were going to give him whiplash.

"Because," he stretched out the word, "I don't want a serious relationship."

"Bullshit." Harry poked him hard in the arm.

"Mom!" His mother shook her head.

"What? It is total crap. The boy has been his own worst enemy most of his life," Harry argued.

"Sitting right here. Right beside you," Derek muttered.

"Harry is right, son. You wouldn't have built this beautiful house if you had no plans to fill it up with a family."

He gaped open-mouthed at his mother. "A single man can't live in a beautiful house?"

"Oh, he can. But that would be a very stupid man," Harry poked him again. "Don't be a stupid man."

He stood, rubbing his arm. "How about I give you both a tour, and then you go harass someone else? Ben is still single. He's all gaga over Bianca Grotta and she's not interested. Isn't she too old for him? Or maybe she isn't."

Both women fell for the bait and started discussing the state of his younger brother's love life as he gave them the grand tour, which ended on the back deck.

"Wow," both women exclaimed at once, staring at the reclaimed arched door frame that Jamie had salvaged from an old church.

The oversized arch had rustic doors attached on either side and had been secured into the ground. It stood at the edge of the property, highlighting the stunning view of the valley below. It was indeed a jaw-dropping focal point. He didn't mention that it had been Jayna's idea.

"That would be a perfect wedding altar," Harry said, playfully slugging him again. "If you hadn't let Jayna dump you, you could have stood right under that arch and married that girl."

"It's never too late," his mom winked.

His eyes narrowed. Jayna had said it would be a unique way to draw the eye to the incredible view. Damn that woman. She had tricked him into building a wedding altar on his property. She probably had a good laugh with Jamie over it.

Relief flooded him when his mother and grandmother left, only to turn into a groan as Tommy arrived.

"Wow, this is quite the place," Tommy whistled as he did a slow turn.

"Thanks. You just missed Mom and Harry." Derek opened the fridge and pulled out two beers.

"Isn't it too early to be drinking?" Tommy asked, but still accepted the offered beer.

"Again, Mom and Harry were just here." Derek twisted off the cap and took a long swallow.

"Ah, that bad?" Tommy pulled out a bar stool at the island and sat.

"Apparently, it's too nice of a place for a bachelor."

"Who decorated it?"

"Why does everyone keep asking me that? Is it so far-fetched to believe I did?" Derek pulled out a stool and sat beside his brother. He couldn't begin to put into words how relieved he was that the relationship with his twin had been restored.

"Yeah! You can't bullshit your older brother."

"You are 6 minutes older than I am."

"Key word being older," Tommy stated. It was a card he'd been playing their entire life.

"Okay, Jayna may have helped."

Tommy nodded. "So, what's up with that? Heard she dumped your sorry ass last weekend."

He needed to change his front door mat from 'Welcome' to 'Go away.'

Chapter 38

Derek

"Go away. No one's home."

"If no one is home, then who is speaking?" Derek leaned against Jayna's closed door.

"If your name is Derek Brennan, then no one is home." Jayna's voice was muffled, but the wooden door couldn't buffer the grumpiness.

"Come on, Jayna, open up." He banged on the door again. "I'm not leaving until you do."

The door swung open, revealing a scowling Jayna. She wore sweatpants and a cropped T-shirt, and her feet were bare. Derek swallowed. She looked just as beautiful as she had in the elegant dress she'd worn the last time he'd been here. However, that time she'd answered the door wearing only a towel. That was the look to beat.

"To whom do I owe this displeasure?" Her tone was sharp, making him grin. He liked this version of Jayna. This Jayna he knew how to handle.

"I…" He what? Stopped by to check up on her? That would go over like a lead balloon. "You…"

"What are you mumbling about, Derek?"

"You can't actually believe it's a good idea to continue dating Lance Romance?" There, he managed to get the words out.

Her scowl deepened. "Is that the only reason you stopped by? You're concerned about me?"

"Is there another reason why you'd want me to stop by?" He shot her the grin that always worked for him.

"Nope. I can't think of a single reason why I'd want you to stop by. Ever!" Her voice raised on that last word.

He blinked. His charm never worked on Jayna.

"And there are so many reasons why I'd want you to leave," she continued.

He blinked again. "Jayna, the guy is a person of interest in a murder investigation. I'm just looking out for you."

"Lucky for you, I'm no longer your concern." She stood, hands on her hips, backing up as he stepped over the threshold into the foyer.

"Jayna," his tone changed to pleading as he closed the front door behind him. "He's not the guy for you. You act differently around him."

"I just smoothed out my rough edges," she said softly, and he heard defeat in her voice.

"But your rough edges are amazing. They set you apart from the other women."

She blinked, her brow furrowing. His brow furrowed as well. He couldn't believe he'd just said that. But every word was true. She was amazing, refreshingly different from any woman he had ever dated before. And Lance didn't understand that. The man did not deserve her.

"Jayna, he's not the guy for you."

"But you are?"

Now he blinked, his mouth dropping open, but no words came out.

"You don't do relationships. You don't do complicated. But you do 'walking out the door' so well. So why don't you?"

"Jayna," his voice cracked with hesitation. Just why was he here?

Because Lance was a person of interest in a woman's murder. And no matter how hard Derek tried, he couldn't stop the worry.

Another thing he didn't do was WORRY!

Jayna had him feeling jealous, possessive, and now worried. But the thought of Lance touching her, kissing those lips, had him seeing red.

The possibility of something bad happening to her prevented him from sleeping the night through.

If Lance was not the upstanding guy that he had everyone believing... if Lance was the one who had killed Greta...

It was unimaginable. However, Burke had told him that Lance had an airtight alibi. So, why couldn't he shake the feeling Jayna was in trouble?

Serious trouble!

Lance was too polished, too well-dressed. The man drank cranberry and vodka! There's no way the guy could handle a round of wing roulette. What did Jayna see in him?

Lance Romance was not the man for her. She needed someone who appreciated her rough edges, as she had referred to all her incredible traits. Incredible traits? He had once found them completely annoying, too. When had he changed his mind? When had he started thinking that he was the man for her?

He hadn't changed his mind, had he? No!

Hell, NO!

Yet here he was, standing in her front hallway, trying desperately to convince her to dump the paramedic.

"Jayna, please."

"Leave, Derek." She pointed at the front door.

"You are so infuriating. I don't know if I want to scream at you for being so dense or just kiss you senseless."

"Neither." She stepped back further. "You have no right."

"Really?" He stepped forward.

"Really!" she hissed as his boots touched her toes.

"I don't like being told what to do," he told her.

"Neither do I." She sucked in a breath as he reached out to tuck an errant strand of hair behind her ear.

"I never noticed," he chuckled and moved his head toward hers.

"Don't," she whispered and stepped back further.

He moved closer, trapping her between the wall and his

body. "Don't what?" His lips were inches from hers.

"Just don't," she said, breathless.

"Don't do this?" he questioned, his lips brushing across hers.

"Yes."

His tongue flicked out, tracing the lines of her full, gorgeous lips. He felt her lips quiver and she released a breath. He could see goosebumps forming on her bare arms. She was equally affected. It was almost paralyzing, this attraction that pulsed between them. And it was more than just attraction.

For a moment, there was nothing but the sound of both their erratic breathing. He was close enough that her breasts were touching his chest. Her nostrils flared. She was pissed which just added to her appeal. He loved the way anger caused her cheeks to flush. He raised his hand to the wall above her head, his head dropping again.

"Yes, don't? Or yes, do?" he whispered as he pressed his lips against hers, gently, just a brief touch. Why had he come here? He was having difficulty remembering. He hadn't come here to kiss her. But now, that was all he wanted to do.

"Don't kiss me. You have no right," she repeated.

"I'd rather wring your foolish neck," he told her as his eyes focused on the quickening pulse in her throat before moving up to lock on her mouth. Her tongue darted out, moistening her lips. It was evident that neither of them wanted to acknowledge this strong pull they both felt to the other. Possibly that only served to fuel it more.

"Derek," she said his name on a broken whisper.

He truly had not come here for any other reason then to make her listen to logic. But she was stealing his ability to think, to reason, to breathe. He needed her. He wanted her. He swore under his breath before his lips crashed against hers.

She groaned softly, her lips parting. That was all the invitation he needed. His tongue was now tangling with her tongue and this kiss was like nothing he'd ever experienced. It felt familiar and so right, like everything he'd been searching for. No woman had ever made him feel like this. He lifted his head, needing air.

Jayna blinked, and as their eyes locked, an unspoken conversation unfolded in that shared gaze—one too honest and raw to be spoken aloud. They both just stared, and it was all there in her eyes what he felt too; a vulnerability that neither allowed anyone to see. His brow furrowed, and the corner of his mouth twitched. There was a sudden urge to say something, anything that would end this separation between them. He didn't need to speak; his gaze said it all—'I didn't mean for this to happen, but I fell for you.' Why couldn't he just tell her that? He knew that was exactly what she was waiting for.

His lips parted, but no words came out. Never had he felt so exposed before. Jayna was peeling back every layer he'd put up over the years. In her eyes, he could see acceptance, and all the regret for pushing each other away, and all the longing he'd been fighting to ignore. 'Just say it, just admit it?' her eyes pleaded.

In that shared silence, the air felt thick with the unspoken words. They were saying silently everything they never would aloud—I miss you; I need you; I could love you. It was a confession hidden in plain sight, wrapped in layers of pride and fear. Neither one willing to take that step over the line they'd drawn by uttering a single word that would break it. They continued to stare, frozen in the bittersweet ache of what might have been—and what still could be, if only one of them dared to speak.

But his only motive was to talk some sense into her. Kissing her had not been the plan. He didn't want to start something real with her. No, he wasn't that guy. He stepped back, breaking the spell.

The same confusion he felt was mirrored in her eyes before it was replaced with a flare of anger.

"Don't let the door hit you on the way out." She moved around him and opened the door.

He shook his head. "I may have called you many things, but

never stupid. Until now."

Moving past her, he brushed his fingers across his mouth and then touched hers. Just to annoy her even more, he told himself. Not because he wanted to touch her one more time.

He paused as he walked toward his parked truck. Peaches. Her hair smelled like bloody peaches today. Seriously, that woman needed to pick a shampoo and stick to it. Then maybe she'd be able to think clearly. It could help her to be more decisive, and to realize that dating a murder suspect was probably not the smartest choice.

And if she had hair that smelled the same, then maybe it would stop wreaking havoc with his equilibrium.

He started walking briskly to his truck.

Peaches.

Who the hell used peach-scented shampoo?

Chapter 39

Jayna

Who the hell did Derek think he was? Showing up at her front door, acting all concerned and conflicted! He called her stupid! He was the stupid one with the stupid handsome face.

He had stood in her hallway questioning her relationship with Lance. Like he had any right! Then he'd kissed her. His lips hadn't just touched her lips, they had devoured them. When he eased back, her vision had blurred for a moment and the ground beneath her feet hadn't felt solid anymore.

'Lance isn't the guy for you,' Derek had told her. His eyes had said he was the one, but there was no way he'd admit that, not even to himself.

It almost sounded like he was jealous before that cocky self-assuredness took over his stupid handsome face. What the hell had that been? The man was so infuriating. The fact that he threatened to kiss her senseless and then had done that very thing left her feeling so undone. It was more than just infuriating that no man had ever made her feel so much. It was unfair. No man had ever kissed her like that. It felt like Derek had reached deep into her soul and filled up all her empty places.

It had been the most perfect kiss from the most imperfect man. How was that possible?

That kiss, against the wall in her front hall had been filled with the promise of forever from the one man who didn't do forever. And that possibly broke her even more than his rejection in high school. What they could be together would be incredible and completely impossible. Derek would never give in.

It tore her apart to realize that Lance could never give her this. That she'd never feel this with any other man. Was she willing to settle when she knew just how wonderful love could be, even if it was with the wrong man?

Lance was the right man, but he did not make her feel this way.

"We have a CTAS-1 coming in, an unresponsive female." Debbie, the ward clerk, clutched the red dispatch phone in her right hand.

Jayna pushed back her chair and stood. "Debbie, can you call RT and alert X-ray to be on standby."

There had been two CTAS-1s so far. Trouble always came in threes—or traumas in the case of the ER. It never failed. The emergency department buzzed with activity as staff hurriedly prepared the trauma room. The harsh light cast eerie shadows, and a shiver raced up Jayna's spine. She glanced at the double doors as Lance and Sonny pushed the gurney through, her heart sinking at the sight of Talia.

"What happened?" Jayna blinked back threatening tears and yanked open the trauma room curtain. She helped lift Talia onto the exam bed.

"The patient was found unresponsive in the coffee shop parking lot by a co-worker. Suspected fentanyl overdose," Sonny explained. "We injected Naloxone—no effect. On the way here, I gave a second dose."

Jayna's hands shook as she cut away Talia's shirt. "Oh, Talia. Why?"

"Her boss said Talia got a text yesterday. Talia's mother changed her mind about letting her see her son. Apparently, Talia took the news badly," Lance offered.

Jayna's stomach churned. She should have checked in with Talia. Why hadn't she? Talia's entire focus had been on regaining access to her son. Her mother rescinding that agreement would have devastated her.

A wave of anxiety threatened to crash over her, but Jayna pushed it aside. Years of training kicked in, and she worked on autopilot. She swiftly attached electrodes to Talia's chest, glancing at the monitor. There was heart activity, albeit low and irregular. Grabbing the oxygen mask, she placed it over Talia's face.

"Get the crash cart, now!" Jayna yelled as the heart monitor began to beep. Talia had stopped breathing.

Dr. Malik rushed in with two nurses. His grim face said it all. "Start compressions."

No. No. Not Talia. Jayna's face remained impassive while inside she fell apart.

She jumped on Talia's chest, positioning her hands correctly and counting each compression aloud. Her arms burned, sweat pouring off her forehead. Lance took over, his hands steady over hers.

No, no, no. Talia had worked so hard to get clean. Jayna had worked so hard to help her stay clean. Everything was going so well. Talia had so many reasons to live, to stay clean. Jayna could have hired a lawyer to help navigate the custody rights with Talia's mother.

Dr. Malik's expression was somber as he stopped Lance. Jayna's heart sank. The odds of surviving CPR were 17 percent. Those odds sucked. Those odds caused her to hate her job.

"Time of death, 7:15 p.m." Dr. Malik glanced at his watch. "Debbie, call the coroner and get me a death certificate."

Jayna's shift ended in less than 15 minutes. If Talia had been found a half-hour later, Jayna would have already been on her way home. Tears blurred her vision as she stared down at Talia's still form. Bowing her head, she whispered a silent prayer for the woman who had given up too soon.

"That's one less addict to worry about," Lance murmured to Sonny. Jayna stared at him, her eyes widening. Unbelievable! She brushed past him and stepped into the serenity garden that bordered the ER.

The garden was beautiful, offering a peaceful escape from a

place that was anything but. Jayna sank onto a wooden bench, letting the tears flow freely. Why had Talia relapsed? Why had she bought fentanyl? Why had she used again after staying clean for so long?

But Jayna knew the answers to all her questions. Talia's sole focus had been on getting her son back. Her mother's refusal had been too much. Why hadn't she checked up on Talia yesterday? That was the true question.

A brown rabbit hopped out from under a shrub, staring up at her. For the past few months, she'd been bringing it carrots, but had forgotten all about the poor defenseless creature. The rabbit sat very still, looking directly at her with accusatory eyes.

"I'm sorry," Jayna choked out. "I'm sorry that I forgot to check on you." She wasn't capable of caring for another life.

"Jayna."

She jumped and looked over her shoulder. "What, Lance?"

"That's one less drug addict to deal with." His voice had been so cold and dismissive.

"I'm sorry. I didn't mean what I said about her. It's just my way of distancing myself. Keeps me sane."

"I didn't mean it either," she said, blowing out an angry breath, "when I said I was ready for a serious relationship."

His brow creased. "You're breaking up with me?"

"Yep."

"Over that drug addict?"

Her eyes squeezed shut as she sucked in a deep breath. "Talia. Her name is Talia, not 'Drug Addict.' And no, she's not the reason I'm breaking up with you."

His eyes widened. "Then it's over Greta? You think I had something to do with her death?"

"No, I don't think that." She softened her tone. She didn't believe he was capable of something so heinous.

The girls at 'Bagpipe-Palooza' were right. Lance wasn't the man for her. This realization had nothing to do with Derek showing up the other evening, all protective and sexy and stupid and annoying and smelling so damn good. He was wrong in so many ways. He'd been wrong about Lance. And wrong for her.

She'd been wrong to think she could save Talia. Wrong. Wrong. Wrong.

This was the wrong time to start a relationship. It was wrong for Lance with everything going on in his life. It was also wrong for her. She wasn't ready. She thought she had been. But she'd been wrong.

It felt contrived to force this relationship because she wanted to settle down, and Lance seemed like the most suitable candidate. It reminded her of her parents' marriage, and she had no intention of duplicating that. Would it be so terrible to remain single? Sure, she envied Nick and Piper's marriage. She was in awe of Leighton and Tommy's rekindled love. However, Talia's death reminded her why she didn't let people in.

She'd let her guard down, feeling a connection with Talia. They both had mothers who'd disappointed them—that was their common tie. And it tore her apart to realize that, like their mothers, Jayna had failed Talia too. She needed to remain alone. That was for the best.

On her way home, she found herself pulling into Patty's Pub and sitting at the bar. The tequila burned all the way down, yet it did nothing to numb her pain. Tears streamed down her cheeks—so unfamiliar. She never cried.

The bar stool beside her scraped as it was pulled back.

"If it isn't my ex-fake fiancé."

"Shut up, Derek. I'm not in the mood."

"You're regretting fake breaking up with me?"

She sniffled and brushed away the tears that she never cried.

"Oh baby, please don't cry over me."

"Get over yourself, Brennan. These tears are not over you!"

"Don't tell me Lance Romance dumped you."

"No, I dumped him," she sniffled loudly and called out to the bartender. "Can I have another tequila, please?"

"So, you're crying over dumping the paramedic?"

"No! It's Talia. The woman I've been helping. She overdosed. She's gone."

Strong arms wrapped around her, pulling her close. Derek's scent enveloped her, and she wanted to stay in that embrace forever.

Forever.

She didn't believe in forever, or being rescued, or comforted. However, for just a moment, she'd allow it. She let herself depend on someone else. Just for a moment. Not forever.

He pulled her tighter, and she sank deeper. It felt so wonderful to be held.

"I'm so sorry, Jayna," his voice was rough, the words of comfort as unfamiliar for him to speak as they were for her to receive.

They were two lone wolves. He didn't look to others for comfort and neither did she. And yet he was giving it, and she was accepting it.

The last of her walls were crumbling. She needed Derek right now. That realization filled her with panic. She shoved backward, nearly toppling them both off the bar stools.

"Whoa." Derek grabbed the edge of the bar with his left hand while his right arm tightened around her.

She blinked and roughly wiped away fresh tears.

"I have to go," she said breathlessly, shrugging off his arm and standing. Grabbing her purse, she rushed out the door.

Chapter 40

Derek

Jayna rushed out the door, and Derek almost followed. Almost. But he hesitated.

The moment he sat down, he'd noticed how pale she was. Her usually vivid blue eyes were almost vacant. This wasn't the larger-than-life Jayna who breezed through life without a care. This Jayna was different. This Jayna had a heart. And it was broken.

A lone tear had slid down her cheek, followed by a second, and then a third. A sob, so quiet he barely heard it, escaped her lips. It was the cry of a little girl who had never been comforted. The brokenness that Jayna hid from the world finally seeped out. It pierced his closed-off heart.

Yet he remained seated. He didn't follow her. If he had, it would change everything. He'd change, and he wasn't ready for that.

Over a week had passed since that night, and he couldn't help but wonder how she was.

She said she'd broken up with the paramedic and knowing that brought him relief. The thought of Lance hurting Jayna had been unbearable. Even the thought of the other man touching her, kissing her, had him seething.

What was that? Did he feel possessive of her? Responsible?

Witnessing her heartbreak over losing her friend had caused his heart to break as well.

He was completely out of his depth here.

He'd only agreed to fake date Jayna, to pretend to have

feelings for her. Easy. Simple. Oh, no! The joke was on him.

He'd gone and fallen for her.

This realization called for whiskey. The stronger, the better. A tall glass of 'get over himself', as Jayna had called it.

A tall glass of 'get over her' would be more accurate. It was exactly what this night called for.

His eyes adjusted to the brightly lit bar as he closed the door behind him. Jamie sat at a table in the center of the room. Was Jayna joining her? He felt a surge of excitement, along with regret that this was the only bar in town. How was he going to get over her if they kept running into each other?

Make that two glasses of "get over her." He should turn and leave. Instead, he walked straight toward Jamie.

"Are you all alone?"

He wasn't asking because he was wondering where Jayna was. He forced a neutral, bored expression to prove that he didn't care or wonder about Jayna. Jamie's lifted eyebrow said she knew differently.

Damn, that woman was intuitive. However, he didn't believe in fortune-telling or whatever the hell it was that she did.

"I'm just waiting on Jayna. She's running late, as usual."

He had no idea why he did, but he pulled out a chair and sat down. "I noticed that about her. She'll be late for her own funeral."

"Speaking of Miss Tardy herself," Jamie laughed when her cell phone rang, and she swiped to answer it. "Yeah, yeah. You're running late."

Jamie paused, listening. "Really? Come on, Jayna, no way that happened."

"Only you," Jamie chuckled and met his eyes across the table. "Jayna claims that she was blow-drying her hair and got it stuck in the air inlet of the hairdryer."

It was on the tip of his tongue to ask what shampoo scent she had used today.

"Derek is keeping me company, so I don't look like a complete loser sitting by myself."

Jamie giggled. "I will not tell him that!"

She set the phone in the center of the table and hit the speaker icon. "Behave, you're on speaker."

"Hey, Derek," Jayna's voice vibrated through the speaker and up his spine. "I think I owe you an apology. I was wrong to get so angry with you the other day when you stopped by."

"Whoa, slow down. I need to savor this. Jayna Sutton is apologizing." He sat forward, leaning his elbows on the table. "Did you hear that, Jamie? I need to confirm I'm not hearing things."

Jayna huffed out an annoyed sigh. "I wasn't wrong about you being an ass! However, I was wrong to be so nasty with you. You just stopped by out of concern, and that was sweet."

The smug smile left his lips. "Take that back. I am not sweet!"

Jayna chuckled, and the sound of a doorbell ringing came through the speakers.

Jamie let out a loud breath and picked up her phone. Her pale blue eyes sparked. It must have been a trick of the light from the cell phone. Eyes did not spark.

"Jayna don't answer the door," Jamie's voice was panicked.

"It's okay, Mom. I know him," Jayna said. "Hey, what are you doing here?"

A crash came through the phone, followed by a scream. The call ended.

What the hell?

"Derek," Jamie's voice trembled. "She is in trouble."

His chair fell backward as he stood. "Call 911," he yelled over his shoulder as he raced for the door.

He knew it. Just knew it! Jayna was in danger. Why hadn't she listened to him?

Derek broke speed limits getting to Jayna's house. Why the hell had she bought so far out? Not only was her house 15 minutes outside of town, but it was the last house on the street. Secluded and not well-lit. It was a dangerous location for a single woman living alone.

Jayna had boatloads of money. She could afford to have better lighting installed, and a state-of-the-art security system. There was a brand-new subdivision beside the hospital. Why hadn't she purchased a house there?

He pulled into her driveway. Both her vehicles were still parked there. He'd barely shifted into park before he was jumping out. Burke's cruiser pulled in behind him. The cop yelled for him to stop.

Burke walked toward him and placed a hand on his shoulder. "Derek, let us do our job."

He stood still, heart thumping, fear racing up his spine. This wasn't right. He should be doing something. Where was Jayna? Who had been at her door?

The front door was propped wide open. He inched closer once Burke and two other officers disappeared inside. The console table in the foyer was knocked over. That was the crash he'd heard over Jamie's phone.

Burke reappeared, stepping onto the front stoop holding a damaged cell phone. "She's not here."

"What do you mean? Both her vehicles are. She was supposed to meet Jamie at the pub."

Burke shrugged. "Looks like there was a struggle. What exactly happened? Jamie told the dispatcher that you were talking on the phone with her?"

Derek inhaled deeply before letting the anxious breath hiss out between his teeth. "She said someone was at the door. Then we heard a crash followed by Jayna screaming."

"Do you know who came to the door?"

"No, she just said she knew him, never said a name."

Jamie. Jamie would know. She knew impossible things.

"Sergeant Burke, there are footprints around her bedroom window." A young officer appeared from the side of the house. "Looks like someone has been watching her for quite some time."

The fear racing up Derek's spine turned into full-out terror.

"It's Lance," Derek spit out. "He dated Greta. She breaks up with him and turns up dead! Then Jayna. She broke up with him, and now she's missing."

"Derek, we cleared him in the Greta Cochrane case. He had a strong alibi."

"Duncan! The busboy at Patty's. He was making Jayna nervous." Derek raised his hands to his hair, grabbing handfuls. But would she have opened the door to him? It had to be the paramedic.

Jamie. He pulled out his cell phone and searched through his contacts. "Who was at Jayna's door?" he demanded when she answered.

"Is Jayna okay?" Jamie's voice was breathless through the speaker of his phone.

"She's not here, Jamie." His jaw clenched. "Who was at her door? You told her not to answer it."

"I don't know."

"Can't you just see who it was? Do some magic or whatever it is you do?"

"It doesn't work that way, Derek. I just had a feeling that something was off."

"Jamie, it's more than just something being off. Something bad has happened to her."

"I know, Derek."

He wanted reassurance from her that he was wrong. He didn't want to hear that he was right.

He didn't want to be right.

"Can you check if Duncan is working?" He met Burke's concerned stare as he waited for Jamie to check on the busboy's status.

"Derek, he never showed up for work tonight. He's not answering his cell phone."

"Damn it." He swiped to end the call and stared directly at Burke. "Why are you just standing there? You have two suspects to be checking out."

"It's not a crime to miss a shift, Derek. And other than the fact that you said he made Jayna feel nervous, I have no reason to believe he is involved."

"You have my gut instinct and Jamie's. She's psychic. She knows things. Go talk to her."

Burke shook his head. "I don't believe in psychics."

Derek turned in a slow circle and screamed Jayna's name. He knew that she was in danger. Why hadn't she listened to him?

Jayna was missing.

Chapter 41

Derek

Jayna was still missing. Over 24 hours had passed without a word.

Derek sat at the bar, his eyes scanning every man in the pub. Burke had asked him to compile a list of anyone he'd noticed watching Jayna. Every man in this bar with a pulse and a functioning libido would have watched her. Jayna was stunningly beautiful. She was funny and full of life. He winced at the phrase. She was going to be alright. She had to be.

His stomach churned, and he stared at the untouched whiskey in front of him. He needed to keep his mind clear. What he needed to do was stop drinking before it became a problem. The past few years, since everything with his brother, he'd been drinking a lot. It was time to quit. His liver would thank him, and Jayna needed him.

His gaze shifted to the small notebook on the bar top. He'd written only two names on the page—the same two he had already given to Burke; Lance and Duncan. He couldn't shake the feeling that she'd never open the door to Duncan. That brought him straight back to Lance.

Burke said Lance had an airtight alibi. Duncan, on the other hand, had missed another shift. The man had disappeared.

This was a complete waste of time. Derek slapped a ten-dollar bill beside his untouched drink, grabbed the notebook and his keys, heading out.

Five minutes later, he pushed open the glass door of the Blythe Landing Police Station. He strolled in, ignoring the officer at the front desk. Derek walked down the corridor toward Burke Winston's office, and he raised his hand to knock on the closed door. Hell with that! He turned the knob and entered.

Burke glanced up from the pile of papers strewn across his desk. "Derek?"

How was the man sitting there so calmly?

"Burke," Derek's jaw clenched. "It's been over 24 hours."

"We are doing everything we can." Burke's voice was a mixture of weariness and concern.

Derek ran a hand through his hair. "Sitting at your desk pushing papers around is not doing everything you can! Every second that passes..." He couldn't finish the sentence.

Burke sighed and leaned back in his chair. "There are officers canvassing Jayna's neighborhood, checking her usual spots, talking to anyone who might have seen something. We're following up on every lead, no matter how small."

Derek's fists tightened at his sides. "What about Duncan? Once again, he didn't show up to work."

"We're looking into that. But Duncan doesn't have any known connections to Jayna besides working at a bar that she frequents. We don't have any evidence to link him to her disappearance."

"No evidence?" The words came out clipped. Derek was barely managing to control the explosion of emotion that was threatening to erupt. "How about the fact that he's vanished? Isn't that suspicious enough?"

Burke nodded slowly. "I agree that it's suspicious, Derek. But we can't act on suspicion alone. We need something concrete."

"Concrete?" Derek spit out. "Jayna is missing. The guy was clearly obsessed with her. He is nowhere to be found. That's concrete enough for me."

A knock sounded on Burke's open door and an officer poked his head in. "Sorry to interrupt, but I need to speak to you. Privately."

Burke raised an eyebrow at Derek, who remained seated.

"Don't get up! I'll just leave MY office." His chair scraped as he shoved it back and stood, sending an annoyed glance at Derek.

The minute Burke left the office, Derek leaned forward and spun the thick file folder around. It was the report on Jayna. He quickly read through it. The same footprints around Jayna's bedroom window had also been found around Greta Cochrane's. The tread matched EMS Station boots issued to paramedics. Size 10. Lance Roman wore size 10. Interesting. The police were investigating the man despite Burke's denial.

The county had donated a surplus of these boots to the Salvation Army Thrift Store. Duncan had bought a pair, according to the store clerk. A search of Duncan's locker at work found a pair of running shoes he'd left behind. Size 10.

He flipped the page. It was Greta's report. Burke must believe the two cases were linked. Derek's hands shook as he continued reading. Large amounts of Ketamine had been found in Greta's bloodstream. The woman had been kept alive for over 78 hours after going missing before she was injected with a lethal dose of Ketamine. Time was ticking.

"You can't read that." Burke grabbed the folder, flipping the manilla cover shut.

"Too late," Derek stood. "So, let's go find Duncan. He's the one."

"He's not the one," Burke said as he eased into his chair. "Duncan's body was found in the trunk of his car. He's been dead for over 48 hours."

"What?" Derek pinched the bridge of his nose. "Then, it's Lance. He would have access to Ketamine."

"And so does every drug dealer in the country. Anyone could purchase it in a back alley." Burke shook his head. "Lance didn't do this."

"Yeah, yeah. You cleared him. But Duncan is dead." Derek swallowed hard. "Do you have any other suspects?"

Burke's mouth remained firmly shut.

"Let's go, Columbo!" Derek stood.

"I don't take orders from you," Burke told him.

"Fine. Stay. I'm going to see Jamie and solve this case."

"You're not a cop." Burke stood as well and grabbed his hat off his desk. "It's not your job to 'solve this case'."

Derek rushed to the front of the station. Burke increased his pace to catch up.

"You'll just mess it up," Burke called after him.

"Or maybe I'll find Jayna," Derek said, pausing by the door to glance at the cop. "I know it's a long shot, Burke, but I can't just sit back and wait."

"And you think that a psychic can solve this?" Burke threw his hands up in the air. "Derek, psychics aren't real."

Chapter 42

Derek

Psychics weren't real. Derek didn't believe in that nonsense any more than Burke Winston did. How he prayed they were both wrong. They needed Jamie's rumored abilities to be real. There was no other way to find Jayna in time.

Jamie's store was locked up tight, but her battered truck was parked at the curb on the side street. Derek pounded on the metal door of her workshop.

"This is a complete waste of time," Burke grumbled beside him.

"Got any better ideas? Any other leads?" Derek shot back.

Burke clamped his lips shut.

"Didn't think so," Derek muttered.

Jamie opened the door on the third knock. "Derek. Burke. Did you find Jayna?"

"You tell us. You're the psychic," Burke said testily.

Jamie shot him an annoyed glance.

"We need your help, Jamie," Derek said, shaking his head at Burke. The cop was being a jerk. "Have you felt anything, or whatever it is you experience?"

"Derek, I'm trying. I really am. It's like there's a wall blocking me. I can't see or feel anything." Jamie let out a heavy sigh. "I wish I could. Jayna is harder to read than most."

"That's because she's hardheaded," Derek said, his voice cracking. Jayna should have listened to him. He knew something was off. He knew that she was in danger.

"You're both wasting my time." Burke folded his arms across

his chest. "Big surprise, she can't tell us where Jayna is. She's a fraud."

"Enough, Burke," Derek snapped. "If Jamie can help, we need to give her a chance."

"I'll stick to old-fashioned police work." Burke grabbed the doorknob. His back stiffened and he turned back, glaring at Jamie. "How do you give people false hope like this? Toy with their emotions? Take their hard-earned money?"

Jamie huffed. "I don't give people false hope or toy with their emotions. Nor do I take their hard-earned money. I only charge for the furniture I restore, and I make a damn good living. I don't need to scam people."

Jamie's nostrils flared as she stared at Burke. "What I do is give people validation. And hopefully, peace and closure."

"Look, Burke, you have no leads. Maybe Jamie can help us, maybe she can't. But I'm going to exhaust every possibility to find Jayna."

Jamie and Burke continued to glare at each other. Shaking her head, Jamie turned away. "You're right, Derek. We need to try every means possible. There's one thing I've never done before, but I'll need your help."

"Name it," Derek agreed.

"Have you heard of a psychomanteum chamber?"

"Psycho what now?" Derek's brow furrowed.

"It's Greek for 'theatre of the mind,'" Jamie explained. "It's a small room used for psychic meditation and introspection. It's believed to amplify psychic abilities and communication with the spirit world."

"Sounds like it should be Greek for 'theatre of the delusional,'" Burke quipped.

Both Derek and Jamie shot him wary looks.

"What do you need us to do?" Derek asked.

"Don't go volunteering my services," Burke continued to be obtuse.

"Too late!" Derek shot back.

"I need a small room built. We can build it in the corner to

246

save time using the existing walls. We'll only need to erect two walls. I have some big sheets of plywood."

"We don't have time to waste building a playhouse," Burke whined.

Ignoring Burke, Jamie dragged a large sheet of plywood toward the corner she had indicated. Derek grabbed the second sheet.

"I can't connect with Jayna directly," Jamie said as they screwed the sheets of plywood together, forming an L-wall. "But maybe I can connect with her through this. It's like creating a bridge between our world and the spirit realm."

Burke grumbled, but he took the jigsaw and cut out a door.

"Jamie, she's still alive. She has to be." Derek fought the panic that threatened to consume him.

Within ten minutes, they had a rudimentary structure built. Jamie secured a full-length mirror against the cement wall and set a wooden chair in front of it. Burke brought in two chairs, placing them away from the mirror, while Derek covered the doorway with a tarp for a makeshift door.

Jamie sat, staring at the mirror, while Burke took a chair in the corner and Derek pulled down the tarp. Shadows filled the room, with only a candle on a small table by the mirror providing light. Derek sat beside Burke, opening his notebook and using the flashlight function on his cell phone for light. Jamie had asked him to take notes.

He wasn't sure what to expect, but a chill raced up his spine as Jamie spoke out loud. Her voice sounded distant, like she was in a tunnel.

"She is frightened. Was frightened." Another chill raced through Derek. Was!

"She shouldn't have stopped her car," Jamie continued in that eerily out-of-body voice. "But she knows him. Feels safe pulling over and opening her door."

"Her car? Jayna wasn't driving," Burke muttered.

"Shh," Derek whispered. They weren't supposed to speak.

"She can't breathe, he's holding something against her mouth and nose. It's dark now. There's a small window. No, it's a door, high up. Cold. She's cold, and it smells moldy and like apples."

"The boots. Not the boots," Jamie spoke in a lower pitch now. "He's excited. Staring in the window. She doesn't know he's there. She's so pretty. Wait, someone has seen him. A man. He's angry, grabbing him. His head. It hurts so bad."

What the hell was Jamie talking about? This was complete nonsense, not that he would admit it to Burke.

"I told you this was a waste of time," Burke muttered. "The boots, not the boots. What the hell does that mean?"

Jamie spun around. "It means something, I just don't know what. I tapped into Greta. She was insistent about the boots. And Duncan. I saw him. It was the same man. He killed both Greta and Duncan."

"Who is it?" Derek sat forward in the hard wooden chair.

"No idea," Jamie said in frustration.

Derek stared at the notes he made. Cloth soaked in chloroform he'd written. Basement or cellar, apple, boots. Greta knew the man as well. The boots, not the boots. What the hell did that mean?

"Complete waste of time," Burke muttered again.

Chapter 43

Derek

It had been a complete waste of time—or had it? Derek kept rereading the notes he'd made. Notes? More like a few cryptic words. He had put so much hope in Jamie's rumored psychic abilities. Yet all she'd come up with was some nonsense about boots and a root cellar with apples. None of it made sense. Was Jayna in a root cellar somewhere apples were stored? "The boots. Not the boots." But Jamie had been adamant that the boots were important. Cryptic nonsense.

Another 24 hours had passed. Jayna was still missing, and Burke was still holed up in his office. Doing nothing. Wasting time.

Derek couldn't shake the feeling that something was off with the paramedic. The police had cleared him with an airtight alibi, but they wouldn't share the details. The guy didn't sit right with him, even if he'd passed the scrutiny of the Blythe Landing P.D. Lance Roman was too polite, too polished, too good to be true. No one was that perfect unless, they were hiding something.

Mabe Lance was a psychopath with a personality disorder, or simply an evil monster!

Derek would swear it on his life—Lance was hiding something. He just prayed he didn't have to swear it on Jayna's life. Damn, if he didn't find her in time, it would destroy him.

Those three weeks spent pretending to be her boyfriend had irrevocably changed him. He'd actually enjoyed being her boyfriend. Fake though it was, it had somehow felt real.

And that realization terrified him. He didn't want a real girlfriend. But he wanted Jayna.

He missed the way her nose crinkled and her laugh with that little snort. She was blunt and over the top. The way she hustled men at pool—it was sexy as hell. She could pound back tequila like it was Kool-Aid. There was not a single woman like her.

"Drinkin' Buddy" came on the radio. He glanced at the display on the dashboard. When had he changed from the rock station to the country station? Jayna had switched it when they'd driven to Toronto for the work gala. He'd never changed it back. Had Gord Bamford met Jayna? This song could have been written about her. He groaned and hit the mute button. He didn't want to have these feelings.

He would find Jayna. Alive! Then he would find a way to reverse these feelings. He just needed to stop finding all her faults charming. Those faults had once annoyed the crap out of him. Why did she have to go and date the next Ted Bundy?

He stopped at the lights in town, glancing down Second Street. Jamie hadn't helped. 'The boots. Not the boots. The boots are the key.' His eyes traveled farther down the road landing on the Ambulance Station. He hit the right signal and turned.

Derek parked just past Jamie's workshop, pulling ahead so his truck wasn't illuminated under a streetlight. It was 7:35 p.m. Just past shift change for the paramedics. He didn't know Lance's schedule or even what he hoped to find. But he had to do something.

All those years of pranking Ophelia came back to him. Using the stealth skills of a TP-ing expert, he eased up to the station and crouched behind a decommissioned ambulance parked at the side of the building. Lance and Sonny sat on the tailgate of another ambulance in the parking lot.

"How are you doing?" Sonny asked, his voice low but still audible in the still night air.

"Alright," Lance muttered, staring straight ahead. "Just can't stop thinking about Jayna."

Derek sucked in a breath.

Sonny nodded. "I know it's tough. But they'll find her. You just need faith." The older man's voice was gruff yet tinged with fatherly concern.

Lance's shoulders slumped. "First Greta, now Jayna. It's like I'm cursed."

Like he was cursed? Or responsible? Derek squeezed his hands into fists. He wanted to plant those fists into the man's face and demand that he tell him where Jayna was.

"You can't blame yourself for what happened to Greta. And Jayna, well, she's a wild one, probably took off with some guy she just met." Sonny shifted on the bumper, crossing his legs in front of him.

Derek's gaze dropped. Sonny and Lance wore matching boots. His eyes moved from Sonny's feet to Lance's feet. After so many years working as a civil engineer, he prided himself on his eye for measurement. Both men wore the same size boots.

His attention moved from Lance to Sonny. The badge on Sonny's chest shone dully in the dimming light. He'd been a paramedic for as long as Derek could remember. The guy must be nearing retirement age—his hair was graying, and his face was weathered. He'd just become a grandfather. No, he couldn't be … could he? Derek's mind swirled. Could he?

"I'm sure Jayna will show up tomorrow." Sonny clapped a hand on Lance's shoulder.

Lance nodded and stood. "Yeah, I hope you're right. My shift is starting, I need to head in. You're lucky that you work straight days now."

"Perks of being an old-timer," Sonny chuckled. "Pay your dues and you'll get there one day."

"Have a good night," Lance said as he walked away.

Derek moved back into the shadows, watching as Lance walked inside the ambulance station. His gaze quickly drifted back to Sonny. Originally, he'd come here to check up on Lance. Possibly follow him, see where the man would lead him. But instead, Derek pressed himself closer to the cold, rusting metal of the old ambulance. He waited with his eyes fixed on Sonny.

The two men were on different shifts now. If Lance had been working when Jayna disappeared, Sonny would not have been. After a few minutes, Sonny stood and made his way to his SUV.

Derek's heart hammered in his chest, and he held his breath, praying that Sonny didn't notice him. The older paramedic pulled out of the parking lot and turned left, away from town. Strange. Sonny lived in the subdivision in town.

Easing away from behind the ambulance, Derek ran down the sidewalk. He yanked open his truck door and jumped in. His hands shook as he started the engine. He left the lights off until Sonny was further down the road. Would Sonny notice he had a tail?

The paved road ended, turning to gravel as they left the town limits behind. Derek's knuckles whitened on the steering wheel as he focused on maintaining a safe distance without losing sight of the blue SUV.

The urban landscape gave way to farm fields and dense patches of forest. How could a family man—a well-respected community member—be responsible for Jayna's disappearance? For Greta's murder? Derek had to be wrong. Yet he continued to follow the glowing tail lights of Sonny's vehicle, continued to follow his gut instinct.

Eventually, Sonny's SUV turned off the gravel road onto an overgrown driveway, kicking up dust and rocks. Derek slowed, then hit the gas. If Sonny had noticed him in the distance, he would expect the following vehicle to continue past. Derek sped up, stealing a glance at the old, dilapidated farmhouse and the apple orchard beside it.

Once he was out of sight, he coasted onto the shoulder, cut the engine, and stepped out. He pulled out his cell phone, about to dial 911, but hesitated. Did Sonny still have his patch phone with him, able to hear incoming emergency calls? And what exactly would he tell dispatch? That he was following the serial killer who was one of their own? He had no proof, just a gut instinct.

Did he even have gut instincts? He was a civil engineer, not a police detective, as Burke had pointed out more than once.

But if he was right, he'd need help. He pulled up the contact list and tapped the call icon. Burke answered his personal cell phone on the second ring.

"What now, Brennan?"

"I think I know where Jayna is. And who took her."

"What now?" the cop repeated, sarcasm replacing irritation. "Did you find another psychic who could actually connect with Jayna?"

"No, just listen. I don't have long to explain. It's Sonny Mitchell, and he just pulled into an abandoned farmhouse on County Road 29." Derek ran up the road, stopping at the hanging mailbox. "Fire number 64921. There's an apple orchard on the property."

"You're following him?" Burke's voice rose. "Derek! You can't follow an innocent man."

"Burke, he's not innocent. He wears size 10 boots. And I just have a feeling." Derek continued running up the uneven driveway staying along the tree line. "Burke, you just have to trust me on this."

He could hear the tapping of computer keys through the phone. "Sonny owns the property, Derek. It was his uncle's farm that he inherited."

Sonny had left his SUV running and had the headlights pointed toward the rear of the farmhouse. Derek felt his pulse pick up. He needed to be careful. Under his feet, the rocks crunched loudly in the quiet night. He caught a glimpse of Sonny's silhouette in the headlights.

He moved to the back of the SUV. Crouching down, he peeked around the tailgate. There it was—the entrance to the root cellar, just like Jamie said. Sonny was lifting the heavy wooden door and disappeared into darkness.

"Sonny just entered a root cellar, Burke," he whispered into the cell phone. "Get here quick. I'm going to…"

Burke swore under his breath. "Don't do anything stupid."

What? Seriously? He was the king of stupid.

"Wait till I get there," Burke ordered, and the call ended.

What was he going to do? His mind was going a mile a minute. It would take Burke over ten minutes to get here. Every second wasted was one closer to losing Jayna. Taking a deep breath, Derek inched toward the cellar entrance. Goddammit, Jayna was in danger.

Chapter 44

Jayna

Jayna was in danger. Her heavy eyelids slowly opened. The remnants of the vivid dream still clung to her consciousness. Her head pounded, and she tried to raise her hand, but it wouldn't move. Panic rose within her. This was not a dream. Why were her hands bound?

Her eyes adjusted to the darkness. Where was she? A fuzzy-headed drugged feeling clouded her thoughts. She inhaled sharply. The air was musty and smelled like apples. A basement, maybe a cellar? The chill of it seeped into her bones as burning fear crept up her throat.

A memory flashed. She'd been running late. Jamie and Derek were on the phone. The doorbell rang. She opened it. Why was Sonny at her door? He shoved in, taking the phone from her hand and smashing it against the wall. Then he grabbed her by the hair, pushing her against the wall. He shoved a cloth in front of her face—she couldn't breathe. Then blackness.

Sonny.

Derek. He would find her. That thought flickered. Why, though? She was nothing to him. She would be the last person he'd send out a search party for. Yet she was certain he would.

Jamie... Jamie. She concentrated, visualizing her friend's face. Jamie would know. Apples. Cellar. "Jamie, please hear me. Help me."

The sound of a door creaking open was followed by footsteps echoing off the cement walls. Her breath hitched, and she strained to see through the murky darkness.

"Awake, are we?" Sonny's voice was calm and deceptively gentle. Eerily gentle. "Guess the last of the Ketamine has worn off."

"Sonny, why are you doing this?" Her voice cracked.

"Why?" Sonny flipped a switch, and a single bulb overhead flickered to life, casting shadows. "You really have to ask, Jayna?"

She squinted against the sudden light, her eyes adjusting to the sight of Sonny's familiar face that was twisted into an unfamiliar mask. He didn't look like the friendly paramedic who brought laughter into the emergency department. This Sonny was nothing like the proud grandfather showing off pictures on his cell phone.

"Lance loved you," Sonny continued, his tone sharpening. "He was a wreck after you broke things off. You destroyed him, Jayna. And you didn't even care."

Her breath came faster, shallower. "Sonny, listen to me. Whatever you think I did to Lance, it wasn't my fault. We'd only been on a few dates. Relationships end, people move on."

"Not him!" Sonny roared, slamming a fist against the wall. Dust particles rained down, and Jayna flinched. "He gave everything to you, and you threw him away like garbage."

"Sonny, please...you don't have to do this," she pleaded, tears pricking at her eyes. "I can talk to Lance. Apologize. We can fix it. Just let me go."

Sonny chuckled softly. It was a sound devoid of humor sending another shiver down Jayna's spine.

"Fix it? Like you fixed it when you broke his heart? You women are all the same. You use men, chew them up, and spit them out when you're done."

Jayna shook her head frantically, struggling to find the right words. This was not the rational Sonny she knew. His eyes were wild. She was not reasoning with a sane man.

"It's not like that, Sonny. I honestly never meant to hurt Lance. Please, you have to believe me."

Sonny stepped closer and crouched down. His face was mere

inches from hers. She could feel his breath, hot and rancid against her skin.

"You think I haven't heard that before? You think I don't know your type? You play the innocent, but you're nothing but a heartless bitch."

Jayna flinched at the hatred in his voice, her sobs growing more desperate. "I swear, Sonny, I'll do anything. I'll talk to him. I'll beg him to take me back. I'll make it right. Just let me go. Please."

"You sound just like Greta. She said all the same things," Sonny's eyes narrowed as his lips curled into a cruel smile.

"It's too late for that, Jayna. Way too late," he whispered calmly. Far too calmly.

He stood, towering over her once more. Jayna's mind raced. She needed to find a way to connect with him. "What about your grandson? You showed me his pictures. You're a kind man, Sonny. You save lives. You don't have to do this."

For a moment, Sonny's expression faltered, a flicker of something almost human crossing his face. But it vanished as quickly as it appeared. "This isn't about me. It's about you. I have seen who you really are. Lance deserves better."

"Sonny," she said softly. She needed to try a different tactic. "You have a family. Think about what this would do to them if they knew."

A flicker of something—guilt, regret—crossed Sonny's face. For a moment, she thought she might have reached him. But it was fleeting; his expression hardened again.

"They'll understand," he said, though his voice lacked the conviction it had before. "They'll understand that sometimes you have to do bad things for the right reasons."

A suffocating wave of desperation surged through Jayna, stealing her breath. "This is wrong, Sonny. Deep down, you know it is."

Silence stretched between them, heavy and tense. Sonny moved to a small table set up in the corner of the cellar. Various medical supplies were laid out neatly. He pulled a glass vial from his pocket and picked up a syringe, his movements methodical and precise.

"Lucky for me, they were setting up for MAID at the hospital yesterday." He held up a vial of Midazolam. "The charge nurse was absolutely losing her shit trying to find it."

Jayna's eyes widened as she watched Sonny draw the clear liquid into the syringe. The man had killed Greta, and he was going to do the same to her.

"It'll be painless. You'll just drift off to sleep. I don't need to explain the process. You know."

She did know. She had assisted in the last medically aided death at the hospital. The patient, an 80-year-old man, was suffering from incurable cancer and tired of the constant pain. Once injected, she'd have less than 10 minutes before her heart stopped beating.

"Help me," she screamed, her lungs burning with the effort.

"Jayna!" a voice shouted, muffled but unmistakable. Derek.

Sonny cursed under his breath, his eyes darting between Jayna and the door. "Stay quiet," he hissed.

Summoning every ounce of strength, she screamed again, "Down here! I'm down here!"

Sonny moved towards her, but his eyes were trained on the stone staircase that led to the door. While Sonny had strapped her hands down, he hadn't bothered with her feet. Big mistake.

Knees. Balls. Nose. Throat. The self-defence course came back to her. Hit a joint. Disable him.

With Sonny's attention solely focused on the staircase, she lifted her foot and connected with his elbow, kicking hard. The syringe flew out of his grasp, skittering across the dirt floor.

"Son of a bitch," Sonny howled, holding his arm.

Nose. She could still hear the self-defence coach in her mind. She raised her foot higher and kicked with all her might.

Crunch.

Sonny crumbled to the ground, blood pouring from his broken nose. He used his sleeve to swipe away the blood and reached behind him, grabbing the syringe.

"It's over, Sonny." Derek appeared at the bottom of the stairs.

Sonny laughed, a dark and twisted sound. "You're just as pathetic as Lance. Running after a woman who doesn't care about you."

Derek's jaw tightened. He moved closer, his eyes moving from Sonny to her. "I'm not letting you hurt her."

Sonny lunged toward Derek with the syringe.

"Derek, the needle, it's lethal," Jayna screamed.

Derek darted to the left when Sonny tried to jab him. Raising his right hand, Derek's fist plowed into Sonny's face, connecting with the already injured nose. The syringe went flying to the ground again.

Jayna watched in terror as the two men grappled, feeling useless with her hands still bound. They rolled across the floor, knocking over jars and tools off the wooden shelving, the noise echoing in the confined space.

Derek landed another powerful punch to Sonny's jaw, stunning the paramedic. He quickly pinned Sonny down, breathing heavily.

"Are you okay?" He glanced over his shoulder after he grabbed a roll of duct tape off the shelf and bound Sonny's hands behind him.

Jayna nodded, tears of relief streaming down her face. "Yes."

The sound of sirens blared in the distance, growing louder. Derek stood up, rushing over to the cot. He grabbed scissors off the table and cut the ties from her wrists.

"It's going to be okay. You're safe now," he said softly.

Jayna's hands were freed, but she didn't move immediately. Instead, she stared at Derek. He'd come for her. She threw her arms around him, clinging to him as if he were her lifeline. "I knew you would come," she sobbed into his shoulder, her voice trembling.

Chapter 45

Jayna

She knew he'd come. Laying on the gurney, Jayna couldn't breathe, couldn't swallow. She couldn't pull her gaze off Derek. She'd felt fear before, but nothing like this. This was crippling. She was terrified that she was dreaming and was still locked in that dungeon of horror.

"Ouch." That worked to pull her back to the present. Her eyes moved to the young paramedic student who was attempting to start an IV.

"Stick me one more time. I dare you!" she hissed and pulled her left arm free. "I'm fine. I don't need an IV."

"It's procedure," the paramedic stated. This was the newbie she'd beaten at pool a couple of months back. Apparently, playing pool wasn't the only thing he sucked at.

"I'm fine," she repeated. She wasn't fine. Far from it. But she needed to keep her composure, otherwise she'd completely lose it.

Someone grabbed her right hand. She turned. Derek. The expression on his face was grim. He had a scratch across his cheek, probably from the scuffle with Sonny.

She tugged her hand free from his grasp because it felt too damn good. He was making her feel safe and wanted. He had come for her, like she knew he would. The thought absolutely terrified her, almost as much as realizing that Sonny was a monster.

"Can you both stop fussing? I'm fine!" she snapped. She didn't want to be fussed over. If she focused on being pissed off that people were fussing over her, then she wouldn't focus on the fact that she'd almost…no, she wasn't going to go there.

"The patient is being uncooperative," the baby paramedic tattled.

Lance appeared at his side. Great! Lance was here, too.

"I'll show you uncooperative." She glared at the snitch.

Burke appeared next to Lance. "I know that you've been through an ordeal, Jayna, but I can't have you threatening the paramedics. They're just trying to do their job."

"Whatever," she muttered and pulled her hand free from Derek's grasp yet again. "Stop mauling me!" What she wanted was for him to wrap his arms around her again and hold her forever. But he didn't do forever. Neither did she. And if she gave in, she would most definitely fall apart. She didn't want to fall apart in front of Derek.

"Well, stop making me worry," Derek snapped back.

"I didn't do it on purpose."

"Right!" That cocky left eyebrow lifted.

"What do you mean, RIGHT?" She tried to sit up on the gurney. Mr. Terrible at IVs and shooting pool pushed her back down. She glared up at him. Rob, according to his name tag. Rob the Knob.

"You probably got yourself kidnapped on purpose, so I'd have to come to your rescue." Derek took her hand in his, squeezing.

She yanked it free.

"Wow! Your ego is almost as big as your head, which is pretty damn big. I have no idea how that scrawny neck of yours holds it up."

"It's so obvious now," he ignored the insult and continued speaking.

She blinked. "What's so obvious?"

"The entire 'oh let's pretend to be boyfriend and girlfriend so I can get with Lance,'" he said in a higher pitched voice. Was he trying to mimic her?

"What now?" Lance looked from Derek to Jayna. "What's he talking about?"

Jayna narrowed her eyes on Derek. "Don't pay any attention to him. He's a drunk and tends to tell tales when he's been drinking."

"I am not a drunk! I quit drinking." Derek shook his head. "Just admit it. You pretended to pretend to make me fall for you."

"I didn't pretend to pretend. See, he's talking nonsense right now. Burke, you should give him a sobriety test before he gets behind the wheel," she told the cop who still stood next to Lance. Then her head snapped back to Derek. "You fell for me?"

"Nope." Derek's lips clamped shut.

"You just said you did."

"Now who's talking nonsense?"

Lance grabbed one end of the gurney and Knob took the other end, lifting her into the back of the ambulance.

"I heard you say it," Jayna tried to sit up again, glancing past Knob, who also had an exceptionally large head.

Lance put a firm hand on her shoulder, forcing her back down.

"Why did you break up with Lance after you worked so hard to be with him?" Derek asked, standing at the back of the ambulance.

"I'm standing right here," Lance reminded her.

She heaved a long sigh. Maybe it was the near-death experience or the fact that Derek had apparently moved Heaven and Earth to find her that caused her to blurt out the truth.

"Because he wasn't you."

Chapter 46

Derek

"Because he wasn't you." Jayna's words echoed as the ambulance door shut.

The breath Derek had been holding gushed out. He felt lightheaded. Everything had just become so complicated. He didn't do complicated. Yet here he stood, heart racing and his breathing erratic as he watched the retreating ambulance.

Burke set a hand on his shoulder. "You did good today."

"Yeah," was all he could manage. His throat burned.

If he hadn't followed Sonny... If he hadn't gone to Jamie … If Jamie hadn't caused his attention to move to Sonny... If he hadn't finally made Burke believe in the unbelievable, then the unfathomable would have happened. He would have lost Jayna.

Sonny was a family man and head paramedic. He was, by all appearances, a decent guy. At first glance he was not the sick bastard he turned out to be.

How was it possible that a monster had been walking amongst them wearing a normal human face? Sonny had been about to administer a deadly amount of Midazolam. Derek overheard the two paramedics discussing the drug. Jayna would have stopped breathing within 10 minutes, her heart stopping as well.

And Derek's world would have stopped.

A world without Jayna would lack color and vibrancy. It wouldn't be one he'd want to be in. A deep frown creased his forehead. What the hell? Talk about complicated. Was he about to do complicated?

He had kept trying to hold her hand. He needed to touch her. And he hadn't wanted to let go.

He didn't want to lose her again.

Poor Lance had looked crestfallen to learn he'd been a pawn in their game. He'd almost felt sorry for the guy.

"Because he wasn't you." Her last words raced through his mind again. They had started his heart racing even faster.

Those words had also broken his heart.

He did not deserve them. He wasn't worthy of them.

He wasn't that guy.

He'd only disappoint her, and she'd already been through enough. Jayna deserved a man like Lance. A man to build a life with, who wouldn't carelessly break her heart like he already had done so long ago.

However, Jayna didn't want a relationship. Sure, she said she did. But the minute she'd gotten Lance, she had that ready-to-bolt look in her eyes. And it wasn't because the guy had been a murder suspect; she'd had it before learning that. She was Jayna Date and Dash. And he was Two-Date Brennan.

She wasn't that woman.

And he wasn't that man.

Chapter 47

Jayna

Derek wasn't the man she'd given him credit for. He hadn't followed the ambulance to the hospital, refusing to leave her bedside. It had been the next day before he'd finally shown up. Seeing him standing in the doorway of her room had caused hope to resurface, only to plunge again. He'd stood there so hesitantly, looking like he wasn't sure if he should enter or flee.

Finally, he walked in and stopped at the end of her bed.

"How are you?" he'd asked politely.

"Fine," she answered.

"Good." He'd shifted from foot to foot.

"Derek!" She was not going to make small talk with him. Not after everything they'd been through.

He met her eyes. Too tired to keep pretending, she didn't bother to hide the hope that they could finally start something meaningful. But the sudden panic in his eyes made it clear that this was the last thing he wanted.

"I'm not trustworthy Jayna. I don't deserve forgiveness or love. I break everything I touch. I will only hurt you."

"You're not afraid of hurting me," she scoffed. "You're afraid of letting me close. If you do, I might see something about you that I don't like. You're afraid that I'll hurt you."

His mouth dropped open, but no words came out.

"That's what I thought."

"Jayna," he said, shaking his head.

This man was strung tighter than a drum. And he was pigheaded.

He didn't feel worthy of her. That thought ripped her apart. The man who, by all appearances, seemed to have way too much confidence, felt unworthy. He didn't believe he deserved love, so he pushed it away, keeping everyone at a distance.

She should have seen it right away. She was an expert at feeling that way.

It's how she felt, too.

She was the poor little rich girl who no one loved. Jayna was lonely. And Derek was too.

The unloved who told the world that love was the last thing they wanted. When in truth, it was exactly what they craved.

"I'm in love with you," she spoke words that had never passed her lips before.

He sucked in a loud, shocked breath.

"You don't know what love is." His words should have sounded harsh. And they would have been if not followed by the next words he spoke, "I don't either."

"That's not true," she defended.

"We both know how to evade love. But neither of us have a clue how to love."

She opened and closed her mouth. The denial died as the truth of his words sank in. His words hurt, but she was even more shocked by the words she had spoken out loud. She had put her feelings on the line, only to be humiliated that he so easily turned her down yet again.

She should have known better.

She knew that his heart was closed off, but now she also saw the truth.

The man was without a heart.

Now she'd given hers to the one and only man guaranteed to shatter it.

She watched him walk away. She didn't attempt to stop him.

Chapter 48

Derek

Jayna didn't attempt to stop him. She let him walk out of her hospital room. Derek had paused just outside her door, listening to the heart wrenching sound of her crying. He'd wanted so badly to go back into her room and be the one to wipe her tears. But he wasn't the wipe-her-tears type. His stomach had knotted as he kept walking and a couple of her tears had leaked from his eyes.

What the hell was wrong with him? He was emotionally stunted and incapable of love. He was not worthy of her.

Sitting on the soft grass, he stared moodily at the pond as the sun cast a golden hue over the still water. So many memories were wrapped up in this place. It was his childhood: this pond and the apple orchard beside it. He, Tommy, and Nick had run wild through the fields, hanging off the low branches of the apple trees, and cooling off in the pond. The air always seemed fresher here, filled with the sweet scent of ripening apples and the earthy aroma of the surrounding fields.

His eyes landed on the dog statue under the willow tree where they'd buried Albert a few months back. The black Lab Tommy had rescued from a ditch turned out to be the best dog ever. Derek could almost hear Albert's joyful bark and see his wagging tail as he jumped into the pond after a tossed stick.

He leaned back on his elbows, staring up at the blue sky, his eyes lowering to the trees. The leaves were starting to change. Among the green were a few yellow and orange. Soon, they'd completely change color and fall to the ground. The pond would freeze over, and another magical summer would be behind him. He could already feel the crispness in the air, a reminder that time marched on indifferent to the moments it swept away.

This summer and early fall had flown by, and it was all Jayna's fault. She had turned his life upside down. When he rushed into that cellar, he had been so frightened that he'd be too late, and he would lose her. The memory of her terrified eyes and the cold, damp walls of the cellar still haunted him. Sonny had stood over Jayna, a wild look in his eyes, holding that deadly syringe. He'd never felt such fear before. It was a bone-deep terror that gripped him and refused to let go. He'd almost lost her.

Then he reverted to his closed-off self. He pushed her away and lost her anyway.

There wasn't much he was afraid of. Yet he was terrified of the way Jayna made him feel. He always ended things before they got too entangled, and he felt relief immediately after. But this time, there was no relief. There was just bitter regret. He should have fought for her. He should never have let her go.

However, he kept going back to the fact that he was to blame for putting her at risk. Sure, they'd only been fake dating. But he'd fallen for her. If he hadn't been too afraid to admit his feelings to himself and her, then she would never have started dating Lance. She'd never have attracted Sonny's attention. It was exactly what he'd done to Tommy, bailing on enlisting and sending his brother to that hell hole all alone. He wasn't trustworthy. He couldn't be depended on by those who loved him.

Scrubbing a hand over his face, he groaned out loud. He had nothing to offer Jayna, but a broken shell of a man. He may present to the world this overly confident, fearless man. But he was too afraid to open his heart. He truly had nothing to offer Jayna; he'd just hurt her more.

That's what he did. He hurt the people who loved him, disappointing them time and again. Jayna had already suffered enough; he didn't need to add to her pain.

A dog barked and pounced on him. "Hey Norbert. I am so sorry you were given such a stupid name." He scratched the dog's ears, feeling a small flicker of joy at the familiar companionship.

"It's not a stupid name." Tommy sat beside him. "Why are you sitting here looking like the sky is about to fall?"

Derek shot his brother an annoyed glance. "Just sitting here. There's no sky falling."

"Are you constipated, then?"

"No! I'm enjoying the peace and quiet." In reality though, the quiet made his thoughts louder, more insistent.

"Mom has Dulcolax if you need it."

"I'm not constipated!" Derek growled. "Is there a reason you've decided to ruin my chill?"

"No, it's just fun," Tommy said, squeezing his knee. "I hear you're a hero."

"Hardly."

"Hardly? You took out a serial killer. Saved Jayna's life." Tommy's voice was filled with pride. "My brother is a certified hero."

Derek turned and stared at Tommy. Every time he thought about how close Jayna had come to losing her life, he felt sick. It was pure luck that he followed Sonny that night. Just a gut instinct. Sonny had killed Greta and Duncan yet hadn't even made it on the police department's radar. The man had simply snapped. But Duncan? He'd been a peeping Tom who had gone unnoticed as well. He just had the misfortune to peep into the wrong window at the wrong time, catching a glimpse of something he was never meant to see. He must have been a loose end Sonny couldn't afford to leave behind.

Derek shuddered, the weight of all that had happened pressing down on his chest, making it difficult to breathe.

He sighed and looked back at the pond, its surface calm and serene, a stark contrast to the turmoil inside him. "I did what anyone would have done. Besides, Jayna had already kicked the shit out of Sonny. I merely had to restrain him."

Tommy shook his head. "Not everyone would have had the guts to follow their instinct. To face down a killer."

Derek shrugged. "I guess."

Tommy's gaze softened. "You did good, Derek. Really good."

"I still hurt her, Tommy. Jayna told me that she's in love with me, and I walked."

Tommy leaned forward, scratching Norbert's ears. "Why did you?"

"Why did I what?"

"Why did you walk?"

Derek shrugged again. "Dunno. I don't do relationships."

"Why?" Tommy asked.

"Why what?" Derek repeated.

"Derek! Can you stop acting like your asshole self for a moment and have a serious discussion?" Tommy let out a frustrated sigh. "Why don't you do relationships?"

"I just don't."

"So, stop."

"Stop what?"

"Seriously, Derek. Stop being an insensitive, pigheaded jerk. Go talk to her."

"What if she tells me to get lost?"

"Who?" Tommy waggled his brows.

"Ha ha. You're frigging hilarious."

Tommy chuckled, then his voice turned serious again. "Does she know how you feel about her?"

"Who?"

"Damn it, Derek. I'm about to plant my fist in your face. If you want my advice, stop being a dumbass."

"I don't recall asking for your advice. I was sitting here, enjoying the quiet, then you and the dog with the stupid name showed up."

"I don't know why I even bother to try." Tommy punched him in the arm. "But you're my brother, and I want to see you happy. So, one more time. Have you told Jayna how you feel about her?"

He shrugged yet again.

"So, that would be a no." Tommy shook his head. "You need to tell her. In clear, concise words. No grunts allowed."

"I don't grunt. And what's the point? I blew my chance with her. She's seriously pissed."

Tommy blinked. "Damn, you are so dense! The point is that you're in love with her."

Now he did grunt.

"You are, Derek! Stop fighting it and start fighting for her."

"I wouldn't have a clue where to start."

"Start by being honest. Tell her how you feel. It wouldn't hurt to apologize for being such a jackass."

Why did his brothers keep pushing him to admit his feelings and to apologize?

"I hurt the people who love me. I can't be depended on." Derek inhaled a deep breath and let it out through his nose. "I bailed on you. I hurt you. I left you all alone."

Tommy stared at him for several long moments. "Derek, you need to let go of the guilt. It is not your fault that I was held captive."

He shook his head, grimacing. "If I had been there, I could have protected you."

Tommy pressed his lips together. "Or you could have died in the blast. Derek, it's not your fault that you weren't there."

"But it was my stupid idea to enlist in the first place."

"You were twelve when you came up with it. We had just joined the army cadets. I thought it was a great idea, too. But you lost interest, I didn't. I really wanted to join the army, to do something great. I didn't sign up because I thought you were joining too. I enlisted because I wanted to!"

Derek closed his eyes, absorbing his brother's words.

"Derek, I chose to go. I have come to terms with it. Despite the horror of those 3 years, it has helped shape me into the man I am today. And I don't want it to destroy the man you could be. We have already lost too much, don't let it take any more years from us. From you."

He nodded. His brother was right. He needed to let go of the guilt. Tommy had forgiven him, now he just had to forgive himself. When he thought his brother had been killed, a piece of himself had crumbled and died that day. He had encased what was left of his heart in ironclad armor, so it couldn't be hurt anymore. It was time to remove the shield.

"I think Jayna is the one woman, no, make that the only woman who could put up with you. If you let her go, then you are even more stupid than I gave you credit for."

Derek shook his head, a slow smile lifting his lips. Tommy was right again. No one except Jayna would put up with his crap. No one understood him like she did. She had no problem calling him on his crap, then moving past it. Not many women would have been able to kick the shit out of their captor like Jayna had. She was truly an exceptional woman.

This feeling inside of him wasn't going away. In fact, it kept growing. He wanted Jayna. He needed her. He wasn't going to meet someone better. There wasn't another woman like her. Obviously, he wasn't going to get over her. If that was the case, then he needed to find a way to make this all right. He had a big decision to make and, like he did with all the big decisions in his life, he made it instantly.

"You're right, Tommy." Derek stood. "Let's go."

Tommy looked up. "Go where?"

"Ring shopping."

"Ring shopping?"

"I need a ring if I'm going to propose."

"Propose?"

"Yeah."

"I didn't mean to ask her to marry you." Tommy's mouth gaped open.

"I'm done wasting time." He started walking up the hill. Tommy ran to catch up. The puppy raced past them both, barking excitedly.

"You can never take your time with anything. You're so

impulsive!" Tommy grabbed his arm. "Just start by asking her out to dinner. See where that leads."

Derek's eyes narrowed. "Are you saying that you think she'll say no?"

"That's not at all what I'm saying," Tommy groaned. "I'm saying that you should date a bit first. Get to know each other better."

"I've known her for over two decades."

Tommy let an annoyed breath hiss out between his teeth. "You're missing an entire step. The whole dating first."

"We dated for a month."

"Fake dated!"

"Oh, it was far from fake," Derek grinned.

"Does Jayna know that?"

"She told me that she loves me." He lifted his palms upward.

"And then you walked out the door," Tommy reminded him.

"And," he drew out the word. "Like you said, I'll apologize for that."

"Derek, you can't just show up on her doorstep with a lame apology and a ring."

"Yeah, that didn't exactly work for Nick." He scratched the two days' growth on his chin. "I'll need something extra."

"Oh, you're already extra enough." Tommy shook his head back and forth. "Just take some flowers, your lame apology, and ask her out to dinner."

"You ARE saying that you think she'll say no!"

"Oh, I'm definitely saying that!" Tommy rolled his eyes. "You have a lot to make up for."

Derek smirked. "Care to place a wager on it?"

Tommy laughed and stared at Derek's dirt-covered pickup. "You're on. If she says yes, I'll wash your truck for a month."

"I want it waxed too," Derek added.

"Hold on." Tommy held up his right hand. "When she says NO, you wash my truck for two months and clean up the dog poop in the yard."

Derek extended his hand. "No problem, because she'll say

YES. And I'm planning to get a puppy too, so add clean up after my dog, who won't have a stupid name."

They shook on it. For the first time since he'd walked out of Jayna's hospital room, he felt hopeful. He would fight for her like Tommy suggested, and she'd agree to marry him. No way was he spending the rest of his life without her or losing this bet.

He wanted what Tommy had, and thankfully, that wasn't his brother's girl as well. For a while, he had become consumed with the idea of Leighton. It wasn't only Tommy at the age of ten who had been drawn to Leighton. He had loved being around her, too. Then she'd made the choice between them, and like everyone, she chose Tommy. Something broke inside him that day. As a result, he became the 'no good' boy, and then man that everyone expected him to be.

But Jayna saw him differently. She saw him as he was, accepted him, and understood that the bad boy act was just that—an act. He could be himself around her, with no pretense. And yet, he'd pushed her away. He had yet again broken her heart, and for that, he would do whatever it took to make it right.

Chapter 49

Jayna

Derek had yet again broken her heart. Jayna knew he wasn't the type to change his mind. He did exactly what he wanted and never did anything he didn't. And the last thing he wanted was to be in a committed relationship.

Even with that knowledge, she'd fallen for him all over again. He'd come to her rescue, a knight in shining armor just like in the fairy tales she had disparaged. She had started to believe in the idea of a soulmate and forever love. She'd allowed the fantasy to build in her mind; Derek moved heaven and earth to find her. It would have made perfect sense for him to follow the ambulance to the hospital, refusing to leave her bedside while confessing his undying love.

Instead, he'd shown up a day later, reluctantly entering her hospital room. He didn't want her. He never had. She saw it in his eyes once he finally made eye contact, before he walked back out the door as fast as his legs could carry him.

He'd warned her not to fall for him. And yet, she had. That made her the world's biggest fool. Not once, but twice. Shame on her this time. She knew who he was, and, sadly, who he wasn't.

He wasn't the guy for her or anyone. Despite her certainty of his feelings for her, she knew he would never give in to them.

What a waste! Together they could have been incredible. But she couldn't force Derek to love her any more than she'd been able to make her parents love her. Maybe she was unlovable, after all.

The late afternoon sun cast a warm glow through the large bay window of her living room, yet she shivered. Despite the room's warmth and tranquility, her mind was anything but calm. She couldn't get warm. She could still feel the chill of that damp root cellar and smell the strong pungent odor of rotting apples. It was a fruit she would never eat again.

The first week, she hurt everywhere. Her wrists were still chafed from being too tightly bound. Her mind wouldn't shut down, and the fear wouldn't go away. She felt frightened and so very alone, even when her friends were with her.

She woke up gasping every night. It was always the same dream, taking her back to that dark, cold root cellar. 'It's too late, Jayna. Way too late.' Sonny's distorted voice and twisted evil face kept replaying. In her dream, Sonny grabbed her arm and sunk the lethal syringe into her vein just as Derek raced down the stairs. Too late, way too late. Derek screamed that he loved her. Finally! But he was too late.

The bittersweet feeling tinged with absolute terror clung to her throughout the day, and the vivid dream waited for her to fall asleep each night.

She was recovering physically from the ordeal, but her emotional wounds still felt raw. And her heart? Well, it was shattered. The truth was, Derek did love her. Just not enough to force him to face his own demons and find a way past them.

While he stood at the end of her hospital bed, she had studied him. She watched as he twisted his hands together, staring at his feet. She'd zoned in on the tight line of his mouth and the heartbreak in his eyes once he made eye contact and finally spoke. "I'm not trustworthy. I don't deserve forgiveness or love. I break everything I touch."

Even though he had made up with his twin, he still felt immense guilt. He still felt like that young boy who could never live up to the expectations of everyone around him. He felt unworthy and was still putting up walls and pushing people away. He was still pushing her away.

He'd never let her in.

She drew in an unsteady breath, rapidly blinking away the unwanted memory, wishing there was a way to permanently erase it. Erase not only Sonny from her thoughts, but Derek as well. Twice she'd let herself believe in him. Twice he'd proven she couldn't. If only she could hate him. That would make it easier to move past him.

Leaning down, she lifted a basket from the bottom shelf of the coffee table. Underneath the photo album from the Mexico trip was the brochure she'd taken from TL Village Mercantile. She flipped it open to the full-page picture of Derek. The smile on his face was so genuine and breathtaking while he posed in front of the new water well. Why couldn't he be that upstanding, kind man here? Why couldn't he live up to his potential and be that wonderful man she knew he could be?

The doorbell chimed, and she jumped, her heart racing. She stared at the foyer and the burning acid of fear creeped up her throat. Opening the front door was difficult. PTSD was the diagnosis the psychiatrist had given her. No surprise.

On shaky legs, she walked into the front hall. A state-of-the-art alarm system had been installed, along with the best deadbolt on the market. She stared at the camera that displayed the front porch. Her mother stood there, elegant in a tailored suit.

Unbolting the lock, Jayna pulled open the door. "Hi."

She stepped aside. Catherine Sutton walked in, her Manolo Blahniks clicking against the hardwood floor. The cloyingly strong scent of Chanel No. 5 overpowered the small space.

"Jayna, darling, how are you?"

Jayna sucked in a deep breath of fresh air before closing the door. "I'm fine."

"Well, isn't this...quaint," her mother spoke the last word with distaste. Her eyes swept into the living room, lingering on the mismatched furniture and rustic salvaged pieces.

"Thank you," Jayna replied, ignoring the insult. "I'm very happy here. It feels like home." She omitted that it felt like the first home she'd ever known. Until Sonny had smashed his way in and … No, she didn't want to think about it.

Her mother gave a tight-lipped smile. "If you say so. But I must say that I envisioned something more sophisticated for you. Have you blown through your trust fund? Do you need more money?"

"I've barely touched it," Jayna replied. "Come on in, have a seat. Can I get you something to drink?"

"No, thank you." Catherine glanced around, finally settling on the couch. "I wanted to see how you were doing after that awful experience."

After that awful experience, as her mother had put it, Jayna was done wasting time and pretending. She was done with small talk and avoiding difficult discussions. She sat down opposite her mother and studied her face. It had obviously been touched up by a skilled plastic surgeon. Not a single line was present. Rather than give Catherine an ageless look, it gave her an emotionless appearance. It suited her.

"Why didn't you spend more time with me when I was growing up?" she asked instead of answering her mother's question. Jayna asked the very question she had been pondering right before her mother had rung the doorbell. "Was I so unlovable?"

Her mother looked taken aback. Or at least Jayna thought she did. It was hard to tell, as her forehead didn't move. "Jayna, that's not fair."

"Fair?" Her voice raised. "Do you have any idea what it was like for me, all alone in that big house with only hired help to care for me? You and Dad were always traveling, always too busy. Why was I never enough to make you stay?"

Catherine let out a long sigh. "Jayna, darling, you had everything you needed. The best nannies, a beautiful home. Anything you wanted, you were given. We gave you the very best life."

"The best life?" Jayna's eyes filled with tears. "Having my parents around when I needed them would have been the best life. I needed you, Mom. Not a nanny."

Her mother met her gaze, her eyes softening. "I did my best. My own parents were always gone, too. I grew up in boarding schools. We just raised you the same way your father and I were raised. I thought you understood that."

Jayna shook her head, her voice cracking. "I didn't. I felt abandoned. And terrified to let anyone close. Terrified, they will leave me too." Like Derek had. "I needed my parents' love and attention, not possessions."

Catherine sighed. "I didn't realize you felt this way. I thought we had given you a wonderful life."

Jayna wiped away her tears. "I need you to acknowledge that you hurt me. That you weren't there when I needed you the most."

"I'm sorry, Jayna, truly I am. I wish I could go back and change things. But I'm here now. If you'll let me, I would like to help."

Jayna stared at the hand her mother held out. "I really need you, Mom. I'm so frightened. I'm afraid to close my eyes, I'm afraid to leave the house. I'm afraid to be alone."

Catherine moved closer and pulled Jayna in for a deep hug. It was the kind of hug that she had craved when she was a young girl waking from a nightmare. Maybe it wasn't too late.

Chapter 50

Derek

Maybe it wasn't too late to win Jayna back. Derek had no idea how he would accomplish it, though. He wasn't a grand gesture kind of guy like Nick, who'd planned the surprise wedding for Piper. Nor was he a spill-his-guts, wear-his-heart-on-his-sleeve type like his twin. He never gushed poetic. He didn't possess a single romantic bone in his body.

But Jayna wasn't the sweep-her-off-her-feet kind of girl. Flowers and romantic gestures would be wasted on her.

So, how did a jaded, unromantic guy woo an equally jaded, unromantic soul like Jayna? For starters, he shouldn't use the word 'woo'. Jayna would call him out on that word choice.

Somehow, he ended up in Leighton's store. Was he looking for inspiration, motivation, or advice? Possibly all three. He wasn't sure. But he was relieved that his relationship with Leighton was comfortable enough to stroll into her store and ask for her help.

Scratching his head, he stood in front of the shampoo display. There were eight different varieties on the shelf. He unscrewed the lid of each one, inhaling. Bottle number five made him smile. Coconut, vanilla, pineapple. It smelled like a tropical beach vacation where the waves crashed in and the Piña Coladas flowed. Sunshine and fun. It reminded him of Jayna. He gathered up all twelve bottles of Summer Beach Vacay off the shelf.

Leighton didn't lift an eyebrow as he set them on the checkout counter. She simply rang up the sale, giving him the family discount.

"That's a lot of shampoo. Never pictured you as the Summer Beach Vacay shampoo type."

"It isn't for me."

Now she did quirk a brow. "Really?"

He side-eyed her. "It's for Jayna."

"Ah."

He narrowed his eyes. "Aren't you going to ask why I'm buying shampoo for Jayna?"

"No."

Leighton was making it very difficult to ask for her advice. "Fine. I'll tell you why."

"I didn't ask."

"It's pretty good!"

She chuckled. "Okay, I'll bite. Why are you buying a dozen bottles of shampoo for Jayna?"

"Because she's not the dozen roses type."

Leighton shook her head. "What? Have you been roof drinking again?"

"No!" Damn, she was making this difficult. "I'm purchasing a dozen bottles of the same shampoo because Jayna is indecisive. She never uses the same shampoo scent, and it drives me crazy. She needs to commit to a scent and stick with it."

Leighton nodded. "Gift bag or basket? Your choice."

His brow furrowed. "What I want is advice." Seriously, was she clueless? "What should I do?"

"A basket."

He groaned. "I don't want advice on paper or plastic. I need advice about Jayna."

Leighton placed both her hands on the counter. "About Jayna's indecisiveness?"

"Leighton! It's about getting Jayna to agree to commit to me."

Leighton's mouth dropped open. "Seriously?"

"Yeah!" First, Tommy had questioned his ability to win over Jayna. Now Leighton was. Or were they questioning his ability to settle down? He pulled out the little black box.

"Is that a ring?"

"Yeah!" he muttered. "It's what a guy uses to propose to a woman. That's why I'm here. I need advice on how to do it."

"So, this isn't about shampoo?" Leighton asked.

He blew out a breath. "No, it's not about shampoo! How can I get Jayna to agree?"

Leighton pulled a basket off the shelf behind her and filled it with pink shredded paper. She carefully arranged the bottles of shampoo, stuck in a candle, and sprinkled rose petals around. "Give me the ring."

He handed over the black box, and she tucked it in the center. Pulling a large sheet of cellophane from the roll behind her, she wrapped it around the basket and tied it with a large red bow. "Give her the basket and have her open it. Then, when she pulls out the ring, drop to one knee and ask her to marry you. Just don't act like your normal idiot self."

"That's it? That's your advice?" He gaped at her. Don't act like his normal idiot self. Fantastic!

Chapter 51

Derek

Fantastic advice! 'Don't act like his normal idiot self.' Not at all helpful. Get down on bended knee. Like that was going to happen!

Derek stared down at the straw mat at Jayna's front door and smiled at the message: "The dog's friendly, but the owner's not. Go away!" His smile faded. What if Jayna told him to go away? There was a very good possibility he would act like his normal idiot self, and she'd tell him to get lost.

He adjusted the basket on his arm and knocked on the door. Jayna pulled it open on the second knock. She looked pissed. Or maybe it was hurt. He was never great at reading expressions. Which ever it was, he had probably caused it.

Her eyes narrowed, and she slammed the door in his face. His first guess had been accurate. She was pissed. And he'd definitely caused it.

He shifted from foot to foot. Should he turn and leave? Leaving would be easier. He could avoid using that stupid 'sorry' word. Although Jayna did deserve an apology and an explanation.

So instead of bolting, he knocked a second time.

"What, Brennan? What the hell do you want?" she demanded, pulling open the door again. She lifted her chin and pinned him with those challenging, gorgeous blue eyes.

"Don't be that way," he scolded.

"I'll be any damn way I please. We're over. You walked out the door."

"I shouldn't have done that."

"But you did. So why are you here now? What do you want?" she testily repeated.

"You."

Her lips parted, but nothing came out. He'd shocked her.

"I want you, Jayna," he repeated.

"You want me?" Confusion mixed with anger flashed through her expressive eyes. Then those baby blues rolled. A Ben-worthy eye roll. "You don't have a clue what you want!"

"I didn't, that's true," he admitted. "But I do now. And it's you."

She placed both hands on her hips and shook her head. "Until you wake up tomorrow and change your mind."

"Nope, not going to happen. And I'm not the indecisive one. You are."

She blinked. "I am?"

"Yeah, and that's the reason for this gift I brought you." He held out the basket that Leighton had expertly wrapped.

Jayna hesitantly took it and turned, walking back into her house. The door was left open, so he guessed that meant he was supposed to follow her. He shut the door behind him and walked down the hall toward the kitchen.

She had set the basket on the island and stared at it, peering inside the clear cellophane.

"Why shampoo? And so many? Does my hair smell?"

"Yep," he answered, laughing at her sudden frown.

"It never smells the same, and it's driving me nuts," he clarified. "You need to pick a scent and stick to it."

"I do?"

"Yes, you do. You need to commit."

"This isn't about shampoo?" Her brow furrowed.

No! It wasn't about shampoo! "It's about your inability to commit."

Her eyes widened. "My inability to commit?"

Chapter 52

Jayna

"My inability to commit!" Jayna's mouth dropped open as she repeated the words a second time. He didn't just say that! "You've got to be kidding me! I'm getting a commitment lecture from Two-Date Brennan?"

"Is it so far-fetched?"

"Yeah!" she scoffed. "What are you really doing here, Derek?"

He propped a hip against the counter and scrubbed a hand over his face. "I messed up, Jayna. I should never have walked out of your hospital room like that. I guess I was just frightened."

"Frightened of what, Derek?" she asked. He'd faced down Sonny, saved her life, but admitting that he had feelings was what frightened him? "Are you frightened of actually feeling something?"

"No, I was afraid of messing things up with you."

"So, instead of taking a chance, you just gave up?"

He shrugged. "I didn't want to disappoint you. I didn't want you to realize that I'm not a guy worth your time."

"Well, congratulations. You succeeded!" Jayna let the sarcasm flow. "I needed you, Derek. I thought I was going to die. Then you showed up, and I began to believe that you really did care about me."

Her chest rose and fell. "I told you that I love you. And what did you say back?"

Again, he shrugged.

"You said," her lips quivered, "that I didn't know what love is, only how to avoid it."

He nodded. "Jayna, all I ever do is disappoint people who love me. I'm not a guy worth loving."

"That's a cop-out," she sniped.

"What can I say, I acted like my idiot self yet again."

She stared at him, waiting for something—anything—to show that he could be a decent guy, a dependable guy. She wished that she could believe in him. "Do you have any idea what it felt like when you walked out of my hospital room? I put myself out there yet again. I offered you my heart a second time, and you didn't want it."

"I did want it. I was…" He threw his hands up in the air.

"You were frightened?" she supplied for him. "And you're not now? You've warmed up your cold feet?"

He nodded.

"I don't know that I can trust you." Jayna shook her head. "I'm going to need something more substantial than just your word. Because your word means nothing to me."

"Ouch." Derek winced. He looked away for a moment, his shoulders sagging. Jayna felt instant shame at the sharpness of her words.

"You're right. Up until now, my word has been meaningless. Yesterday, I didn't deserve you. But today, well, today I do. I will do whatever it takes to deserve you."

She opened and closed her mouth. No words came out. She was speechless. He'd shocked her. How she wanted to believe him, but she was fresh out of second chances.

"Derek, you saved my life and then broke my heart all within 24 hours."

After all she'd been through, she realized that she was done wasting time. The counseling was helping with not only finding a way out of the crippling fear caused by Sonny, but also coming to terms with feeling unlovable.

She deserved to be loved and refused to settle for anything less.

"You've ruined me." His face scrunched up like he'd sucked a lemon. "You wrecked me. Turned me into one of those guys."

"What kind of guy would that be?" She'd bite.

"The kind of guy who does serious."

She stared at him. Was this the best she was going to get out of him? "Just admit already that you have feelings for me," she snapped. "Admit that you fell for me while we were fake dating."

"Can't we just skip all the mushy stuff? Do we really have to talk about our feelings?" He made air quotes as he spoke the last word.

Jayna pursed her lips and crossed her arms over her chest.

"Okay!" He lifted his hands up in defeat. "I didn't NOT fall for you."

"Wow! Sweep me off my feet," she snorted. "Guess I'll NOT toss you out on your ass. For now!"

Within a few months, the Neanderthal had actually started to resemble a real man. Give him a few more months, and he might even be able to gush love quotes. She laughed out loud at that thought.

"What's so funny?"

"Nothing." That would be a stretch to imagine the ape gushing about love. She'd settle for him being able to say 'I love you' without the sucked on a lemon face.

"So, you were really worried about me? I heard that you made Burke's life hell while I was missing. You even dragged him to Jamie's workshop for a psychic reading."

"Yeah, well, whatever," he stuttered and produced another sucked lemon face. "Just don't attract the attention of any more serial killers, and we'll be fine."

"But it was so romantic the way you rushed into that cellar and saved me. My knight in shining armor."

Just when she'd completely debunked the entire white knight persuasion, Derek Brennan had to go and destroy her theory that forever love, and soul mates were fake.

But he'd always been that way. No one could tell him that something was impossible. He'd have to prove them wrong.

"Well, I could hardly leave you there. I was just starting to get used to having you around," he shot her that lopsided, dimple-popping grin. "Tommy pointed out that you're the only woman who could put up with my crap. Apparently, I'd be crazy to let you go without fighting for you."

Her eyes rolled up. "And that's what you're doing here? Fighting for me?" She pressed him again. There was a human inside there somewhere; she just had to dig it out. She would probably have to dig all the way to China to find it, though.

"Open your gift." He pointed to the elegantly wrapped basket that sat on the kitchen island.

"Later." She kept her hands on her hips.

"Why do you have to be so difficult? Just open it."

"I'm difficult?" her voice raised.

"Damn it, woman, open the basket." He pushed it closer to her.

"I don't feel like it." She pushed it back. It was the Tequila shot all over again. And she hated to back down.

He grunted and tore open the plastic wrap, pulling out a little black velvet box. "I can't believe you're going to make me do this."

Her eyes widened. No, it couldn't be. It looked like a ring box. No! And then he dropped to one knee in front of her. NO!

"Jayna, you are the most irritating woman I have ever met."

Her eyes narrowed. Was he going to propose or insult her? "Says the most annoying man on the planet."

He blinked, brow furrowing. "You know that I'm not good at this. Jayna, just take this stupid ring and marry me."

He popped the lid on the box, revealing an exquisite princess-cut diamond ring.

"You're proposing?"

"Yeah. What the hell do you think is happening here?"

She shrugged, her eyes moving from his stupid, far-too-handsome face to the incredibly beautiful ring. "You don't do serious, complicated, or marriage."

"That was yesterday. I changed my mind today."

"Hmm."

"What does hmm mean?"

"It just means hmm." She lifted her shoulders, forcing a bored expression on her face.

"Does hmm mean yes?"

"Damn, you're so pushy." A defiant smile lifted the corner of her lips.

"You really have to make everything so difficult," Derek grabbed her hand. "Jayna, are you going to wear this ring or not?"

Her forehead creased into a deep V. It was a lot to take in. The Neanderthal was on bended knee in front of her, holding a sparkling ring. He looked like he was about to vomit.

This was going to be the best she'd get out of him. "Guess so. It's not like anyone else has asked."

He pulled her hand closer and slipped the ring on her finger. "You are so wishy-washy."

"Wishy-washy? Are you an 80-year-old woman? No one but a grandma uses that phrase. Wow, you really know how to make a woman swoon," she said, her voice laced with sarcasm.

Derek stood up, dusting off his knee as if the whole ordeal had been a minor inconvenience. "Can you stop making fun of my vocabulary?"

She looked up at him, her smile softening. "For a moment there, I thought you might actually say something romantic."

"Hey, I got down on one knee, didn't I? That's pretty romantic."

She laughed, shaking her head. "I suppose it is."

He wrapped his arms around her, pulling her close. "Besides, you like me just the way I am. Admit it."

"Yeah, yeah," she muttered, burying her face in his chest. "You'll do."

His chest rose and fell beneath her head, his heartbeat so steady and reassuring. His arms tightened around her. She felt safe and protected for the first time since Sonny had crashed into her house. Derek made her feel safe and the realization hit hard and sudden. This man was in love with her, even if he couldn't say the actual words. He wanted her. He did love her.

"Okay, Mr. Almost-Romantic," she said, pulling back slightly while still holding on to him. "Can you say the L-word just once?"

"Really? Getting down on one knee, buying a diamond ring— a very expensive diamond ring—and asking you to marry me wasn't enough?" He lifted her chin and stared into her eyes.

"Nope."

"Are you always going to be so demanding?" His voice was deliciously low, and her stomach twisted.

"Yep." Her toes started to tingle. His right hand swept over her cheek. The light touch sent shock waves through her.

His hand moved to her chin once more, cupping it. "I love you, Jayna."

His head dropped and his lips covered hers. She had no idea how she didn't collapse onto the floor. Maybe it was because his left arm was wrapped around her, holding her up. This man could seriously kiss. This man who was all hers. The word love flowed off his tongue like it wasn't foreign or distasteful. He meant it.

He pulled away, grinning, and took his cell phone out of his back pocket. Holding the phone over her hand, he snapped a picture of the ring on her finger.

"Why'd you take a picture?" she asked.

He smirked, pocketing his phone. "I need proof to win a bet with Tommy."

Jayna raised an eyebrow. "A bet?" Her temper started to rise as well.

"Yeah, Tommy didn't think I had the guts to propose. And he didn't think you'd accept."

"You made a bet with your brother? Is this proposal real?" Was this guy for real?

"Of course it's real. I'm miserable without you. I can't stop thinking about you all the time!" His voice was filled with annoyance. "I mean, you are seriously the most annoying chick I have ever met. It's easier to marry you than to get over you."

"Wow, Brennan. You need to start writing for Hallmark."

He pulled her close again, dropping his head for another toe-curling kiss. "Okay, I gotta run. I need to see a man about a dog."

"A dog? Isn't the saying 'see a man about a horse'?"

"A horse? What do I want with a horse?"

Before Jayna could say anything else, he was heading for the door. "Seriously?" She called out to him, but he had already left. Who did that? Who proposed and then ran out the door? Derek Brennan did. It was so typical that the guy never did anything predictable. And it was ironic but summed up the man perfectly.

She stood in her kitchen. He was just messing with her. He would rush back any second. She stared at the basket filled with a dozen bottles of shampoo. Of course, the man wouldn't show up with a dozen roses.

She tapped her foot and glanced at her watch. "Seriously?" She walked down the hallway and yanked open the door. His truck was gone. Then she looked down.

Her front door mat was gone as well.

With a growing sense of curiosity and mounting irritation, she pulled out her phone to access the security camera feed. Rewinding the footage, she watched as Derek bent down, picked up the mat, tucked it under his arm, and strode to his truck.

"Unbelievable," she muttered and couldn't help but laugh, speaking out loud. "Of course, he proposes and steals my door mat."

Chapter 53

Derek

Derek had proposed, on bended knee no less. Then stole her doormat, which looked damn good in front of his mahogany door. He chuckled again, 'The dog's friendly, but the owner's not. Go away.' It was perfect. His phone dinged with an incoming text.

<Did you steal my doormat?>

<I did> He thumbed a reply and hit send. If she wanted it back, she could come and get it.

He stepped back and took a picture, capturing the mat along with his front door. He sent the picture along with another text. <It looks better at my front door. And you don't have a dog>

Ding. <Neither do you>

Derek scooped up the German Shepherd puppy and set her on the doormat. He quickly snapped the picture before she scampered off after Tommy's puppy.

<I do now> He typed and sent his reply along with the new picture.

Three dots appeared on his phone screen, indicating that Jayna was typing. Then they disappeared. He chuckled. She was speechless, which was quite the feat. Glancing at his watch, he gave her 15 minutes. Exactly 14 minutes later, her truck pulled into his driveway.

Predictable.

"I can't believe you!" Jayna had barely climbed out of her pickup and was already ranting. "Where do you get off proposing, running straight out the door, and stealing my brand-new doormat?"

His heart skipped a beat. Jayna had always been gorgeous, but an angry Jayna was a sight to behold. Her cheeks flushed a very becoming shade of pink and her blue eyes deepened in color. As she stepped closer, the sun caught her flaxen blonde hair. For a brief moment, the long curls turned golden. Wow. She took his breath away.

"Hey, fake fiancée who is now my real fiancée!"

"Oh, don't get ahead of yourself. I can give back the ring."

Tommy dropped the soapy sponge back into the bucket. "If this engagement is off, then I'm not washing your truck."

"And that's another thing!" Jayna pointed at Tommy, who stood next to Derek's pickup. "Who makes a bet on their proposal?"

"It was his idea," Tommy held up both soapy hands and then pointed at Derek.

"Snitch." Derek shook his head.

Jayna stalked up the front path to the deck where he stood. The new puppy and Tommy's puppy charged toward her, tails wagging, barking that high pitched joyful puppy bark.

"Hi you two." She bent down and scratched Norbert's head and then scooped up the German Shepherd puppy. "Hey little guy."

"Girl," Derek supplied.

"Hey little girl, you sure are cute. What's your name?"

"Chaos."

"That's a really stupid name." Jayna kissed the puppy's soft head.

"Told you so," Tommy added.

"Stay out of it," Derek snapped, then pointed. "You missed a spot."

"Where?"

"The other side."

"She looks like a Bella." Jayna sighed, holding the puppy up, staring into her face.

"No dog looks like a Bella," Derek grumbled. "Definitely not a badass German Shepherd."

"She's not a badass, she's a sweetie." Jayna turned her attention from the puppy back to him. "Her name is Bella!"

Jayna sank onto the first step of the deck, hugging the puppy to her. Was she crying? His chest felt tight, panic surging. Was she here to return the ring?

"What's wrong?"

"You bought a puppy." She was crying.

"You don't like puppies?"

"I love puppies," she sniffled.

This is why he didn't do relationships. Women were complicated. He glanced over at Tommy and lifted his hands. What was he supposed to do?

Tommy pointed at Jayna. Derek shrugged, shaking his head. "Comfort her," Tommy mouthed and made a circle with his arms, imitating a hug.

Damn it. Jayna was a tough chick. She'd pretty much taken Sonny out before he stormed into the cellar. Blood had been pouring from the psycho's nose. But a puppy had her bawling her eyes out?

He sank down beside her, draping his arm across her shoulders. "So, what's the problem?"

She inhaled deeply. "Couples start with a puppy before they have kids."

"You don't like kids?"

"Kids are fine. It's just me. I won't make a good mother," her voice cracked. "You were raised by these great parents. I mean, look at Tommy. He was a great kid and turned into an incredible man."

"That is true," Tommy spoke up.

Derek shot him an annoyed glance, then turned back to Jayna. "What about me?"

She harrumphed. "Well, they did the best they could with you."

Tommy let out a loud laugh, and Derek glared at him again.

"Jayna, you will be a great mother. You are nothing like your parents."

Jayna sniffed again, rubbing her cheek against the puppy's soft fur. "You don't know that. I could be a disaster. What if I turn into them?"

"You won't," Derek said firmly. "You've already proven you're different. You work for a living, and barely touch your trust fund."

Jayna let out a shaky breath. "But a puppy, Derek? That's a big step."

"We don't have to figure everything out now. We'll just figure it out as we go along. Together."

She looked up at him, eyes still glistening with tears. "You really think we can do this?"

"I know we can," he replied, his voice steady and reassuring. "One step at a time. We start with Chaos, then we'll see if we decide to pop out a kid or two. Whatever you want Jayna, sign me up."

Jayna glanced down at the puppy, who started licking her face. "You can't call her Chaos. It's like tempting fate."

"We aren't naming her Bella," Derek confirmed, a small smile tugging at the corner of his lips. "And I get to name our kids, too."

She smiled through her tears, hugging the puppy closer. "Oh, that's not going to happen."

Tommy cleared his throat loudly from behind them. "Does this mean I'm off truck-washing duty?"

Jayna shook her head, roughly wiping away the tears. "Definitely not. You're washing my truck when you're done with Derek's."

"Seriously?" Tommy muttered, pulling the soapy sponge out of the bucket.

Jayna stood up, cradling Bella in her arms. "Derek is helping."

"I am?"

"You are. I can practice my parenting skills on you. Pick up where your parents left off," Jayna laughed at his confused expression. "You made a bet on our engagement. Not cool! Then you stole my doormat. Also, not cool! Consider this punishment for your bad behavior."

Tommy laughed again and tossed the soaked sponge at him. Derek caught it, soapy water splashing into his face. Damn, he really didn't think this entire engagement thing through. He now had a puppy and a fiancée. A real fiancée. And a bossy one at that. Had this been Jayna's plan all along when she'd proposed the fake dating scheme? She did have a wedding altar installed in his backyard.

Jayna set the puppy down on the grass. "Come on, Norbert and Bella," she called to the puppies and ran to the edge of the property where the archway stood.

"Her name isn't Bella," Derek called after her.

"Is too," Jayna turned, running backward. The smile on her face nearly dropped him to his knees.

"Admit it," he yelled, pointing at the arch. "That is a wedding altar you and Jamie built."

"I'll admit no such thing." The grin on her face said otherwise.

Tommy squeezed his shoulder. "The puppy's name is Bella, and that is a wedding altar which you will be marrying that girl under. Just give in. It's much simpler."

He could only nod. The arch was definitely a wedding altar, and he was definitely going to marry Jayna under it.

Epilogue

Jayna

Derek was marrying Jayna under the 'wedding' arch at the edge of his property. It had been beautifully decorated for the occasion. Twining vines and white tulle cascaded down the sides, gently billowing in the soft breeze. White roses, peonies, and eucalyptus leaves had artfully been arranged and crowned the top of the arch.

"I now pronounce you husband and wife. You may kiss your bride," said the minister.

"Admit this was your plan all along?" Derek whispered.

"I'll admit no such thing!" Jayna whispered back. "Now shut up and kiss me so we can seal the deal and get the party started."

"Stop being so bossy," he retorted, pulling her close.

"Stop being an ape." She stepped closer.

"I'm not an ape." His head lowered.

"That's debatable." She stood on tiptoe, wrapping her hands around his neck. "Just kiss me already."

And he did. He kissed her senseless, kissed the legs right out from under her. He set the Bunsen burner to full blast and stirred up all the tingles. Wow, the man could seriously kiss.

The minister loudly cleared his throat. Guess this wasn't a church-appropriate kiss. Good thing they weren't in a church. Reluctantly, she pulled back. "To be continued later," she whispered.

Derek nodded enthusiastically.

"I present to you, Mr. and Mrs. Brennan," the minister announced.

"Sutton-Brennan!" Jayna corrected.

"I'm not a hyphenate kind of guy," Derek grumbled. They turned and smiled at their guests, who burst into loud cheers.

"Why not? It's such a double standard," she muttered out the side of her mouth. "Lucky for you, I'm not big on my family name."

"It is lucky for me! Jayna Brennan. I love how it sounds." He shot her that lopsided grin that popped the lone dimple.

"Lucky for me," she tried to sound sarcastic, but it fell short with such a huge smile on her face.

They walked between the white chairs set up for their guests, smiling and accepting all the well wishes. It was a small affair, with just close family and friends in attendance. Derek's parents and grandparents beamed, as did her parents on the other side of the makeshift aisle. There were even two movie stars in attendance. Nash Logan and his wife, Calla, sat beside Kylie and Jovanny Grotta.

Derek had set up a large wedding tent in case of rain, but

the weather was absolutely perfect. The cloudless blue sky transitioned to a clear evening sky filled with a thousand twinkling stars. Along with the music of the live country band, crickets added their own serenade.

Jayna smiled as she stared around at their close-knit group of friends. Jessica had made it back from Sierra Leone just in time. Her friend sat at the table, her eyes trained on the billionaire cameraman, Sam Marek. There was an intense frown tugging down the corners of Jessica's pretty mouth, and Sam kept stealing glances her way. Something was going on between those two.

Jamie pulled out a chair beside Jessica, setting down two glasses of white wine. Jamie's neck twisted, and she shot a disparaging look at Burke, who was leaning against the bar. He glowered back at her. Intriguing and even more intriguing.

What exactly was going on with her two best friends and these men? Something was definitely brewing. Maybe it wasn't quite time to take down her matchmaking shingle. Now that she was a believer in true love and forever, her matchmaking skills had surely evolved as well.

It wasn't fair that she was the only J to be blissfully happy.

Derek wrapped his arms around her waist from behind and kissed the top of her head. She sighed.

"Hey Bella, girl," Derek said, as he leaned down and patted the 70-pound German Shepherd who squatted at their feet. She had been making rounds, shamelessly begging for ear rubs from all their guests.

"Great wedding," Burke said as he walked toward them.

"Thanks." Derek stepped beside her, keeping his left arm around her waist.

"I know it's your wedding day and all, but I still need to ask. Do either of you have any idea how a doormat that reads 'Dog's friendly but the owner's not' ended up on Ophelia Meddler's porch?"

"Nope," Derek answered, brow furrowing. He shrugged and looked at Jayna. "How about you, honey? Any idea?"

"Not a single one," Jayna answered.

Burke narrowed his eyes. "I seem to recall seeing a doormat matching that description at your front door the last time I was here to play poker. I just checked, it's not there now."

"Wow, that's quite the coincidence," Jayna stated. "Come to think of it, I did notice it was missing."

"Maybe it was that kid Bobby McDermott. Nick said he's been pranking the Meddler quite a bit lately," Derek offered.

Burke pursed his lips. "Twelve-year-old Bobby McDermott? He would need to ride his bike five miles outside of town to reach your house, then steal the mat and somehow ride his bike back with it under his arm."

"Hey, a good prank is worth the extra effort." Derek grinned. "That wouldn't have stopped me at his age."

"I knew if you two joined forces, this town would never be the same." Burke shook his head. "I can only hope you don't plan on procreating."

Derek raised both eyebrows.

Jayna placed a hand on her belly. "You're the first to know, so don't go blabbing it to anyone."

Derek's hand tightened around her waist, and he leaned closer, kissing her temple.

"I have another twenty-two years before I can retire." Burke let out a loud groan and threw his hands up in the air. "The spawn of Two-Date Brennan and Jayna Date and Dash, I just can't."

"You could take a different job," Derek suggested. "Heard the county is looking for a meter maid."

Burke glared, mumbling as he walked away. "Guess I could always move. Change police departments."

"If it's a boy, we should name him after Burke," Derek pulled her into a tight embrace.

"Oh, he'd love that." Jayna lifted on tiptoe again and kissed her husband.

The band started to play Reba's 'Forever Love' and Derek pulled her onto the dance floor. Maybe the song wasn't so bad after all. It was time to change her anthem from Consider Me Gone to Forever Love.

***Author's note.

Thank you for joining me on this journey through 'Forever and Other Lies'. Your support and readership mean the world to me.

I'm excited to share that this book is just the beginning of the 3 Js series. Look out for the next installment, 'Soulmates and Other Apparitions', coming in the winter of 2025. In this sequel, Burke continues his investigation into the Sonny Mitchell case and, much to his dismay, must enlist the help of psychic Jamie Whitney. Will these two be able to overcome their dislike for the other and not only uncover the shocking details of Blythe Landing's serial killer but find love as well?

'The 3 Js series' also connects to the 'What If series', where you can dive into the love stories of other beloved characters. Be sure to check out what happens with Kylie and Jovanny, Piper and Nick, and Tommy and Leighton. The 'What If' series offers a unique and fun alternate storyline to the Blythe Landing series.

If you want to read more with Derek as the male lead, he has a completely different storyline in 'I Still Drive Your Truck'. Kylie, Jovanny, Nick and Piper also have completely different stories. I mean, who doesn't love an alternate ending? Why not an alternate storyline?

Thank you once again for your support. I hope you enjoyed 'Forever and Other Lies', and I can't wait for you to see what's next in the series! Be sure to follow me on Facebook—Sherri Storey – romance novelist, and on Instagram at sherristorey1. Click linktree and sign up for my author newsletter so you don't miss out on new releases and offers.

I would very much appreciate a review if you could take a few minutes to leave one. Reviews help others find their next favorite read and encourages an author to continue writing.

Happy reading,

Sherri Storey

About The Author

Sherri Storey

Sherri Storey pens swoon-worthy romances that make you believe in love all over again. Drawing inspiration from her own cozy town in Ontario, Canada, Sherri infuses every page with the charm and quirks of small-town life. But don't let her homey roots fool you – her favorite pastimes involve jetting off to tropical beaches, where she lounges on the sand, cocktail in hand, dreaming up her next unforgettable storyline. So, if you find a bit of sun and surf between the lines, you know where it came from!

Made in United States
Orlando, FL
29 January 2025

57943347R00171